You, Me, and Forever

OTHER TITLES BY LAURA PAVLOV

The Blushing Bride Series

Rosewood River Series

Magnolia Falls Series

Cottonwood Cove Series

Into the Tide

Under the Stars

On the Shore

Before the Sunset

After the Storm

Honey Mountain Series

Always Mine

Ever Mine

Make You Mine

Simply Mine

Only Mine

The Willow Springs Series

Frayed

Tangled

Charmed

Sealed

Claimed

You, Me, and Forever

Laura Pavlov

 Montlake

Published by Montlake, Seattle

www.apub.com

Amazon, the Amazon logo, and Montlake are trademarks of Amazon.com, Inc., or its affiliates.

EU product safety contact:
Amazon Media EU S. à r.l.
38, avenue John F. Kennedy, L-1855 Luxembourg
amazonpublishing-gpsr@amazon.com

ISBN-13: 9781662525438 (paperback)
ISBN-13: 9781662525445 (digital)

Cover design by Hang Le
Cover photography by Madison Maltby Photo
Cover image: © MrPrize / Shutterstock

Printed in the United States of America

And then one day, there you were, shining brightly.
Showing me that I wasn't meant to stay in the dark.

JmStorm

CHAPTER ONE

Montana

The sun was shining, the sky was blue, and the birds were chirping almost harmonically. The surrounding mountains sat in the distance, looking more like a painting than the actual landscape in Blushing, the small Alaskan town I lived in. Normally, this would have been enough to put me in a good mood. I was that girl—the perpetually positive, glass-half-full-if-not-overflowing, write-in-your-gratitude-journal-every-day type of girl.

But life had thrown a few curveballs at me lately, and even this beautiful day couldn't pull me out of my funk.

I stalked into the office, and both Violet and Blakely turned to look at me as they huddled around the front desk.

"I'm guessing the meeting didn't go well?" Violet asked. My best friend and I owned the Blushing Bride, the only wedding planning business in Blushing.

Even though all I wanted to do was go pout in my office alone, I came to a stop and sighed.

"They want to get married in four months." I shrugged.

"You've pulled off shorter timelines than that," Blakely said, smiling. She was our office manager, and she kept everything running smoothly for Violet and me. She kept our schedules straight, booked meetings with prospective couples, and basically organized our professional lives.

"That's not the issue," Violet said as she tapped her lips with her pointer finger. "Let me guess, they want to get married at the Seaside Inn?"

"Yep. They have their heart set on it," I groaned. "Apparently, Barbie has been dreaming of getting married there since she was eight years old. She had an absolute meltdown, even though she already knew that the Seaside Inn wasn't an option because everyone in town knows it's been purchased. But she made a point to tell me that this is the worst thing that's ever happened in her life, and she couldn't believe I wasn't able to work some magic and pull off a miracle. She followed it up by calling me a 'dream crusher.'"

"A 'dream crusher'? Come on." Violet shook her head with disgust. "That is the most ridiculous thing I've ever heard. And what eight-year-old kid is planning her wedding? She didn't even know if she'd live here as an adult back then. She needs to take a chill pill and calm her pretentious ass down. Maybe you should suggest she read a Ruth Bader Ginsburg book and channel her inner feminine power. There are bigger issues in life than choosing your wedding venue. Come on. The groom didn't bail on her. Worse things have happened. And blaming you for something that's out of your control is ludicrous. She's got all the makings of a bridezilla, and we haven't even signed her yet."

"We did sign her. Apparently, the dream crusher is still the best option out there." I sighed. "Being the only option makes our odds pretty high."

Blakely and Violet both laughed, but I wasn't in the mood to join in, so I turned to head to my office.

"Slow down, girl," Blakely said before holding up a bag from the Brown Bear Diner. "We've got chicken salads. Come on, let's eat."

I was a sucker for their chicken salad.

I followed them into our office's little kitchen area, where we often ate lunch. We'd renovated this cool old house downtown when Violet and I had decided to open the Blushing Bride together right out of college, over five years ago. I'd dragged my bestie back to the small town where I'd grown up and sold her on the business plan.

This office was everything my Pinterest heart desired, and we'd spent the last few years renovating it to be everything we wanted. Wallpaper covered in pink and white peonies flanked the walls in the front office, and a large crystal chandelier hung over Blakely's desk, where she greeted customers.

Violet and I had our own offices down the hall, both decorated in our own chic styles, and we had a conference room to meet with clients as well. The kitchen area was a bonus; that was where the three of us ate lunch and talked shop most days.

We did our brainstorming below a large whiteboard that hung on the wall.

"Thanks for grabbing lunch," I said.

"I know it's been a lot lately, with all the ups and downs, but I'm fairly certain I've diagnosed what's going on with you," Violet said as she grabbed us each a bottle of sparkling water from our pink vintage refrigerator.

My friend was a woman of all trades. She was a problem-solver. A self-proclaimed healer. And, most of the time, a bit of a know-it-all.

But she owned it, and I trusted her with my life.

"I can't wait to hear this." I poured my dressing over my salad before closing the lid and shaking the container several times.

"I've never heard of it, but Vi claims it's a real thing." Blakely forked her chicken and took a bite before giving Violet a look to let her know the floor was hers.

"You're suffering from a horrible case of vajabbies. But not to worry, there's a cure."

"What is vajabbies?" I groaned, already knowing that I didn't want to hear the answer.

"Well, let me review what we have going on. We're busier than ever, thank you, Harry Simon!" she said. Harry Simon, the biggest pop star of our generation, had married his longtime supermodel girlfriend, Bailey Clark, without any paparazzi finding out about it before the nuptials took place. Because who would have ever suspected that the Hollywood "it" couple would run off to Blushing, Alaska, to tie the knot? So, ever since word had gotten out over a year ago, business had been nonstop. "And then our most popular venue gets sold to some billionaire asshole who doesn't care about our town or our business."

"Thanks for the reminder," I grumped.

"I'm really not a fan of grumpy Montana." Blakely reached for her water and took a sip. "I mean, you're allowed to be grumpy now and then, but this has been a few weeks. That's usually Vi's job."

"Thank you, I wasn't quite done bitching yet," Violet said, pursing her lips. "This brings me to my vajabbies diagnosis. We got the horrible news about the Seaside Inn, and then that wanker ex of yours posted a photo with his new fiancée. Wham, bam, that's a shit ton of stuff to deal with all at once."

"Is this supposed to be helpful?"

"Monny, you've been broken up for six months, and you have not had sex with anyone since."

"What are you, keeping track of my sex life?" I rolled my eyes.

"There's nothing to keep track of. You're clearly in a dry spell, and your vagina is pissed off and crabby. Which means you suffer from a toxic case of . . . vajabbies."

Blakely used her hand to cover her smile.

"Our business is booming," I said, "and everyone wants to get married at the Seaside Inn, where freaking Harry and Bailey tied the knot. And now that venue will be gone in one month. I'm trying to reschedule a lot of angry couples at the moment for their upcoming weddings that they thought would be happening there. So yes, I am pissed off and crabby, but it has nothing to do with my vagina." I stabbed my lettuce like it was a personal offense to me and popped it in my mouth.

The nerve of her to go there with me right now.

"Monny."

"Vi," I said, arching a brow. "Do not make this a thing. It's offensive."

"Listen, we're under a lot of stress, trying to find more venue options. I've been on the phone all day working on this. But at least if you were having sex, it wouldn't feel like the world was ending. Seeing that Phillip got engaged was the icing on the cake. You're hurt, but we're here for you. You know that."

"I'm not upset about Phillip." I reached for my water.

I am a little upset about Phillip.

Not because I cared that he was getting married. It just stung a little that he'd moved on so easily. We'd dated back in high school and then broken up when we'd gone to different colleges. After I'd moved back to Blushing to open our business, he and I picked up where we'd left off. It wasn't magical or that kind of relationship where you get hit with the butterflies—but it was comfortable.

Apparently, I like comfortable.

But Phillip had been traveling to California for work often, and out of nowhere he decided that he no longer wanted to live in Blushing anymore. In fact, he didn't want to live in Alaska anymore.

I had a business here. One that had just started booming a few months before he'd made this life-changing decision.

I had a life here.

I wasn't willing to leave. He wasn't willing to stay.

It was all very amicable six months ago.

And then he moved to California and posted a photo with his new girlfriend, Angel, less than a month after he'd left—a woman who worked at his company, whom he'd mentioned a few times when he'd traveled there.

"I'm having dinner with a few of the guys from the office . . . and Angel."

"I have a coffee meeting with my coworker, Angel."

"Angel's fine, but a little annoying. I miss you."

Fast-forward to last week, when he'd posted engagement photos with Angel.

Six months to the day after we'd broken up.

Clearly she wasn't as annoying as he'd claimed.

Did I want to marry Phillip?

No. Not anymore, at least. Our relationship had run its course.

But I was hurt that he'd found someone else so quickly and easily, while I'd basically poured myself into work. It also hurt that he was engaged to a woman he'd spent time with while we were together, which made me question if he'd cheated on me during our relationship.

It shouldn't have mattered now, because we weren't together.

But it made me question myself.

And now I'm a bitter wedding planner, which is never a good thing.

"I don't think she misses him at all." Blakely shrugged as she dropped a slice of lime into her sparkling water. "You always seemed bored with him."

"Thank you," I said, forcing a smile at her before shooting Violet a hard look. "It's not about Phillip. I was okay when we broke up. We outgrew one another."

"Well, thank God for that, because even his name is problematic. 'Phillip Moon'? I mean, can you imagine having to write 'Montana Moon' for the rest of your life?" Violet had always made fun of the name when he and I were together.

"It sounds like the name of a movie." Blakely shrugged.

"Oh, please," my best friend said over her laughter. "It sounds like the name of a porn star. Can't you just hear some big, oiled-up, hairy man slapping someone's ass and shouting out, 'Take it like a good girl, Montana Moon'?"

My head tipped back, and it felt good to laugh. "Well, now the porn star name is Angel Moon."

We were all laughing, which was how it usually was when the three of us were together.

"Anyway, he was a loser, Monny. He never supported your dreams." Violet held her hands up to stop me from interrupting. "I know, you don't hate him. Hating people is a waste of time in your world. It's all amicable. I get it. But he was a selfish dude, even if you hate saying anything bad about anyone. And the timing of his relationship is questionable. I never trusted him, and I think deep down you didn't either. So now you've been buried in work ever since, thanks to our favorite celebrity wedding—but I've managed to go on plenty of dates. The tourists are out in full force now, with it being the summer solstice. And the quickest way to get your mojo back is to find yourself a hot tourist and have a one-night stand that reminds you how good sex can be."

The summer solstice was a big deal in Blushing, because the sun stayed out for nearly twenty hours a day at the height of it. And since our town had become somewhat famous over the last twelve months, the tourism was out of control pretty much year round now.

Hence the reason some jackass rich dude had bought the inn. He recognized the potential. Hell, everyone with social media or a television would know things were booming here.

"I agree. And we're all single at the moment. Let's go out tonight and find Monny a smoking-hot loverrrr!" Blakely shouted, and we both gaped at her.

"Clearly, you don't get out enough, either, because that was—a lot." Violet chuckled.

"Listen, I'm just stressed about finding some new venues," I said. "We do the majority of our weddings at the Seaside Inn, and that's where my mind is right now. I'm not looking for a one-night stand. I'm looking for a new, cool location."

"Says the girl who's never had a one-night stand." Violet smirked. "How many things have you tried because I told you how fabulous they were, and now you love them? This is no different."

"Are you seriously comparing Tater Tots and Manolo Blahniks to sex with a stranger?" I laughed.

"Girl, those crispy taters and red-heeled goddesses have nothing on a hot, steamy fling. Or just a good make-out sesh with a hot guy to get your confidence back. Plus, we're good for all events scheduled in the next four weeks, and several of the ones beyond that have already been moved. Who knows, maybe the new owners at Seaside will make this an even better venue that we can utilize?"

"The St. James Corporation doesn't care about our weddings. They are a massive company out of New York City. They destroy their competitors and probably eat small children for breakfast. I hardly think providing us a wedding venue will be a priority." I sighed.

"I think we'll be fine," Violet said. "We have other options, and those will work until we figure out a new game plan. Plus, maybe this will be an opportunity for us to invest in a venue that we could own. Then we wouldn't have to worry about it being sold out from under us."

Violet wasn't normally an optimist, but I was the yin to her yang, and with me spiraling, she was trying her best to shine some light on the situation. But the reality was, we couldn't afford to purchase a venue at the moment. Yes, we were doing well financially, at least in terms of anything a new company faces. We were saving money every month for the business, but purchasing a venue large enough to host a wedding would be a whole different ball game. You needed a lot of land for outdoor ceremonies, as well as a structure to offer accommodations for guests who had traveled here. We weren't in a position to invest a million dollars into a boutique hotel on the water, not that we could even find anything for that price.

Like I said, Blushing was booming at the moment, and real estate was a hot commodity. I'd been lucky enough to purchase a small home of my own last year, which had been a goal of mine.

But purchasing land and a hotel was a whole different story.

"I like the idea of you buying the venue," Blakely said. "You two are badass boss bitches."

More laughter.

"That takes time and money. We need to have more options to offer clients, and time is not on our side," I groaned.

"Okay, I hear you," Violet replied. "But the first solution is to bring our little ray of sunshine back to life. You're walking around like someone stole your Gucci bag. Tonight, the three of us go out. We find you a sexy tourist who you'll never have to see again, and you let him do naughty things to you and relieve some stress. It will be the final needed closure with Phillip, the asshat. It'll be the last step to moving on in every aspect of that relationship once you've finally hooked up with someone outside of Boring Moon Man. Then tomorrow you'll come back a new woman, all sated and relaxed, and we'll solve all of life's problems together."

Blakely said, "You could just go and flirt with a guy. You don't have to take him home. I mean, I've watched too many *Dateline* episodes to do something that crazy. I wouldn't go home with a rando—he could murder you or hold you captive. And obviously there are no locals that you're interested in, so it would have to be a stranger."

Violet sighed dramatically. "You are the world's worst cock block."

"We don't have cocks," I reminded her.

"But someone does, and you're both blocking him. There hasn't been a murder in Blushing ever, has there?" Violet was googling it on her phone now. "Nothing comes up. Tourists come here for an escape. Small towns are too gossipy. They'd never get away with it. Plus, I've dated plenty of tourists, and I've never had an issue."

"Listen, I'm not going to be pressured into having sex. I will go out tonight. I will put on something sexy and flirt my ass off, if it means tomorrow, you promise that we'll put our heads together and figure out this venue situation."

"Do I get to pick your outfit?" Violet asked.

"Sure."

"Can we use aliases?" she pressed.

"Fine. I know how much you love to pretend to be someone else with tourists." I chuckled.

"Ohhhh, I'm so here for this," Blakely said. "We can use fake names and come up with much more exciting careers than we currently have."

"Hey. We like this career," Violet said over her laughter.

"I know, but it's all part of the secret identity. Let's reinvent ourselves for just one night and have some fun." Blakely grabbed our empty salad containers and tossed them in the trash.

"I'm in," Violet said, and they both turned to me.

"Okay. I'm in." I shook my head.

Why did I feel like I was going to regret this?

CHAPTER TWO

Myles

My company had taken ownership of the Seaside Inn a few days ago, and the current owners had negotiated with me to rent back the place for a month so they could see through some obligations for weddings and other events they'd scheduled.

This was also their personal residence, and they couldn't get into their new home for another couple of weeks. I knew that it would take me that long to get permits in place. I'd decided to fly in and speak with the contractor in person, as we'd only met via Zoom thus far, but he'd come highly recommended. I'd spend a few weeks here getting everything ready to go before I bulldozed the place down to the studs.

I'd bought this property sight unseen, because when I saw a diamond in the rough, I went after it. My company had purchased a hotel in Anchorage last year that was thriving, but Blushing was all over the news, and everyone and their mother was talking about it.

I didn't like to miss out on opportunities. This bed-and-breakfast could be accommodating far more people than it was currently serving. The place had eight rooms and a restaurant that was apparently very popular. But it was the land that was the real gem. It sat on an acre of oceanfront property, and I planned to build a much larger structure once I'd torn it down.

I'd spent my afternoon talking with Howard and Lydia Barnes, who'd owned the inn since it opened over thirty-five years ago. They were well past retirement age, and they were ready to be done working so hard.

So I'd made them a generous offer.

I walked the property, and the views were unbelievable. The place was even better in person than it was in the photos. I'd sent my assistant, Connor, out here to scope things out after we'd made the offer, and he'd been impressed.

But even that hadn't prepared me for the potential here.

I spent the rest of the day crunching numbers, jotting down ideas, and taking a few calls for other projects we currently had going on.

I'd rented a house a few doors down from the inn, and I'd be staying there for a few weeks and working remotely. Now that I was in Blushing, I had some new ideas about expansion that I'd need to run by my architect, Jackson, before we took our final plans back to the city. He also happened to be my best friend, and the best in the business, and I knew he'd work his magic to maximize the potential.

My phone buzzed, and I picked up when Connor's name flashed across the screen. "Hey, how did the closing go?"

Connor Wilkes basically organized my entire life, and the dude didn't miss a beat. I trusted him immensely.

"As smooth as always," he said.

My family owned one of the largest commercial real estate companies in the country. My grandfather had inherited it, and I'd taken over a few years ago. I'd expanded quite a bit since then.

"Great. I'm calling it a day over here. It's getting late, but you wouldn't know it because the sun doesn't fucking sleep here."

It was almost 9:00 p.m., and you'd think it was the middle of the day.

"Yeah, the first few days are going to be tough to get any sleep until you adjust. When I was there, I found a great place for a quick drink and some good food. It's a tourist hangout, so everyone was on vacation."

"I hate that. That means there's going to be a lot of sloppy drunks." My tone was dry.

"Nah, it was a big enough spot. You can get a booth in the back or sit at the bar. The party was outside, because it sits right on the water. Let me check my notes," he said as he paused. He was the most efficient guy I'd ever met aside from myself.

"I don't need you to check. This place is the size of a postage stamp. I live in Manhattan, for fuck's sake. I can just walk the mile-long downtown here and find a place."

"Here it is. It's called the Moose Brew," he said, and I knew he was using his cough to cover his laughter.

"'The Moose Brew'? Seriously?"

"Dead serious. And the food was amazing. I've already warned you that there's a moose that cruises around town, so be careful when you're out at night," he said.

"Well, that shouldn't be hard, since it never gets dark. It should be fairly easy not to miss a goddamn moose."

"Go get a cocktail and a steak. You'll thank me later," he said.

"All right. I'll talk to you in the morning."

I hadn't had time to grocery shop yet since arriving earlier today, so going to the Moose Brew was probably a good idea. I walked the short distance to the main drag with all the restaurants and shops, and I quickly deduced which one was the Moose Brew because the place was going off when I walked up. I could see how packed the back patio was. That was clearly where everyone wanted to be.

I was in the mood for a good meal and a little peace and quiet, so I decided to sit inside at the bar. There were fifteen to twenty people in the bar area, and the restaurant had a fair amount of people as well, but it was large enough that I could keep to myself.

"You don't want to venture outside to the chaos?" the bartender asked as he set a napkin down in front of me. "There's a DJ out there."

"Nah. I prefer it in here at the moment," I said.

"I'm Benji. I own the place." He extended a hand.

"Myles. Nice to meet you." I hoped that would be the extent of the conversation. I had some emails to go over, and I wasn't big on small talk.

"What can I get you?" he asked as I perused the menu. I appreciated his ability to read the room that I wasn't looking for a friend.

"I'll take an old-fashioned and a T-bone steak, cooked medium, with a Caesar salad on the side."

"You got it." He tapped on the wooden bar top.

I spent the next twenty minutes sipping my bourbon and responding to emails. I'd sent a list of things for Jackson to look into, insisting that he get his ass to Blushing in the morning to walk the property with me. I took a quick call from my brother, who I spoke to every day, even though he worked long hours as a brain surgeon. Benji set my steak down in front of me, and I ended the call and dropped my napkin in my lap.

I looked up to see two women smiling at me from the other end of the bar. I gave them a curt nod and turned my attention to where the music was booming from the patio. A woman with long dark hair and golden tan legs caught my eye as I cut into my steak. I couldn't make her face out from here, but her shoulders were notably tense, which kept my attention. There was a man hanging all over her, and it was obvious she wasn't interested.

I took another bite and looked back down at my phone to see a message from Jackson that he'd be here tomorrow. I looked back up to see the woman holding her hands up to the man, who was clearly inebriated. It appeared that she was telling him to step back with her body language.

I was moving to my feet, ready to get involved, when she forced a smile and walked inside toward the bar. She wore a white fitted tee and a denim skirt with a pair of cowboy boots, and she looked sexy as hell.

Her cheeks were flushed, eyes dark, and lips plump.

Her gaze locked with mine before she quickly looked away. She moved past a group of people sitting at the bar, and she turned to stand just a foot from where I sat. The bartender appeared to know her, and they both laughed before he stepped away to make her a cocktail. I couldn't take my eyes off her.

She startled when the asshole who'd been harassing her outside came up behind her and wrapped his arms around her, locking them around her chest. She quickly turned and pushed him back.

That was all I needed.

I was done watching this jackass hang all over her.

I was on my feet, and my hand gripped his shoulder firmly. "She's made it clear she's not interested."

Her dark eyes shot up to mine, and I saw the surprise there, but she also appeared relieved.

"Who the fuck are you?" the drunk asshole said, his words slurring as he wobbled on his feet.

I leaned close to his ear. "I'm the guy you don't want to piss off. The only way this ends well for you is if you walk the fuck away from her right now and don't come back."

He blinked a few times and then held his hands up. "Yeah, yeah, fine, dude. I wasn't that interested anyway."

I didn't speak another word. I just stared at him till he tucked tail and got the fuck out of there.

I moved back to my seat and took a sip of my drink without saying a word to her. She walked toward me, martini in hand, pink lips parted as her gaze locked with mine.

"Thank you," she said as she stood in front of me.

"Not a problem."

"Is this seat taken?" she asked, and I didn't miss the way her hand shook the slightest bit, and she held her chin up as if she was trying to appear confident. The type of business that I did required me to read people.

Read their body language.

Find obvious tells that let me know if they are nervous.

She's definitely nervous.

I shook my glass, moving the ice from side to side, before taking the last sip and motioning for her to sit. "I take it you didn't appreciate that asshole hanging all over you."

"Yeah. He wasn't taking the hint. I think he was pretty loaded."

"Not an excuse to push himself on a woman," I said. I held up my glass when Benji made eye contact with me to let him know that I'd like another. "Get one for the lady as well, please."

Her eyes widened, and she smiled. "Oh. I just got one, but thank you. I don't think my friends will be ready to go anytime soon, so I can sit in here and enjoy these cocktails. What's your name? I'm guessing you're from out of town?"

She acted like she wasn't used to getting hit on, which seemed impossible to believe, especially considering I'd just had to get involved with the last dude who'd taken his shot.

"Yes. I'm Myles, and just visiting. How about you? Are you a local?"

She smiled, and it was clear she was thinking her answer over as Benji walked over with our drinks.

"I'm Dominique Venezuela," she said, quirking a brow as if she was proud of her answer, which was clearly bullshit because no one said their name with that kind of thought or excitement. "I'm just here visiting as well."

Benji was smiling at her, making it even more obvious that she was bullshitting me.

I picked up my glass as she held hers in her hand. "Nice to meet you, Dominique Venezuela."

"Nice to meet you, Myles." She clinked her glass to mine and took a sip. "What do you do for a living?"

"I do a whole lot of things. How about you?"

"I'm a . . ." She paused to clear her throat. "I'm a diamond dealer."

I chuckled, because she'd piqued my interest, which was rare. She was clearly full of shit, but undeniably charming.

"Nice. That's a solid business. So what exactly is involved in that?"

She finished off her martini and set the glass down. "You know, imports and exports. We're very busy with all the ports, Myles."

"I'm sure you are. And you're just visiting Blushing as well?"

"Yes. I'm here on a girls' trip with my two best friends. I head back to Chicago tomorrow. So I'm just here for the night."

"Then I guess I'm lucky that you're just here for the one night, and I happen to be in the seat next to you at this bar."

She chuckled and shook her head before reaching for the cocktail that I'd gotten for her. "I guess you are."

We spent the next hour making small talk, which I normally despised. But this woman was witty and funny, and for whatever reason, I was enjoying myself. I ordered us another round and asked Benji to bring a couple of waters, because I got the feeling that she didn't drink often by the way she gulped her drink and how her words were slurring the slightest bit.

Two women walked our way, and it was clear that they were intoxicated—they were shouting her name and shaking their hands around.

"Dominique, we couldn't find you," the blonde said, raising a brow as she perused me from head to toe. "Hey there, good looking. I'm Marilyn Monroney. The pleasure is all yours."

For fuck's sake.

This one was clearly using a bullshit name, too, but she owned it and had zero hesitation.

I extended my hand to her. "Myles. Nice to meet you, Ms. Monroney."

"Myles. That's a cool name," the other woman said before she proceeded to hiccup a dozen times as she laughed. "Sorry about that. I'm Dr. Pamela Pepper. Are you here on business or pleasure?"

"Dr. Pepper, huh?" I looked at the woman sitting on the stool beside me, and her teeth sank into her bottom lip like she knew they were busted. "That's quite a name. What type of doctor are you?"

"I'm a penguin heart surgeon."

"Wow. I didn't know that was a thing," I said. "You both seem to have such interesting careers."

"Dominique, you weren't bragging about your diamond business, were you?" the blonde asked.

"You know, I just told him about all the imports and exports that I do," she said with a smile.

"Yes. Our girl is quite the savvy business lady," Dr. Pepper said, and I did my best not to blatantly laugh.

"We were going to head out," Blondie said. "What are you going to do?"

A look passed between them that I couldn't quite read.

"I, um, I'm having a good time, actually." Dominique turned to look at me in question, as if she was asking if I would stay with her.

I couldn't help but smile and nod. I wasn't in any hurry to leave, which was saying a lot because I normally liked to get in and out of a place.

"Myles, is it?" Marilyn leaned forward, eyes all business now.

"Yep. That's my name." I smirked.

"Well, Myles . . ." She glanced over at her friend and then back at me. "I track this girl's location on my phone, and you should know that I'm the chief of police in the Big Apple. Yep, you heard that right. I run the show in New York City, so I've got everything about you right here in the vault." She tapped her temple, and I laughed.

Partially because I lived in New York, and I knew the current chief of police, and it was most definitely not the woman standing in front of me.

And partially because Dominique was looking at me with the most mortified look on her face, and I fucking loved it.

At the moment, I didn't even care that she'd given me a fake name.

We were just having fun, and she was sexy as hell, and I wasn't ready for this night to end either.

"I wasn't planning on breaking the law, Chief Marilyn Monroney. Just enjoying some drinks with my favorite diamond dealer." I winked at the dark-haired beauty sitting next to me.

"Wow . . . he's so gorgeous," Dr. Pepper whispered incredibly loud, which made them laugh.

They kissed their friend on the cheek, and Marilyn turned toward me one last time.

"Myles," she called out.

"Yes."

She just held up two fingers and pointed them at her eyes and then back at me. "I've got eyes everywhere."

"I'm begging you to stop," Dominique groaned as she took the last sip from her glass.

Once they were gone, we just stared at one another. I didn't normally take random women home with me from a bar. I had women in the city that I took to dinner or spent time with. I hadn't been in a serious relationship in a few years. My last one ended poorly, with Gigi throwing a bottle at my head and calling me a selfish bastard when she'd wanted to move in together and I wasn't ready.

Hell, she was probably right. Maybe I was a selfish bastard. Relationships were big distractions, and I didn't do distractions. I was always honest about who I was. Gigi had been fine with our arrangement when it started, but she'd changed her mind somewhere along the way. That's when problems usually arose.

When one person wanted to change the rules and the other didn't.

For me, there was no gray area when it came to relationships.

I had my life set up exactly the way I liked it.

I dated plenty, and sure, I liked the company of a beautiful woman—going to dinner, light conversation, a good fuck—and then we'd part ways.

No drama. No complications.

But for whatever reason, this woman had my attention.

And I always trusted my gut.

"So," she said. "Do you do this often?"

"Do I do what often?"

"Go to a bar and pick up a woman."

"Is that what I'm doing, Dominique? Am I picking up a woman in a bar?"

She sighed. "I don't know. But I kind of hope so."

I took the last sip from my rocks glass and set my credit card down for Benji to close out my tab. "I'll take the check."

Because she didn't need to ask me twice.

CHAPTER THREE

Montana

I was doing this.

I was going home with a random guy that I'd just met in a bar.

A ridiculously good-looking man. One you'd expect to see on the cover of a sports magazine.

I was extremely attracted to the man. But I knew nothing about him.

Am I really doing this?

He took my hand after he'd closed his tab and led me out of the bar. When we stepped outside, he turned to look at me.

"I get the feeling you don't do this often?"

"That's—true." I cleared my throat, trying not to appear nervous. "You know, with all the imports and exports, I keep very busy."

One side of his mouth turned up, he had a prominent dimple on one side of his face, and he was incredibly attractive. Tall, with dark hair, green eyes, broad shoulders, and just the right amount of scruff peppering his jaw. He wore a white button-up and a pair of dark jeans.

"I'm sure it keeps you very busy. Listen, there's no pressure here. If you want me to walk you to your hotel, I'm happy to do that. If you'd like to come home with me, I've got an Airbnb around the corner."

Shit. I'd told him that I was from out of town, so taking him to my house wasn't an option. It would be obvious that I lived there.

This was going to be a one and done.

A hookup.

A one-nighter.

It was better to keep it casual, and not tell him anything.

"What would going home with you entail?" I looked up at him.

I wanted this.

If I were to ever have a fling, this would be the guy. He was almost unfairly good looking. There was an edge and confidence to him that made him appear very off limits. And I was drawn to him.

So why not throw caution to the wind and spend one night with an unattainable, sexy man?

I'd never see him again.

I was twenty-seven years old, for God's sake. I'd only been with two men in my life up until now. Both long-term relationships.

Why not live a little?

"Going home with me means whatever you want it to mean." He leaned down, tucking my hair behind my ear as he moved closer.

Do it.

Kiss me.

Please kiss me.

His green eyes locked with mine as if he were reading my thoughts, and then he closed the distance between us. His mouth crashed into mine, and my lips parted immediately as his tongue slipped in. He was gentle at first as he explored my mouth, one hand in my hair and the other on the side of my neck. He tilted my head to the side to take the kiss deeper.

I'd never kissed a man that I didn't know well.

I've also never been kissed like this, so maybe I've been doing it all wrong.

My fingers tangled in his hair, tugging him closer as he groaned into my mouth.

Voices came from behind us as a group of people left the bar, and he pulled back and looked at me. "The ball's in your court, beautiful."

"I'd like to go home with you," I said, blowing out a breath because I couldn't believe I was doing this.

He took my hand and started walking.

"You're not married, are you?" I asked. I'd obviously already checked his ring finger for any jewelry or tan lines, and neither were there. But one can never be too safe.

He chuckled. "No. You?"

"Nope. Do you have a girlfriend back home?"

I doubted this was typical one-night stand conversation, but I was nervous.

And this was what I did when I was nervous.

He walked up the steps of the gorgeous home on the water and pushed the door open. It was the Johnson estate, and I was shocked a single guy would rent this place. He obviously had money if he could afford this.

Once we were inside, he turned me so my back was pressed to the door, and he placed a hand on each side of my face. "If I had a girlfriend or a wife, I wouldn't be taking you home. That's not my style."

"Okay," I whispered as my heart thundered in my chest.

"How about you, Dominique. Do you have a boyfriend back home, where you import and export all the diamonds?" His voice was gruff and laced with tease.

My legs and hands were tingling from the buzz running through my body, and it was hard to think straight.

I shook my head. "My last boyfriend just got engaged to another woman—one of his coworkers."

"His loss."

"I don't know about that. She teaches yoga on the beach in California, and she's really pretty in that 'I don't even have to try' kind of way." A nervous laugh left my lips.

I was oversharing. This was what I did.

"You're beautiful. Personally, I think most would find a diamond dealer to be way more exciting than a yoga instructor." He smiled, and I desperately wanted him to kiss me again.

"She's probably super bendy," I said, and my voice was barely recognizable as it came out all breathy.

"How long ago did you and he break up?" he asked, the question surprising me as his thumb traced the length of my jaw.

"Six months ago. You should probably know that it's been a while for me. You know, with having sex. I've been sexless for a while now." I looked up at him before reaching for the button on his jeans. I was done talking about my annoying ex and the lack of sex I'd had. This gorgeous man was here and ready for whatever I wanted to do—so I was going to do it.

His hand wrapped around my wrist, and he stopped me. "There's no rush. I plan to take my time with you."

Yes, please.

The next thing I knew, he was lifting me off the ground, and my legs wrapped around his waist, my jean skirt bunching up high on my thighs. He carried me down the hallway to the bedroom, dropping me on the bed with a little bounce.

"If this is too much, you just tell me, okay?" he asked, hovering above me.

I could still taste his whiskey from our kiss on my tongue.

"I'm ready for too much," I blurted out, and he chuckled this gruff, masculine laugh.

His fingers traced up my calf, my thigh, and moving beneath my skirt as I sucked in a breath. His lips were on mine, and he kissed me as his fingers continued to run up and down my leg.

We kissed for the longest time, and my body was on fire. I tried to thrust forward to get him to move his hand where I wanted it. I finally pulled back, unlocking our lips long enough to look at him. No words were exchanged, as if he knew what I was asking for.

His hands teased the outside of my lace panties, and I gasped.

He stroked me over the fabric, slowly, as his lips found mine again. Our tongues tangled as his fingers stroked me between my thighs.

I was bucking into him, desperate for more, when his fingers slipped beneath my panties.

"You're so fucking wet, beautiful." He pulled back, his heated gaze on mine. "When was the last time you were touched?"

"I told you that I broke up with my boyfriend six months ago," I said, feeling mortified and pathetic at how desperate I sounded. My body was betraying me, letting him know how much I wanted him. My hands covered my face, and he tugged them down.

"You don't hide when you're with me. I don't care when you were last touched—I just want to know what you need and how to make you feel good."

"It's been a long while. We weren't really doing great before we broke up, so even when we had sex, it was pretty rushed and uneventful those last few months." I shrugged. I was never going to see this man again, so I had nothing to lose.

I was just a sex-deprived diamond dealer from Chicago where he was concerned.

"That's a shame," he said. "So how about I make you feel good tonight?"

I nodded. He stunned me when he grabbed my hips and flipped me over quickly. I laughed as he unzipped the back of my skirt, and I lifted just enough for him to tug it down my legs.

"Good Christ. This ass is a work of art," he said after tossing my skirt on the floor. He ran his fingers over my butt cheeks. He took his time kissing each side before slowly rolling me over so I was facing him again. He tugged off both of my cowboy boots and let them fall to the ground.

I'd never been undressed by a man before, and taking off my own clothes moving forward would be a disappointment.

I just watched him as he leaned down on the bed and kissed my calves, taking turns as he gave his attention to each leg. And then he was kissing my thighs, and he paused when he got to the apex, pressing his nose to my core and groaning. He spread my legs wide, and he buried his face between my thighs, right over the lace of my panties.

I couldn't breathe. I pressed myself against him, wanting the lace gone. Wanting his mouth on me.

His lips on me.

His tongue on me.

As if he could read my mind, he tore the side of my panties and tossed them on the floor. I pushed up on my elbows and looked at him. No man had ever ripped my panties from my body.

"I'll replace them. I need to taste you right fucking now."

I nodded. *The hell with the panties.*

And then he licked me from one end to the next, and I fell back against the mattress. The sensation was so overwhelming that I couldn't stop the moan that left my lips.

Has anything ever felt this good?

I tangled my fingers in his hair as I bucked against his magical mouth.

And he teased me with his tongue and sucked my clit, taking me to the edge so fast I did everything in my power to hold on.

I squeezed my eyes closed, my fingers tugging at his hair, as I continued riding his face. My breaths were the only audible sound in the room.

I was panting and moaning, and I couldn't stop myself.

And just when I thought it couldn't get any better, he sucked my clit hard just as a finger slipped inside me.

My entire body tingled as I bucked against him with a desperation I'd never experienced.

He slipped in another finger, and that was all it took.

I lost any sense of control.

Bright lights exploded behind my eyelids, and I went right over the edge as I cried out his name.

And he just kept working his fingers in and out, his mouth sucking harder, as I rode out every last bit of pleasure.

And when everything slowed, he pulled back and smiled up at me. His lips shiny from my pleasure. He pulled his fingers out and slipped them into his mouth and sucked.

Oh. My. God.

"You're so fucking sweet. I could stay between your thighs all night."

No man had ever spoken to me like that.

But he had no hesitation. There was not a self-conscious bone in this man's body.

Speaking of bones.

He was pushed up on his knees, looking down at me, and I reached for the button on his jeans, and he didn't stop me this time. Once I'd maneuvered through the button and the zipper, I shoved the denim down along with his boxer briefs. My eyes widened at the sight of him.

Long and thick and hard.

"Have you never seen a dick before, Dominique?" he asked as a lazy smile spread across his face.

"Not one that looks like that."

He chuckled as his fingers moved to the hem of my white tee, and he tugged it over my head and tossed it on the floor. I struggled to get the button open on his dress shirt before he tore the shirt open, followed by the sound of buttons clanking against the wood floors.

"You're not the most patient man, are you?" I gaped at him as he pulled the shirt from his body and let it drop to the floor.

"Patience isn't my strength." His hands moved behind my back, and he unbuttoned my bra before gently sliding it down my shoulders. "You're fucking gorgeous."

Has anyone ever looked at me the way this man is looking at me right now?

It wasn't that I thought I was unattractive, but this man was looking at me like I was the most beautiful woman he'd ever laid eyes on. Maybe this was just how people acted with one-night stands. All the flattery and all the praise before you walk away and never speak again.

And I'm here for it.

Yes, I was still slightly intoxicated.

Yes, I would probably be mortified tomorrow morning that I'd done this.

But right now—I wouldn't want to be anywhere else.

How long had it been since a man had made me feel good?

Since a man had made me feel wanted?

Since a man had made me feel anything?

He leaned down and flicked my hard peaks with his tongue before swirling around the tip and then covering each breast with his mouth. I was floating on air from my orgasm, and this was almost too much.

"Myles," I groaned. "Do you have a condom?"

He pulled back to look at me, studying me like I was a puzzle that he wanted to solve, which was making it hard to focus on the giant penis that was pointing right at me.

There was something in his gaze.

Hesitation, maybe.

My heart raced because I was fairly certain that he was about to reject me.

"You've never had sex with someone that you weren't dating, have you?"

Um . . . hello, buzzkill.

"What? That doesn't matter, I want this." I reached out and wrapped my hand around his erection and stroked him a few times, and he groaned. My mouth watered at the sight of him, where he hovered on his knees above me. I'd never been a big fan of the blow job, but for whatever reason, I was desperate to wrap my lips around him.

"You can't look at me like that, with your hand wrapped around my cock, and lick your lips." His voice strained as he spoke.

I shifted down lower on the bed, positioning myself just beneath him, before angling him toward my lips.

I wrapped my arms around his hips and pulled him forward as I took him in between my lips, inch by inch.

This was by far the most erotic thing I'd ever done. I watched his arms flex above me as he held himself there, and he shifted his hips forward and then back.

Slowly at first.

He let me set the pace as I kept my hands on his hips and guided him.

In and out.

His breathing escalated, and a groan left his mouth.

And I took him deeper.

Faster.

His tip hitting the back of my throat each time he thrust forward.

Over and over.

His breaths were labored, and it turned me on. I wanted to pleasure him the way that he'd pleasured me.

It made me feel powerful and sexy and I took him deeper.

"Fuck!" he shouted as a guttural sound left his lips.

He pulled out before I could process what was happening as he stroked himself with a few quick motions and he came on my chest.

I'd never been more turned on in my life as I ground up against his thigh.

His free hand moved between my legs, and he rubbed little circles along my clit while he continued to stroke himself.

And that was all it took.

I followed him into oblivion and went over the edge for a second time.

CHAPTER FOUR

Myles

Holy shit.

I'd had my fair share of sex. My fair share of blow jobs. My fair share of one-night stands.

But this . . . this was next level.

I'd never get the vision out of my head of me hovering above her as she opened those plump pink lips and let me fuck her mouth.

Her innocence was obvious, and it was easy to see that she'd never done anything like this before. There was something in her eyes when I studied them. Hesitation, maybe? I barely knew the woman, yet I could tell this was a lot for her.

I pushed off of her and made my way to the bathroom, where I grabbed a washcloth and covered it with warm water before wringing it out and making my way back to the bedroom.

She was lying there with her dark hair falling around her. It stood out in contrast against the white sheets on the bed. Her chest was still rising and falling, and I felt good knowing that I'd made her come twice without even dipping my dick into her.

I loved pleasing the woman I was with, but pleasing this particular woman was somehow much more satisfying. There was this look on her face, as if that had never happened before.

As if no one had ever touched her or looked at her the way I had. It turned me the fuck on.

But my gut told me not to push, and I always trusted my gut. I grabbed my briefs on the way back to the bed and pulled them on before sitting on the edge of the mattress and pressing the warm washcloth to her chest. I cleaned her up, and she cinched her brows together and watched me.

"You all right?" I asked as I set the washcloth on the nightstand.

"Am I all right? Um, I'm fabulous." She sat up, taking the sheet with her and covering her gorgeous tits. "Why'd you put your undies on?"

"My 'undies'?" I laughed. "They're briefs."

"Fine. Briefs." She shrugged. "Was this not good for you?"

"Are you fucking serious? That was the world's greatest blow job, and it was hot as hell."

"Yet you put your briefs on before we've had sex." She cleared her throat, and she suddenly appeared wounded.

I tucked her dark hair behind her ear. "I know the last time you had sex was with a guy you were dating. I don't want you to do something you'll regret. My ego is far too big to be anyone's regret."

She groaned. "My first fling has a moral compass? This is a total bust. Isn't this your thing? Do you normally turn down sex with a one-night stand?"

She was funny and cute as hell, and I was dying to bury myself deep inside her. But my instinct told me not to go there. For her sake—which was outrageous, considering I barely knew the woman.

"I'll tell you what, Dominique Venezuela," I said, my lips turning up in the corners because we both knew that wasn't her name. "It's late. Let's get some sleep. If you wake up in the morning and want to have sex, you just climb right on."

Her eyes widened. "You want me to spend the night? Isn't that sort of against the rules for a one-night stand?"

"It's after three in the morning, so the sun will be coming up soon. There's no reason to leave in the middle of the night. And there are no rules with hookups. You make them up as you go." I slipped into bed and pulled her down against me, her back against my chest. I liked the feel of her soft skin, and the way her hair smelled like strawberries and honey.

"Do you normally cuddle with people you hook up with?"

No. I normally go to their home, and I get the fuck out of there after everyone's gotten off.

But I wasn't ready for her to leave yet.

"It depends. And morning will be here soon enough."

"If I forget to tell you in the morning, thanks for a great night, Myles," she said, her voice sleepy, as her hand came over mine. "I hope you have a great life."

"Go to sleep. Chatting is not part of one-night stands." I kissed the top of her head.

Her breathing slowed as she nuzzled against me.

And sleep took us both.

It was probably the deepest I'd slept in a while.

The sun forced my eyes open, and I groaned at the fact that this fucking place had very little time without the sun shining. I stretched my arms over my head and reached for my phone to see that it was later than I'd expected—it was almost seven o'clock in the morning. The sun had been up for a while, but I'd been dead to the world.

Flashbacks of the night before flooded my thoughts as I sat forward and glanced around. The spot beside me was empty, and I glanced at the floor around the bed to see that all her clothes were gone.

I pushed to my feet and made my way to the bathroom to brush my teeth before padding out to the spacious family room and kitchen. There was no sign of her.

A piece of paper on the counter caught my eye.

Miles,

Thank you for everything. I had to leave early, as the diamond business never sleeps. I hope you have a great life.

XO, Dominique Venezuela

I'd never had a woman I'd hooked up with wish me a good life so many times. *Yeah, I get it. It's a one and done. I know the drill.*

I'd wondered if she'd take me up on the offer to have sex today, but I was glad that I'd refused her last night, because my gut had been right. I had a feeling she'd regret it, and that wouldn't sit well with me.

I ran a hand through my hair as I flipped the paper over, a small part of me wishing she'd left a phone number. But she was leaving town today, and I had no idea where she really lived, or what her real name was, since I was fairly certain that everything she'd told me was fabricated.

Lying was always a big turnoff for me, but somehow her telling me the wrong name hadn't offended me. It felt more like a game she and her friends were playing than a form of manipulation.

I shook it off as my phone rang, and I saw that it was Jackson. *Duty calls.*

"Hey, did you look over my ideas?"

"Yep. I'm on it," he said. "I think you can get even more rooms on the property and go bigger than we'd originally planned without losing too much green space, because there's just so much to work with. Anyway, just wanted to let you know that we'll be landing soon."

"Sounds good. I'll jump in the shower and pick you up when you get here."

"See you soon."

Jackson and I had grown up together, and we were like family. He'd worked on the majority of our commercial projects, and the dude was a brilliant architect.

I made my way to the bathroom, hoping for a quick shower, but considering I had a wicked case of blue balls this morning, I spent a little time giving myself some relief from the thoughts of the woman I couldn't quite get out of my mind just yet.

I got dressed, made a cup of coffee, and shook it off.

I swung by the airport to pick up Jackson after he'd landed. Thankfully this island had a private airport for those who wanted to get on and off by something other than a boat.

He whistled when we pulled up in front of the Seaside Inn. "You're right. It's even better in person. Look at that fucking view."

"Yep. It's something. And with all the tourists flocking to this place, they can't accommodate half of them. So a lot of people stay in Anchorage and just come hang out here because it's the place to be right now, apparently." I parked in the small parking lot beside the inn.

"So we need to get this going sooner rather than later."

"Definitely. We can't do anything for a month because apparently they committed to hosting another wedding here in a few weeks, and there wouldn't be enough time to get that one rescheduled. They wanted us to wait six months, but thankfully I was able to negotiate it way down. It's going to take nine to twelve months to get this project up and going, and if we can time it to happen by next season at this time, we'll make a killing."

"You do have a good vision when it comes to this shit," Jackson said.

"Says the dude who draws everything we build. You're the talent here. I'm just the one who takes that plan and puts it into action." I pulled the door open and stepped inside.

"Myles, it's nice to see you again," Howard said as he walked over to greet us. "I was hoping you'd come by this morning. I want to introduce you to the couple getting married here, seeing as you technically own the place now."

I didn't feel a need to mention that I already owned the place, and he was just renting it back from me.

Nor did I feel the need to meet locals, though that didn't stop him from trying each time I saw him.

I had a business plan that had been very successful to me thus far, and chatting with the locals was not part of it. Sure, we'd be hiring employees from Blushing to work on the construction, as well as employees to run the place once it opened.

But Howard wanted to introduce me to the people getting married here this month, and the caterer and the party planners and all that shit that I didn't have any interest in. This was going to be a luxury resort, not a wedding venue. Sure, they could rent a banquet hall if they wanted to, but that would be a very small portion of the business we were building. We'd have a five-star restaurant on site, and we'd hire the best if they were here, or we'd find them and move them here.

That's how the St. James Corp. does business.

"Sure." I gave him a curt nod and held out my hand to the man beside me. "This is Jackson, the architect on the project. Jackson, this is the man we purchased Seaside from, Howard."

They shook hands and made small talk as I told the older man that I was going to take Jackson outside to walk the property.

"This is small-town living, brother. You're not used to having locals in your business, because you've never taken on a project like this in a town of this size." Jackson chuckled as we stepped outside and he took in the property.

"Yep. I'm learning that quickly. I'm going to spend a few weeks here and meet with the contractor and figure out how we're going to get supplies brought in and come up with a game plan. We'll probably need to bring a lot of things over by boat."

"Damn. You sure you're up for this? This isn't New York, Myles, or even Los Angeles or Vegas, or other areas we've taken on projects like this. It's a small town, more remote—things are going to be more challenging."

"Yes. I'm more than aware. There's apparently a moose in town who you just sort of ignore, and Howard and his wife Lydia appear to know everyone in town, so I get the feeling they think I'll be the same way." I scratched the back of my neck.

He chuckled and clapped me on the shoulder. "It's good for you. You've always been in the city, and maybe it's time you spend a little time in nature. You could try smiling every now and then. People like that."

I flipped him the bird, and we spent the next hour talking through our ideas. He was going to make a few tweaks to the plans, and I glanced at my phone to check the time.

"All right, we've got that meeting with Charlie from Huxley Construction. Let's go see if he's here. Howard said we can meet in the dining room and go over everything there."

We made our way inside, and Charlie Huxley was standing there talking to Howard. Well, Howard was talking, and Charlie appeared to be trying to get the conversation to come to an end after he'd looked up to see us walking his way.

We made the brief introductions and pulled him away so we could go chat on our own.

"Are you from here?" Jackson asked him as we sat down at the large table, and I pulled my laptop from my briefcase.

"Born and raised." He scratched the back of his neck as he stared at the screen, and his eyes widened. "This is going to be a big one."

"Yeah, and now this guy wants to go even bigger, and add another wing on the west side."

"Damn. You don't mess around."

"Is this something you feel comfortable taking on?" I asked. "I told you I've got a crew we can bring out and house here for a few months, as we want to get things going right away."

"Yeah, I've got this. And we're going to need the extra crew to get this done in the timeline that you want. I've got some guys in Anchorage that'll be happy to work on this, and my crew of eight to ten guys here, but this is a lot. Especially if you're set on opening by next season."

"I've opened hotels that were four times this size in the same amount of time, so I think it's doable," I said.

"It's doable, assuming we have what we need regarding the crew and we can get all the supplies here in time. Those are the holdups that kill a project timeline. But if you're on top of that side of things, and supplies aren't an issue, I can manage the guys and stay on track. I thought doing the forty-five rooms was going to be a lot, but now we're increasing this to a sixty-room hotel." He shook his head. "It's a lot larger than anything we've had here. I mean, the current inn is the largest accommodation that Blushing has to offer at the moment."

"I think it's necessary," I said as he studied the drawing on my computer screen, and Jackson pointed out where we'd add the fifteen-room wing on the west side.

"Hey, Myles. That couple I told you about is here, and I'd love you to come meet them."

For fuck's sake.

"Yep. I'll be right there, Howard," I said, trying to hide my irritation.

Once he walked away, both Charlie and Jackson chuckled.

"He's probably the nicest man you'll ever meet," Charlie said. "But the dude can talk. And he wants everyone in town to be best friends. I tend to keep to myself, but Howard and Lydia won't stand for it."

I pushed to my feet. "All right. Let me get this over with. You two can work out the logistics."

I walked toward the entrance, where Howard was waving me over.

I startled when I saw the woman standing next to the man that Howard was speaking to.

I knew "Dominique Venezuela" was a bullshit name, but was she seriously here to get married?

Had I completely misread this woman?

And why was I so pissed off about that?

CHAPTER FIVE

Montana

"I thought Dad said that the new owners weren't coming here until after you moved out?" I said to Howard. My father worked at the inn as the head chef, and this place was like a second home to both of us.

"He surprised me yesterday and decided to come check the place out. And he's here with his architect to meet with Charlie to go over their plans." Howard beamed at me and Jesse Barker, the groom-to-be.

Did he seriously think that I would want to meet this guy? The man who was literally going to devastate the business I'd spent the last five years trying to build? The man who planned on bulldozing the place where my father had worked my entire life?

"Great," I said. I was sleep deprived, and now I was meeting the asshole who had bought the inn. The man had only given us four weeks to use the space, even though we'd booked weddings here for the next twelve months.

Thanks for nothing, Moneybags.

Could this day get any worse?

"Here he is. This is the infamous Mr. St. James. Myles, this is Montana Kingsley and Jesse Barker."

Myles?

Myles St. James?

Apparently, this day can get worse.

My gaze locked with sage green eyes, and I could still taste his whiskey on my tongue when I closed my eyes.

I'd had a fling with the enemy.

A one-night stand with the man I despised.

Two of the best orgasms of my life came from the devil himself.

I'd never had a fling. I wasn't that girl. I was never supposed to see this man again.

I'd sneaked out of his home this morning, doing the walk of shame in my jean skirt and sexed-up hair and missing my panties that the man had torn to shreds.

He didn't even flinch when he looked at me, and I tried desperately to act like a professional.

"Nice to meet you, Jesse," Myles said, his gaze on the man beside me as he extended a hand. "I hear you and your fiancé are planning to get married at my fine establishment."

You've owned the place for five minutes, St. James. Don't act like you have anything to do with how wonderful it is.

"Yes. We're so thrilled that we made the cutoff, since my girl was set on getting married here and wouldn't consider tying the knot anywhere else." Jesse looked down at me and winked.

He and his fiancé, Susannah, were friends of mine, and we'd grown up together.

Myles turned to look at me, his features giving nothing away.

Hell, maybe he didn't recognize me, as I was looking pretty haggard today, and for whatever reason, all I could think about were his chiseled abs and unusually attractive penis.

I wasn't even a fan of the penis normally, but this man was built like a Greek god.

But when he looked at me, all I saw was disdain.

I could feel my cheeks heat.

"That's wonderful news, Jesse." His voice sounded overly friendly as he turned his attention to me and extended a hand. "Montana, is it?"

I cleared my throat, remembering that I'd lied about my name.

I was going to have an epic fight with Violet later, because this had all been her horrible idea, and now I was in the world's most uncomfortable situation.

"Yes. Nice to meet you, Mr. St. James." A zip of electricity ran through my body at the contact, and I pulled my hand away quickly.

"Do you have a sister? You look so familiar," he asked with a cocky smirk on his face, and I wanted to crawl into a hole.

"Nope. Nada. Just me. No siblings."

"I see. So how long have you two lovebirds been together?" he asked, glancing from me to Jesse, and I realized that he thought I was the one getting married.

I pursed my lips. "I'm the wedding planner, not the bride."

Jesse laughed hysterically, as did Howard. As if me being the bride was the most comical thing they'd ever heard.

I hate everyone today.

"Montana dated my best friend all through high school and then again over the last few years, so we never dated. Though I do think I tried first, and you shut me down," Jesse said, and I gaped at him.

"Anyhoo, it's nice to meet you, but we need to get outside and meet Susannah, *the bride*. She's out there with my partner, Violet, discussing the layout for the tables."

"Well, considering I own the place, I'd like to see how you set this up. I'll join you outside," the bastard said.

Howard clapped his hands together and smiled. "Well, isn't this wonderful. Everyone's been so nervous about you coming to town, Myles. Especially Montana here. She's practically cursed your name every day for weeks."

Thanks, Howard.

The man was more like a grandfather to me, and I loved him, but he was a perpetual oversharer.

"Yeah, we've all heard it. You're basically the devil over at the Blushing Bride," Jesse said with a laugh.

I shot them both a warning look and forced a smile. "Don't be silly. We're thrilled about you moving here and knocking down the most historical building in our quaint town and putting up a high-rise hotel that blocks the views for everyone who lives here."

Jesse and Howard just chuckled and started walking toward the door leading to the yard in the back.

Myles moved beside me, leaning down close to my ear. "The diamond business must be slow if you're booking out weddings in small-town Alaska. Or was this all part of your plan to get me in the sack and try to change my mind about the hotel?"

I watched as the door closed once Jesse and Howard were outside before turning to the jackass beside me. "Are you kidding me right now? I would never have gone home with you if you'd shared your last name. You made it sound like you were here for the night—I didn't know you were staying."

"Hey, you're the one who lied about your name and your business and the fact that you fucking live here. Let's not throw stones when we live in glass houses, you little honey badger."

"'Honey badger'? Seriously?" I hissed.

He leaned down again, his lips grazing the edge of my ear. "Your pussy tastes like honey, and you're a sneaky little badger."

I couldn't speak; my mouth was hanging open when he pulled back and smirked.

"Honey badger got your tongue?"

"Let's just get through this incredibly awkward moment, and then we never need to see one another again," I grumped as I stormed toward the door.

Violet's eyes widened as we made our way outside, and I could feel his big body hovering behind me. I'd shared the details of my wild evening last night with the girls this morning over coffee and bagels. I'd told them that we hadn't had sex, but that the man had still managed to rock my world.

"Mr. St. James. We had no idea you were coming to town," Violet said, eyes wide as she extended a hand to the man beside me.

"Really? I thought with all those impressive police connections, you'd know everyone coming in and out of town. I'm guessing your name is not Marilyn Monroney?" He smirked, keeping his voice low as Howard talked with Jesse and Susannah and pointed out at the water.

"I mean, it's not my professional name, as I try to keep my police chief status on the down-low." Violet chuckled, because she thought everything was funny.

"I'm guessing Dr. Pepper is in surgery with the penguins?" he asked, and I glared at him.

"Is this funny to you? This is a disaster. I had no idea who you were." I shook my head and threw my hands in the air.

"Listen, you little deviant—I didn't lie about my name or what I did for a living. This disaster is your doing. So suck it up, buttercup." He turned his attention to Howard when he called him over, and he walked away.

I squeezed my eyes closed and counted down from five. It was a little trick my father and I had always done since I was a little girl. When I opened my eyes, Violet was smiling.

"I kind of like him," she said.

"Like him? He's the enemy, Vi."

"And you did naughty things with the enemy." She chuckled as Susannah called my name, and we moved in their direction.

"Myles thinks the tent should be over here because of where the sun sets. You'd have the perfect view," Susannah said as she batted her lashes at him.

"I agree with Myles," Jesse said.

Of course they agree with the handsome billionaire.

They were all looking at him like he was the best thing they'd ever seen, and it infuriated me.

"Well, the sun doesn't set until ten p.m., and the reception starts at five." I glared at him before turning my attention back to Susannah.

"If you recall, you wanted the tent situated so that you would have the perfect view of the water and the mountains, which is right over there, where we'd originally planned to have it."

They nodded, and Howard left to go inside when Lydia called for him.

"I'm guessing the party will just be getting started at ten p.m., when the sun goes down," Myles said, and they looked back at him.

"And you'd be incorrect. We have a noise ordinance downtown, and things need to shut down before ten p.m. I'd think your billion-dollar corporation would have done its research before building a monstrosity here."

"Ahhh . . . it's sweet of you to worry about my company, Ms. Kingsley. But I noticed last night that no one appeared to enforce the noise ordinance, because things were going off at the Moose Brew well after midnight." He tapped his finger against his chin. "Come to think of it, I thought I saw you there last night?"

Susannah, Jesse, and Violet were looking between us like we were a tennis ball going back and forth across the court.

"Oh, she was there," Jesse said. "I left early, but you and the girls looked like you were out to have a good time."

Susannah laughed. "Jesse came home and told me he heard you guys were using fake names with the tourists last night, and pretending you had these elaborate careers."

Five.

Four.

Three.

Two.

One.

"I hope that's a joke." Myles shook his head with disapproval, and I wanted to throat punch him. "I believe lying about your identity is a crime in most states."

"So is bulldozing historical pieces of property."

"That's actually not true. And the Seaside Inn will be bigger and better than ever when I'm done with it."

"Charming." I oozed sarcasm as I rolled my eyes.

"I believe it will be, yes."

I let out a long breath. This conversation was not professional, and I had clients I needed to focus on. Not my hot one-night stand gone bad. "Mr. St. James, I'm sure Jesse and Susannah are not interested in the future plans for the inn, and we've still got some things to go over for their big day. So if you'll excuse us."

"Actually, if you don't mind, Montana, I'd love to see the plans. You said the architect is inside now with Charlie, right, Myles?" Jesse said like they were the best of friends after talking for all of three minutes. Susannah was still swooning at the arrogant billionaire like a lovesick teenager, and her fiancé didn't seem to mind one bit, because he seemed equally impressed.

"Yeah. We trust you to work your magic, Montana. But the new inn design is all everyone is talking about, so we'd love to take a look, if you're willing to give us a sneak peek." Susannah didn't take her eyes off Myles.

Violet shot me a look before speaking. "Absolutely. We've got everything handled. You go ahead and take a look at the drawings, and we'll handle the details for the wedding."

Myles winked at me before turning to walk away.

I was fuming.

"Just hold it in until they're back inside the hotel," Violet said, voice completely calm as we both stood there staring at the water. She glanced over her shoulder and then looked back at me. "Okay. The coast is clear. Let her rip."

"How freaking dare he tell them where to put the tent and then steal our clients. Who does he think he is?" I huffed. "He's an arrogant, cocky bastard."

"Well, he didn't really steal our clients. They sort of begged to go inside with him. And I'm fairly certain he is more than aware that he's a rich billionaire who rocked your world last night."

I gaped at her. "He hardly 'rocked my world.'"

"Two orgasms and you didn't even have sex. That's the definition of 'world rocking,' babe. But I am surprised that you still seem to be suffering from the vajabbies, because your resting bitch face is a whole vibe today."

"I thought you were on my side," I groaned as I turned and stalked back toward the inn, and she followed.

"I'm always on your side. And I think this might work to our favor."

"How does any of this work to our favor?" I asked, my head still pounding.

"You know the saying: 'Keep your friends close and have a fling with your enemies,'" she said with a laugh.

I turned to look at her. "I almost had sex with a man I despise. I finally let you talk me into using a ridiculous alias, and I got caught. And now my clients are in there tripping all over themselves to see that bastard's plans to tear this place down. And for the record—that is not the saying. It's 'Keep your friends close and your enemies closer.'"

"Always such a stickler for detail." She chuckled.

I glanced around the lobby of the inn as we made our way to the door. My dad was off today, and I was glad because I wouldn't want to see him right now. He'd know something was wrong, since he knew me too well.

I paused to look at the staircase. The place where my Christmas stocking had been hung every year of my life. My chest squeezed at the thought.

This man was going to tear down my favorite place in Blushing, and I hated him for it.

He might have been able to win over everyone else in town with his money and his charm, but I wasn't going to be one of them.

CHAPTER SIX

Myles

"Thanks for coming out on such short notice. You think you can tweak those drawings and get them back to me in the next few days so I can take them to the city?" I asked Jackson as he cut into his steak.

"Yep. I can get that back to you by end of day tomorrow," he said after he'd finished chewing.

Benji walked over and asked if we wanted a refill on our beers.

"Sure. Two more sounds good. But let me ask you something, Benji," I said.

"Of course." He leaned over the edge of the bar and folded his hands together.

"I'm fairly certain you heard the woman I left with last night tell me that her name was Dominique, and if I were a betting man, I would guess that you knew that wasn't her name because she's a local."

"Dominique Venezuela?" Benji said over his laughter. "The woman who was here with Dr. Pepper and Marilyn Monroney?"

Now it was Jackson's turn to laugh. I gave Benji a slow nod. "You didn't think you should give me a heads-up?"

"Not even for a second." He chuckled. "You seem like a man who can handle himself just fine. I didn't think you believed that was her name for a second. Especially the way I heard you repeat it to her several times like you knew it was bullshit. And it was nice to see Montana cutting loose for once. That girl works too hard. I was happy Violet and Blakely got her out for some fun."

"So you do know her?"

"Everyone knows her. She grew up here. Her dad is the best cook in town. He works at the Seaside Inn. She practically grew up there," he said, tapping the table with his knuckles two times. "Let me grab you those beers."

"Montana? This is a woman we've met?" Jackson asked as he bit off the top of his french fry. "You've been here for a day. That's not like you. You're usually all business."

"I am all business. She's someone I met last night at the bar. It was no big deal." I took a long pull from my beer after Benji set it down. "She gave me a fake fucking name and said she was from out of town, but I saw her at the inn today when we were there."

Jackson leaned back in his chair and clapped his hands together twice as a big smile spread across his face. "The player got played?"

"Please. I knew that wasn't her name, because she fucking changed the tone of her voice every time she said it."

"Yet you took her home?" He raised a brow. "That's not usually your style to pick up a woman in a bar."

"Well, I sure as fuck wasn't escorting anyone to a black-tie event last night. I came here for dinner and ran into her. It was nothing."

"Seems like it." He smirked. "Is that why you asked the bartender about her?"

"I was curious if he knew that she was lying to me about her name and about living here."

"Well, obviously he knew, but the bigger question is, Why did she lie about it? She never gave it up, even this morning when she left?"

"She left before I woke up. And no." I held my hands up. "I didn't sleep with her."

But I'd wanted to.

"So why didn't you ask her why she'd lied when you saw her today?" he pressed.

"Because I don't give a fuck. You know how I feel about liars. I grew up with one. I tend to avoid that shit once someone shows me who they are. I should have called her out right when I met her. Why would I give a shit what her name was? She had no reason to lie to me. But I left it alone because I never planned to see the woman again." I shrugged, glancing down at my phone to see a text from Gigi.

Jackson looked over my shoulder. "There's someone you should plan to never see again. That woman has been trying to get her hooks in you for years."

Gigi Wellington and I had known one another for a long time. She was someone I attended events with occasionally, and we'd spent an evening together here and there. But I hadn't been out with her in a few months because she'd made it clear that she wanted it to be more than it was. I would never intentionally lead anyone on. I didn't do drama or complications. I was honest about what I had to offer, and it wasn't much if you were looking for something serious.

"Whatever. She's just saying hi. I've put some distance there."

"Good luck with that. She's a woman on a mission when it comes to you."

I held my hand up for Benji and pulled out my credit card, and he left to close out the tab. Jackson was taking the private jet home to the city tonight, and I had a few hours of work left to do.

"Benji, right?" Jackson asked when he handed me my credit card slip and a pen to sign.

"Yes. Benji Carlson." He extended his hand, and Jackson shook it and told him his name.

"Well, it seems your friend Montana left something at Myles's place, and he'd like to reach out to her. I figured it being a small town and all, you might know the best way to reach her."

What the fuck is he doing?

Benji smirked before pulling out his phone and raising a brow at me. "You want her number, don't you?"

"What? No. This is just Jackson being an asshole." I shook my head.

"You'll need it anyway. You bought the Seaside Inn. That's where she throws ninety percent of her weddings. You've kind of destroyed her business without even realizing it. So, you should probably reach out and see if you can work something out for her. She's been scrambling, trying to find new venues for the weddings that had been reserved there."

My phone was sitting on the bar, and Jackson reached for it and handed it to Benji. "This man is all business. He'll want to make things right."

Benji typed what I assumed was her contact information into my phone.

"I don't need to make anything right. I agreed to honor the wedding that was scheduled there this month. The others will just have to be moved to other venues until we're done with construction. When I bought the place, I made sure that the contracts that had been signed had a clause stating that if the place were to be sold, the weddings that were scheduled would not be honored. The clients signed that contract. It's not Montana's fault that the venue sold."

"I hear you, but look at the size of this town. It's not like there are hundreds of other options," Benji said.

Cry me a fucking river.

This wasn't personal. People bought and renovated and expanded property all the time. That's the real estate game, and I played it well.

Benji set my phone down on the bar.

"She seems like a resourceful girl. I'm sure she'll be fine." I pushed to my feet.

"She's very resourceful. Built that business from the ground up with her best friend. But I sure as hell hope you hire her dad when you reopen, because the quickest way to get on Montana's bad side is to fuck over her father." He whistled.

"Who the hell is her dad?"

"Daniel Kingsley. He's been running that kitchen over at the inn since Montana was born."

I groaned. All the employees had been given plenty of notice that the place was closing down and that we'd soon begin construction. They were all welcome to reapply once the doors opened again next year. I wasn't going to hire people just because they'd worked there before. I wanted the best, and there would be an interview process.

"I'm sure Howard and Lydia are giving great severance packages to their employees."

"They've only got three employees, and Daniel's been there the longest. He's pretty much run the whole place for them."

I pushed to my feet. I didn't want all these backstories. When I purchased buildings in the city, I didn't know anything that went on behind the scenes. I didn't know who'd worked for them or how long they'd been there.

The place would be vacant when I took over, and we'd start construction and rebuild.

Maybe coming to a small town had been a bad idea.

"All right. Thanks for the info. I appreciate it." I nodded as Jackson and I made our way outside.

We drove to the island's airport, and I clapped him on the back and thanked him for coming today.

"I'll send over the new drawings tomorrow. Call me if you need anything. And call the wedding planner. You know you want to." He held his hand up in a wave and jogged toward our private jet.

I drove back to my rental and stepped inside. I sat down at the table and opened my laptop to see another email from Howard.

The man loved to email me. This had been going on for weeks, ever since we'd started the negotiation and through the closing.

He was reminding me that the women from the Blushing Bride were going to be stopping by this week to take some measurements, as the tent they'd rented was larger than usual and they needed to map out some of the logistics for the outdoor ceremony. Apparently, this next wedding was going to be a large one.

I'd already known that, because he'd told me multiple times. None of this was something I needed to be updated on, but I just thanked him and said it wasn't a problem.

I read through the email from the contractor. Charlie wanted to meet with me again this week to discuss some materials that he thought would be easy to access and fit well in the design.

I tapped my fingers against the desk a few times before picking up my phone.

I chuckled when I saw what Benji had typed for her contact information: *Montana the Hot Girl from the Bar.*

I changed it to: *Honey Badger.*

I wouldn't want to forget the way we'd met.

Me: This is Myles St. James. I just received an email from Howard that you needed some time over at the hotel this week. I don't have a problem with that.

Honey Badger: How did you get my number?

Me: I reached out to some friends to ask if they knew a good diamond dealer and they recommended you.

Honey Badger: This town is too trusting. And FYI, I know I'm allowed to be at the hotel over the next few weeks. How else would there be a wedding if I couldn't prepare for it?

Me: Do you have this attitude with everyone that you work with in the wedding industry?

Honey Badger: No, Moneybags. I save it all for you.

Me: Let me get this straight. YOU lied about your name. YOU lied about where you live. YOU lied about what you do for a living. And I'M the bad guy?

Honey Badger: Correct. I shouldn't have lied that night. But you were the bad guy before you even arrived here. You very well may put us out of business with your quest to make more money than anyone needs.

Me: That's a bit dramatic. Marriage is about a union, not the venue.

Honey Badger: Spoken like a man who's never been married. The venue is huge. And people book their weddings a year in advance, so I'm scrambling to find a new venue for more than eighteen weddings that we had scheduled at the inn over the next year.

Me: Once the new property is built, you are welcome to book there.

Honey Badger: How generous of you. Once you build your hideous eyesore, you're happy to let me book there and make you even richer? Good to know.

Me: Of course. That's how I make my living.

I chuckled. I knew I was pissing her off, and for whatever reason, I was enjoying it.

Honey Badger: For the record, just because something is huge doesn't make it better.

Me: Me and my dick disagree. Big is typically better.

Honey Badger: You're such an egomaniac. And I am curious, why didn't you tell me your full name last night? Was it because you knew I wouldn't have gone home with you?

Me: You're serious?

Honey Badger: Dead serious.

Me: I've got news for you, sweetheart. I don't have to trick a woman to get her to come home with me. And for the record, you never asked my last name. Only one of us lied about who we were and that was you. Hence the reason you are listed in my phone as Honey Badger. A little sweet, a little salty.

Honey Badger: How original of you. You're listed in my phone now as Rich, Arrogant Prick Who Thinks He Walks on Water.

Me: That's a mouthful. Oh wait . . . you can handle a mouthful, if memory serves.

It was a low blow. But she was pissing me off. She was the one who'd lied to me. Not the other way around.

Honey Badger: I barely remember. I was just pretending I enjoyed it. I wanted to see how much I could inflate that big head of yours.

Me: Which one? I think they're both rather inflated.

Honey Badger: Fuck you, Myles.

Me: I think you wish you could. But I shut that down, didn't I?

Honey Badger:

Well, that went well.

I dropped my phone on the table and scratched the back of my neck. I typed in "the Blushing Bride" and searched her business.

The woman acted like she was running a Fortune 500 company, for God's sake. It was a wedding business. People got married all the time. She was taking things a bit too seriously.

Her website was very professional, and I quickly learned quite a bit about her and her company from the "About Us" page. Montana Kingsley and Violet Beaumont were co-owners who'd met and attended college together in Colorado, and were self-proclaimed "besties." I focused on the section about Montana, where she shared that she was raised in Blushing, Alaska, with her father. No mention of her mother or any siblings. She said that she loved helping plan other people's happily ever after, though she herself hadn't found her own quite yet.

Well, using a ridiculous fake name and lying about where you live and what you do for a living isn't going to be the best way to meet your soulmate.

She shared her favorite hobbies, which were running, painting, and reading. Her favorite books were *Little Women* and *Pride and Prejudice*. And her favorite movies were *The Godfather* and *Rocky*, because she grew up watching them with her father.

Color me intrigued.

The woman was equal parts aggravating and interesting.

And for whatever fucked-up reason, I wanted to know more.

◆ ◆ ◆

I'd been spending a lot of time at the inn over the last week since I'd arrived, and I'd briefly been introduced to Daniel Kingsley, but seeing as it was late and dinner was long over, I decided it was time I had a conversation with the man.

"Hey, Daniel. I had the short ribs for dinner tonight, and I'd be lying if I didn't say that they were the best I've ever had," I said as I stood across from him while he wiped down the counter.

"Yeah?" He nodded. "That's good to hear. I'm going to have a glass of wine; why don't you join me?"

He moved to the refrigerator and poured us each a glass of wine before motioning for me to take a seat at the small table in the corner. It was quiet, which was in great contrast to the madness that usually happened in the kitchen during lunch and dinner shifts.

"Everything I've eaten from this kitchen over the last few days has been top notch. I'm impressed." I took a sip of the chilled chardonnay. "And I'm not easily impressed."

"I'm assuming you've eaten at plenty of fine-dining restaurants, so I'll take that as a compliment."

"As you should." I set my glass down. "So, Howard tells me that you have a job lined up in Anchorage?"

"I do. They're giving me free rein of the kitchen and the menu, so we'll see how it goes."

"You don't mind commuting back and forth?"

"Nah. I've lived here my whole life. It's a short boat ride over."

I reached for my glass and took another sip. "It's going to take some time to get this place up and running, but if you'd like to run the kitchen here, I've sampled enough over the last few days to know that we'd be lucky to have you."

"I appreciate that, Myles. I've got to think about right now and keep the lights on at home, you know?" He chuckled. "But I'll keep that in mind when you open the doors."

"Well, I'll come find you if not. You're talented. I see why everyone in town wants to eat here," I said.

"You sound like my daughter. Did she ask you to come in here and stroke my ego before you head home for the night?" He smirked.

I rubbed the back of my neck. "I'm fairly certain your daughter despises me."

I'd continued finding reasons to text her over the last week, since I'd come to enjoy getting under her skin.

It was so easy to do.

He laughed. "Yeah, you didn't have much of a chance with her after you bought the Seaside Inn. She's a sentimental one, and this place means a lot to her. So, you were enemy number one before you even arrived."

"Yet you don't seem to hate me?"

He took the last sip of his chardonnay and set his glass down. "My daughter is as loyal as they come. She cares about this town, about this place, about Howard and Lydia, about the locals—about me." He shrugged. "She's just got a heart that's too big for her own body. I don't believe the sale of the inn is personal, so I'm not offended by it. It's just business. But my girl doesn't look at it that way."

Just hearing this man speak about his daughter made it very clear how much he adored her.

I couldn't imagine my father speaking about me this way.

"You two are close?"

"It's always been me and her against the world, I guess. But she'll be all right when all is said and done. How about you? Are you enjoying Blushing, or are you missing the city?"

"Well, I like it here more than I thought I would. Probably because I'm eating well." I chuckled, and his head tipped back with a laugh. "But I do think this hotel is going to be good for the town. Provide a lot of new jobs and opportunities for the locals, and a place to stay for the tourists."

"I'm sure you're right. And most of the people in town are excited about the new place. Just give Montana some time. She'll come around," he said as my phone vibrated with a text from his daughter.

Speak of the devil.

Howard stepped into the kitchen and asked Daniel about a shipment that was supposed to come in today, and I pushed to my feet and thanked him for the chat. I glanced down at my phone.

Honey Badger: I will be at the inn early in the morning to measure for the dance floor. I would appreciate if you would stay out of my hair.

Me: Interesting that you had to text me to ask me not to bother you. I think you miss me.

Honey Badger: In your dreams. I just don't want to be harassed every time I arrive there.

Like I said. I'm enjoying getting under her skin.

Me: I can't make any promises.

Honey Badger: 👍

Me: 🖤

I didn't know if it was because she'd texted me first, or if it was because I knew I'd irritated her once again, but I walked out of the inn with a big smile on my face.

And tomorrow couldn't come soon enough.

CHAPTER SEVEN

Montana

"This looks amazing, Dad," I said three weeks later as my father plated the samples of the appetizers for Jesse and Susannah's wedding. They'd already selected the menu, but my father was a perfectionist when it came to food presentation, and he wanted to prepare some samples for me.

"Yeah? Wait till you taste them," he said as I picked up the bite-size piece of watermelon wrapped in mint and feta and popped it in my mouth.

"Oh my gosh. These are amazeballs," I groaned, reaching for the napkin to dab my mouth.

"Looks like I timed it just right," Myles said from behind me, and I whipped around to see him saunter into the kitchen like he owned the place.

Well, technically, he does own the place.

But I still despised him, even though I'd fantasized about the bastard every day since the night we'd spent together.

He was hot as hell and had magical lips—but unfortunately that didn't make him any less of a pompous ass.

"Myles, my man, give this one a try," Dad said, and I shot him a look.

It annoyed me that my father liked the man so much. Myles was the reason that my father would be commuting to work at a restaurant in Anchorage until he found a gig back in Blushing. This man had single-handedly put him out of work; yet leave it to my dad to be completely enamored with the guy.

"I'm always happy to sample," Myles said as he reached for a strawberry–goat cheese crostini. "Wow. That's fucking fabulous."

"These are the appetizers for the wedding next week," Dad said.

Myles and I both reached for a prosciutto-melon skewer as his finger grazed mine. I pulled my hand back quickly and popped a piece of cantaloupe in my mouth.

"Damn, Daniel. This is really good."

I finished chewing and glared at him just as my father thanked him for the compliment.

"Why do you think everyone wants him to cater their wedding?" I asked. "That's part of the appeal of the inn. It comes with the best chef in town."

Myles studied me for a long moment before turning to my father. "You said you've already got something lined up for when the doors close here next week. You know I was serious about you coming to work for me when we get the new place open. I know we've talked about it, but I hope you're taking the offer seriously."

I gaped at my father. "He offered you a job? You didn't think to tell me that?"

Dad chuckled. "I didn't know I needed to run every opportunity by you."

"Of course you do. We're a team, remember?" I huffed. "But it would be working for a large corporation, and you wouldn't be able to create your own masterpieces."

"Says the woman who has never owned a large corporation herself." Myles's voice was clipped. It had been three weeks of awkward run-ins and snide comments.

Snippy texts that really served no purpose.

He'd texted two weeks ago to tell me that he was watching *America's Most Wanted*, and he wanted to know if "Montana Kingsley" was even my real name, because he was fairly certain he'd just seen me on his TV screen as a wanted felon.

I'd responded with the honey badger emoji and the middle finger emoji.

Last week he'd texted to ask if I could get him a deal on a diamond tennis bracelet for his mother's birthday via my imports and exports business.

I'd reminded him that he had more money than he knew what to do with, or he wouldn't be building a monstrosity in our town, so he could figure it out himself.

He'd responded with the dollar sign emoji.

This had become our shtick, and as much as he annoyed me, I would be lying if I said I didn't enjoy bantering with the man.

"I just think that a large hotel is going to have a menu that appeals to the masses. This is a small inn. He's been allowed to create the menus that he wants because it's a boutique hotel and it allowed him the creative freedom. Are you telling me that I'm wrong?"

"I'm telling you that you know nothing about the hotel business. You just want to hate me, so you are going to disagree with everything I say because you're angry. You're thinking with emotion and not like a businesswoman."

"Or I just happen to dislike you and disagree with you at the same time." I placed my hands on my hips. "Both can be true."

"All right," my dad said. "Hank needs me in back, and you two are killing my creative juices per usual with your bickering. How about you each go to your respective corners." He shook his head. "Myles, I appreciate the offer, and when the time comes, if you're still interested, we'll talk. But I can't wait for work until next season, so I'll take this job and we'll play it by ear." Dad put his finger up to stop me from interrupting, because that's exactly what I was about to do. "Baby girl, I love you, but I'm a grown man. I'm very capable of making decisions for myself."

My chest squeezed at his words. It had always been my father and me against the world.

"I know you can. I just know how hard it is for you with the inn shutting down."

"Hard for me, or hard for you?" He kissed the top of my head. "I'm actually looking forward to a change."

My father walked to the other side of the kitchen and through the double doors, and I glared at Myles. "I thought you were supposed to be out of town for the day?"

Howard had told me that Myles had taken the private jet to the city because he had some business to take care of back home.

"Are you keeping tabs on me, HB?" Sometimes he chose to shorten the annoying nickname he'd given me, so I'd adopted the same strategy.

"I just noticed you weren't lurking around trying to put your nose in my business, MB." I turned to walk out of the kitchen, and he followed. "Of course you would get a big head about it."

"You sure like to talk about my big head, don't you?" His voice was laced with humor as his fingers wrapped around my forearm, and I came to a stop. My back was pressed against the wall in the hallway leading to the entry of the inn.

The space was small, and the smell of bergamot and black currant flooded my senses.

"I don't care about your big head," I snarled. "Either one of them."

He leaned forward, one hand on each side of the wall, caging me in. "So you do remember?"

My heart raced, and my mouth went dry. "Is that what you want? You want me to say that I remember that you have a big peen?"

He stared at me. "A 'big peen'?"

"Just calling it as I see it." I chuckled.

He sighed. "Have dinner with me."

"Why?"

"I want to talk to you about something business related, and you're always so hostile, so I figured dinner would be a more relaxing setting."

"I'm not going home with you," I said, tipping my chin up.

"I wasn't asking you to come home with me."

I rolled my eyes and glanced down at my phone to check the time. "Fine. Dinner. No drinks. This is business. I'll give you one hour. I've got plans tonight."

"Do you have a big diamond deal going down this evening?" His voice was gruff.

His face was close to mine, and I squeezed my thighs together at the dull ache residing there from his nearness.

I hated that I looked forward to seeing him every day.

I hated that I was disappointed when I'd heard that he was out of town when I'd arrived this morning.

And I hated that I'd made up more excuses than necessary to stop by the inn when I knew he'd be there.

"Maybe."

"Or a hot date?" he pressed.

"It's none of your business. You've got one hour, Moneybags."

"Great. I'll drive." He stepped back and motioned for me to lead the way.

When we made our way outside and he opened the passenger door, I paused, one brow raised. "The only reason I'm agreeing to get in your car is because I didn't drive here. I walked. Where are we going?"

"Where it all started. The Moose Brew." He had the audacity to lean over and reach for my seat belt, and I slapped his wrist away.

"I can buckle myself, you pompous ass."

He snapped it into place. "This is the hostility I'm talking about, Montana. I'm doing something nice for you, and you act like I'm committing a crime."

He pulled back and shut the door hard before stalking around the fancy jet-black sports car he'd rented.

Why did he have to be so damn sexy? Even his angry walk was a turn-on.

Broad shoulders and long legs on full display before he slipped into the driver's seat beside me.

"I wasn't accusing you of committing a crime. I was telling you that I know how to buckle my own seat belt."

He didn't respond as he drove toward the bar just a block and a half away. We should have just walked.

When he pulled into the parking lot, he turned to face me. "I wasn't trying to piss you off. I didn't see you reach for your belt, and it was just my instinct to buckle it for you."

Well, that was unexpected.

"Why?" I asked as I reached for the button and tugged my seat belt away.

"Because contrary to what you think, I would like to get you to the Moose Brew in one piece. I look forward to being insulted over the next hour."

It was hard to be angry at someone for wanting you to be safe, but I kept my tone light. "It's Blushing. We're driving one block. I wouldn't have guessed you to be such a worrier."

He pushed out of the car and came around to open my door and offered me a hand. "You don't know anything about me, other than what you've decided in your head."

He let me lead the way inside and held up a hand to Benji when he waved at us. "We're sitting in the booth," he said.

"So bossy." I laughed.

I slipped into the booth, and Benji came around with two menus. "We don't need those. We've only got an hour. We'll take two steaks, two salads, and a large bottle of sparkling water with some limes."

"How do you know that I want the steak?"

"Because the night I met you here, you told me that it's what you always order," he said, and Benji waited for me to give him a curt nod, because he also knew that's what I always ordered, and he knew I preferred it to be cooked medium well.

He chuckled and walked away before dropping off a large bottle of sparkling water, along with two glasses and a dish of limes.

"And you know what I drink now?" I said as he unscrewed the top from the bottle and poured it into my glass.

"You said no drinks."

He made good points, per usual. Which only annoyed me more.

"So why are we here?"

"I am opening the largest hotel in Blushing, and you own the Blushing Bride. We should be working together, not against one another." He reached for his water and took a sip.

"So you need my business?"

He smirked. Maybe it was the cocky, sexy way that he tilted his lips, or the way his sage green eyes shone that had my legs squeezing together on instinct.

I wasn't normally a woman who reacted to the opposite sex this way. Probably because I'd been with the same guy for so long that we'd just grown comfortable with one another.

Or it could be that this man just had more sex appeal than any human should be allowed.

Yes. Yes. That's definitely it.

Once again, I blamed him and his annoying sex appeal for making me feel like a horny, out-of-control teenager every time I was around him.

"I make it a point not to need things, Montana. But I also don't pass up opportunities."

"Your hotel is going to be the hottest tourist attraction in Blushing. But you think my weddings are going to be an opportunity that you don't want to miss out on?" I wasn't buying it. He didn't need me, and we both knew it.

Why were we even here?

"That's a fair point. And sure, having the exposure of weddings at the resort will be good for business. But more importantly, it's an opportunity for you."

"Why do you care?" I asked, pausing when Benji set our plates down in front of us. He winked at me before walking away.

Myles thought about my question as he rolled up the sleeves of his dress shirt, exposing his forearms. I internally groaned that the man even had sexy forearms. How was that possible? He cut into his steak and popped a bite in his mouth before motioning for me to eat.

The bossy bastard can't help himself.

He waited until I took a bite before he spoke. "I don't know why I care, but I do. And I'm a man who trusts his gut, and my gut tells me to insist you take this opportunity."

I rolled my eyes, even though I couldn't hide my smile. "Maybe it's guilt because you know that you're bulldozing a beautiful property, and at the same time you're sort of ruining my business."

He chuckled. "I don't do guilt. It's not my thing. I don't base decisions on emotion. I base them on facts and numbers. And how does this 'sort of' ruin your business? That doesn't make sense to me. It either does or it doesn't."

"Listen, not everyone is looking at everything in dollars and cents," I said, reaching for my water.

"Well, then, they aren't trying to make money, and that's their prerogative."

"Most of my weddings choose the Seaside Inn because of the nostalgia that comes with the property. It's one of the oldest structures in Blushing. So, yes, I've found other venues for the weddings that I've been forced to move, but they aren't better than the Seaside Inn, and that bothers me."

"The clients don't think they're better, or you don't?" he asked, his gaze locked with mine.

I thought it over. After the initial blow of letting our couples know that they'd have to move venues, everyone had been fine with it. Most had moved to the Parkers' bed-and-breakfast up the street, and though the view wasn't quite as impressive, it was a close second. And the Parkers had offered discounted pricing, since they were just thrilled to get the business from us, and my father would still provide the catering out of their kitchen.

"I don't."

His lips twitched. "Attagirl, Honey Badger. You're passionate. I like that. But does it actually hurt your business that the weddings will be moving to a different venue? Are you losing bookings?"

"No. But I had an easier time selling the Seaside Inn to clients because it's just special."

"And it will be special again. Even larger in size, which means you can book more weddings than you have before, because we can accommodate that. More guests can stay at the resort for destination weddings. This is not a bad thing. And we will get this built quickly. It's what I do. So I don't understand the hostility."

"Because tearing that place down is emotional for me," I said, suddenly feeling defensive and frustrated.

"Business should never be emotional."

"Maybe that's because you don't have a heart." I shrugged.

I expected him to get angry and snap back.

But he didn't.

His gaze softened. "You're not wrong about that."

CHAPTER EIGHT

Myles

"That's your answer?" she said, and for whatever reason I wasn't offended by her statement. I could be cold when it came to business. I knew that.

I'd learned from the best.

My father was a heartless bastard.

"How about this. You tell me why it's emotional for you that I'm tearing the structure down and building something that will be larger, accommodate more people, and function much better. Not to mention it will be modern and up to date."

"Well, there's your problem. I hate modern and up to date. I like character."

"Montana, this is business, not a dating app. Bringing a property up to date and having more space and better function is the key to making this more successful. Tell me why you are so emotionally attached. I want to understand it." I set my silverware down and folded my hands together.

Why do I fucking care what she thinks?

Seeing her every goddamn day was making me crazy. I'd gone on a business trip today and was supposed to spend the night there, but I wanted to get back.

This woman was so far under my skin, and I couldn't figure it out.

"I grew up there," she said, eyes wet with emotion. "My dad has worked there since I was born, and I've literally spent my entire life there. I learned to play the piano in that entryway, and mine and Dad's initials are engraved on the side of that old banister in the place that Howard and Lydia hung our stockings every year over the holidays. I have this here." She paused and tilted her head down to show me the tiniest scar in her hairline before continuing. "I tripped when I was seven years old and split my head open on the fireplace there. I've gone through heartache and happiness inside that inn, and my business boomed, which in turn helped Howard and Lydia's business boom. And you're just tearing it down like it means nothing."

A sharp pain hit my chest.

I shook it off.

I knew better than to think I was in charge of other people's emotions, but hearing her say this—it made me feel things I wasn't used to feeling.

Guilt? Fuck no. I didn't believe in that shit.

Empathy. Maybe a little.

I didn't want to be my father, but I also avoided vulnerability, and I'd been successful at it most of my life.

"You gave them the opportunity to retire, Montana." I leaned forward, waiting for her to look at me. "I looked at their books. Those weddings are the bulk of their income, which has more than tripled since you opened your business a few years ago. In turn, that means that I paid them three times what I would have before they started working with you. You gave them a fucking gift, and you're not seeing it."

She blinked several times and looked away. "They do seem happy about retiring. I know they're tired. I just—I love that place, you know?"

"I get that. But that doesn't mean the new hotel won't be something you love as well."

"Can I ask you something?"

"You can ask," I said, my voice laced with humor. "I'll let you know if I'm going to answer."

"Why did you want to buy the Seaside Inn?"

"Because I saw potential. I've always been drawn to potential." It was the truth. And for some reason, I saw something in Montana Kingsley that had drawn me to her.

"But you must have been drawn to the charm, so why not keep that and just expand on it?"

"I wasn't drawn to the charm of the inn." I shrugged. "I didn't even fly in to see the property before I purchased it. I didn't need to. It was the land, the views, the fact that Harry fucking Simon chose to get married here and put this small town on the map. Blushing can't keep up with the tourists who are flocking to come here now, and they're staying in Anchorage and taking a boat over to hang out in this cool hot spot that everyone in Hollywood is gushing about. I saw an opportunity."

"And life is all about opportunities for you?"

"In business, yes." My gaze found hers, and I couldn't look away from her plump lips. "But every now and then it happens outside of business, just not very often."

Her tongue swiped out along her lower lip, as if she knew exactly what I was thinking. "Did you just refer to me as an 'opportunity'?"

"I wouldn't say that. But I would say that you have been . . . unexpected."

"More like your worst nightmare, huh? You had no idea you'd have to see me again."

"I'm not the one who snuck out without leaving a phone number."

"You don't strike me as a guy who gets phone numbers and does repeat business, so I'm sure you were just fine with it," she said as she caught her lips between her teeth and looked away.

"You don't know a whole lot about me, HB. You've just decided that you hate me because I'm the one who bought the inn."

"Fine. I know nothing about you. So let me ask you a few questions."

"Give it your best shot," I said.

"Is real estate a family business?"

"Yes. My grandfather taught me everything I know, and I made the decision to take over his company when he passed away. That hadn't been the plan, but it was something I was passionate about from a very young age, and I had a vision to expand our growth outside of New York."

"What was the plan before you took over the company?" she asked, her gaze searching mine.

"I was a third-year medical student when my grandfather got sick, and I took a leave of absence to take over for him. The plan was to become a surgeon like my father, but it was never what I wanted to do. This was the right move for me."

"Was your father okay with your decision? Or did he want you to finish medical school?"

I chuckled. "My father is very single minded, and he has tunnel vision. It's his way or the highway. Even though this company that he looks down at is what made his wealth initially. His father, my grandfather, started the St. James Corporation from the ground up and built it into the largest commercial real estate company on the East Coast. His investments and business decisions put him on the Forbes 400 list, which has benefited my father and our family greatly. But he'd never acknowledge that."

"I sense some hostility there?"

"My father is a brain surgeon, and that profession comes with a certain—confidence. So yes, he's done very well for himself, and he's been written up in magazines as a world-renowned surgeon in his own right, and he enjoys having his ego stroked. And even after years of having it drilled into my head that being a brain surgeon was the only career choice to consider, I realized that it was not what I wanted to do. Obviously he didn't approve. But I no longer felt the need to get his approval after my grandfather got sick. It made me look at my life differently, I guess. At the end of the day, I wanted to build things, create things, so that's what I did."

"That's admirable, Myles," she said, smiling just the slightest bit.

"My father would disagree. But thankfully my brother Samuel followed in his footsteps, so he has that."

"Myles St. James, are you telling me that you're sort of the black sheep of the billionaires?" She clapped her hands together.

"Is this funny to you?"

She nodded. "Yes. It's like one of those Netflix shows about wealthy families. You've got the arrogant surgeons, and the noble real estate developers, all making a ridiculous amount of money and fighting this internal turmoil about living up to familial expectations." She shrugged.

"'Familial expectations,' huh?" I laughed.

"You see, when you're raised in a tiny house with just your dad, and you spend your weekends learning how to change tires on a car and taking the canoe out on the water—life is fairly simple. I've never had familial expectations, because Dad and I just support one another's dreams. Always have. I knew I wanted to be a wedding planner before I went to college. I never wavered. He never tried to change my mind. So, I wake up every day and I do what I love. It's not a bad way to live. And it sounds like that's what you finally did."

Damn. She had a way of making things seem a whole lot less complicated than they actually were.

"It's not a bad way to live, Honey Badger." I smirked.

"So are you close with him now? Were you able to move past it?"

"This isn't a one-sided conversation. How about you answer a few questions first."

"I've got nothing to hide. Ask away," she said as she forked a carrot and popped it in her mouth.

"You live in Alaska—why is your name Montana?"

"That's your question?" she laughed.

"Hey, I didn't judge your questions."

"Fine. It's not the happiest story, so prepare yourself." She sighed, setting her fork down and dabbing her mouth with her napkin. "My parents met in college at the University of Montana. You know the tale.

Boy meets girl. They fall in love. Girl gets pregnant. Dad drops out of college to raise the baby, while Mom continues to chase her dreams to become an attorney. Dad moves back home with the baby that she insisted on naming Montana, because she clearly has no imagination. He has support from his family there, and he raises her on his own. Obviously, they grow apart over time. And Mom never joins them after she graduates because she falls in love with someone else."

"You're shitting me."

"I shit you not, Moneybags."

"She never came to Blushing?"

"Nope. Not once. She wrote him a letter letting him know that she had moved on and told my father that keeping me had been a huge mistake. She gave him the choice to keep me and continue raising me on his own, or she suggested he could give me up for adoption. I was a freaking child at the time. The woman is clearly not very maternal." She shook her head with disgust. "He doesn't know I know that story, by the way. I found a letter that she wrote him. So anyway, it's always just been me and Dad. But I get to have a name that was chosen by a woman who wishes I was never born."

"Fuck her."

Her lips turn up in the biggest smile she'd ever given me. "Yes. Fuck her, Myles St. James."

"And for the record, I like your name. It's unique."

"You don't have to feel sorry for me because my mom ditched me. I've had a great life. I have a dad who has loved me enough for two parents. I grew up in a small town that I love, and I've built a business that's thriving."

"I don't feel sorry for you." I shrugged as Benji walked up and cleared our plates, and I handed him my credit card.

"So now it's your turn to answer my question."

"All right. Remind me what the question is," I said, knowing perfectly well what it was.

But she'd just been brutally honest with me about her childhood, and I didn't want to shut down now.

"Were you able to move past things with your dad?"

"It's complicated. My father has not been very present in my life or my brother's, because he works a lot. And that's okay. But he's neglected my mother in a way that bothers me, he's pressured my brother into a life I'm not so sure he wants, and he despises me for being the one person who he can't control—yet he demands that our family be united for social events and holidays, and it all feels a little disingenuous to me. And it's hard to put a family together that's been broken for a long time. But, I guess you could say that we're a work in progress."

Her eyes told a story. Montana Kingsley was all heart, and she was showing it to me right now.

Empathy and sadness flooded those dark-brown eyes as she sighed. "I'm glad you have your brother beside you. Do you have any other siblings?"

"Well, I'm fairly certain we have at least one other sibling that hasn't been acknowledged. Like I said, the man is a brilliant doctor, but his moral compass is damaged beyond repair." I shrugged. "But that's a story for another day. I think that was enough sharing for one day."

"Thanks for telling me that. I wouldn't have guessed you a big sharer." She chuckled.

"You'd be correct."

"Why'd you tell me all this?"

"Same reason you shared what you did with me. Sometimes you just trust your gut."

Her gaze narrowed as she studied me. "Did you bring me here because you want to be friends?"

"Is that what you want? For us to be friends?"

"I guess it's better than enemies." She shrugged. "I mean, I hope you weren't expecting me to go home with you after this dinner and have a repeat of what we both know was a mistake."

"You sure it was a mistake?" I asked, my tone gruff and flirty. Why was I pushing this?

"Yes. We can barely stand each other most of the time. And you don't even live here, so it could never be more than a friendship."

Well, that's not completely true.

It was possible to be more than friends with someone, without being in a serious relationship. I'd had a few ongoing, no-strings-attached situations over the years with a few different women. They usually ended with me being called an asshole, but it didn't mean that a casual relationship wasn't possible.

Benji walked over and handed me my credit card, and I thanked him before signing the receipt and slipping my card in my wallet. He held up a hand in goodbye as he walked away, and I leaned forward, my face close to hers. "You do know that people can have a good time without making it complicated."

"If you recall, you were the one who stopped things that night, Myles." She raised a brow.

"Because I could tell that it was a big deal for you. Even if you were begging me for it."

She laughed. "I never begged. God, I hate you sometimes, St. James."

"I think you like me sometimes too."

She sighed. "I'm actually grateful that you stopped things when you did. It would have made things more complicated for me. I'm a relationship girl, you know? I don't do the casual thing. That was a first for me."

I could see the struggle there. Her vulnerability and honesty.

I gave her a nod. "I understand. So, we're friends. I've never had a female friend that I didn't fuck."

She smiled and shook her head. "You just really say what you think, don't you?"

"Always." I pushed to my feet, and she followed.

"Well, I'm glad we're on the same page. And I have lots of guy friends, so I can take the lead on this. Plus, it behooves us to be friends, since I'll probably be throwing some weddings at that monstrosity you're building."

As I held the door open, I leaned down close to her ear, the smell of strawberries wafting around me. "I'll follow your lead, but I'm not going to lie. That pussy of yours is impossible to forget."

She startled and turned to look at me, eyes wide. "You've got a filthy mouth, Moneybags."

"Yeah? I think you like it."

I placed a hand on the small of her back and guided her to my car, and this time when she slipped inside, she didn't hesitate when I pulled the seat belt across her body, my knuckles grazing her breasts just before I snapped it in place.

I climbed into the driver's seat, and we drove in silence for a few blocks.

"Thank you for saying that, even if you're completely crude in your delivery and it's clearly outside of the normal friendship boundaries," she said with a chuckle.

"It's crude to tell you that you have an unforgettable pussy?" I laughed as she guided me to her house, pointing out where I needed to turn along the way. "I'll keep that in mind, because I've never told a woman that before."

"You expect me to believe that?" She rolled her eyes before telling me to take the next right.

"I have no reason to lie. You're an aggravating woman, no doubt about it. But that pussy of yours—it's spectacular."

Her mouth hung open. "Myles! If you want to be friends, this ends now. We've spent weeks hating one another. Let's just tone down the sexual innuendos. I'm right up here on the left, the white house on the corner with the red door."

I pulled into her driveway and turned to look at her.

Cheeks flushed. Eyes heated. Teeth sinking into her juicy bottom lip.

She was definitely struggling, just like I was.

I didn't know why I couldn't let it go.

I want her.

When was the last time I'd wanted someone this badly?

I couldn't remember a time, honestly.

75

"Fine. Maybe I'm just a flirty friend," I said as she pushed her door open, and I stepped out and hurried around the car.

I followed her up to the front porch. "Thanks for dinner. I'm glad we made a truce. And thank you for the inappropriate compliment. I would appreciate it if you don't say it again, but for tonight, it was nice to hear."

She offered me her hand, and I took it.

She held my gaze for the longest time. I leaned down and kissed her cheek.

"Good night, friend."

She sighed and then turned to put the key in the door as I walked backward down her steps from the front porch toward my car.

I heard her laughing as she shut the door.

She wanted me to play by her rules.

And that was just fine.

Because I knew what I wanted, and I wasn't backing down.

CHAPTER NINE

Montana

"Oh boy, look who stopped by to say hi," Violet said over a fit of laughter. "Clifford Wellhung is staring at us like he wants to make an appointment."

I looked up from where I was signing a few contracts for upcoming weddings, and I laughed at the sight of Clifford, the local brown moose who cruised through town like he owned the place.

Clifford was what everyone in town called him, but "Clifford Wellhung" was the name that Violet called him.

Because she was crude.

Because Clifford was definitely rocking a set of balls that were impossible to miss.

He'd been around for years, and if you didn't mess with him, he wouldn't mess with you.

He stared in our window for a few seconds before he turned and walked toward the courtyard across the street, where he often lay beneath the large oak tree.

The views from our business were my favorite. I could see the water in the distance, and the mountains behind it. It calmed me in a way, and I'd been feeling much better lately.

I don't know if it was the fact that I had a new sexy friend whom I was either running into or talking to via text every night.

I'd never had a friendship like this.

We talked. We flirted. We fought. We laughed.

Rinse and repeat and do it all again the next day.

And I actually looked forward to it. Even if I was ridiculously busy this week planning this wedding, Myles St. James had somehow become my favorite part of the day.

I'd never admit that to anyone else, but it was the truth.

I hadn't heard from him today, which was not the norm, and I was trying not to let it bother me.

It didn't matter.

I had things to do anyway. It was a typical busy Friday.

"Speaking of well-hung men . . . ," Violet said, just as the door chimed.

"Well, well, well, if it isn't my three favorite frauds," Myles said as he crossed his arms over his chest and his eyes found mine. I felt a burst of butterflies in my stomach, but I tried hard to act unaffected.

His dark hair was cut short on the sides and a little longer on the top. He wore a white fitted tee, dark jeans, and a pair of brown boots. He'd grown comfortable here in Blushing, and I tried to remind myself that he wasn't staying.

"Well, well, well, if it isn't our favorite billionaire," Violet said.

"Is it normal for that moose to hang out by your window?" he asked, and I couldn't help but laugh because the look on his face was hilarious.

"Have you never seen Clifford before?" I asked.

"You've named him? I've seen that fucker hanging out in the center of town, and I stay out of his way. I didn't know he had a name." He ran a hand over his jaw, and the way it felt when he'd buried his face between my legs flooded my memories.

Did it just get hot in here?

"Yes, his name is Clifford," Blakely said as she turned to put a few files in the cabinet. "Monny actually named him years ago, and the name stuck with everyone in town."

"Is it his real name, or is this his alias?" he asked, his attention on me, and I didn't miss the way Violet and Blakely were looking between us as if they'd noticed.

"It's his real name. Clifford Wellhung, actually. He's a Scorpio, and he enjoys long walks on the beach and square dancing with the ladies on Saturday nights." I smirked.

He smiled, that dimple on full display. And when Myles St. James smiled, it did something to me. I worked hard to act unaffected around this man, but it was becoming more challenging with each passing day.

"Good to know. I'll have to hit him up to meet me for a drink sometime." His gaze locked with mine. "You got a minute? I wanted to run something by you."

"Sure. We can go to my office," I said, handing the file with the contract to Violet as she raised a brow.

I led him down the hallway and into my office, then shut the door behind us. Myles took the seat across from my desk. He glanced around. "It's so . . . girly in here."

"I like to call it French—it's romantic and chic. I made a vision board of this office long before I went into business for myself."

"What the fuck is a vision board?"

"It's a place to dream, Myles. To be creative and think about what you want."

"And it goes on a board?" he asked, like this was the most outrageous thing he'd ever heard.

"What? Don't billionaires make vision boards on Saturday nights for a fun family activity?" I teased as I pointed to the wall to the left that held three of my favorite vision boards. They were covered in magazine clippings of everything that I loved and wanted for my life.

"Yeah." He rubbed his neck. "The St. Jameses aren't big on arts and crafts. Not really our thing, but I think it's cool."

He pushed to his feet and walked to the wall that held the boards and studied them, one at a time. "You like to paint and read. You clearly like the water, and you enjoy shopping because you've got a lot of boats and shoes and purses on here."

I chuckled. "Yes. All my favorite things."

"You've got a large piano in the center of this board," he said, pointing to the one in the center. "That's sort of what I wanted to talk to you about."

"The piano on my vision board?"

"No. The piano at Seaside. Would you like to have it?"

"Would I like to have it? Are you selling it?"

"No. It's old, and it's not for sale. But Charlie and I were talking about demo next week, and I remembered you mentioning that you learned to play on that particular piano. I thought you might want to keep it. You know, as a memory from your childhood."

I stared at him for the longest time. "I can't let you give it to me, but I could buy it from you. I just assumed you'd sell it to an antique dealer. I think it's worth a lot of money."

"It's not for sale, Montana. It's yours if you want it." He cleared his throat.

"You're pretty good at this friendship thing, you know that?"

He pushed to his feet. "Don't get ahead of yourself. I still think about that pussy of yours daily, so I'm not that good at the friendship thing."

I groaned. "You're ridiculous."

"I've got to get back to work. I'll let him know that you want it."

"I'm not sure how I'll get it moved, but I'll call around and see if I can find someone," I said, pushing to my feet and following him to the door.

"Don't worry about it. I'll have it delivered to your house for you."

Before I could stop myself, I lunged at him. I wrapped my arms around his neck and hugged him. "Thank you for thinking of me. It means a lot to me that you're letting me keep it. It'll mean a lot to my dad too."

When I pulled back, his features were softer than usual. "Yeah, well, I'm heading back to the inn to give your father shit about making vision boards on Saturday nights."

"Don't knock it till you try it, Moneybags. You like building things. You might just surprise yourself."

He walked out toward the front office and turned around to look at me one last time. "Maybe you'll have to show me how it's done."

"Oh, she'll be happy to show you how it's done," Violet said, taking his words completely out of context, and I gaped at her.

"I'm going to hold her to it, then." He winked and stepped out of the office.

And we all three stood there in silence for a few seconds.

"Holy fucking hotness. That man makes Clifford Wellhung seem like he has no swagger."

Blakely reached for a few Skittles from the candy jar that always sat on her desk and popped them in her mouth. "He sure does. And what did he do to you in the office? Your cheeks are pink, and you look a little sweaty."

"Stop. It was business."

"Business regarding your vajabbies diagnosis?" Violet asked as she walked around the desk.

"I've been so much better lately. I no longer suffer from the vajabbies, but thanks for the reminder." I reached for a few Skittles.

"That's because you've probably been getting a good workout from your vibrator with your new bestie hanging around you all the time."

"Vi, let it go. He'll be gone as quickly as he came."

"That's what she said," Blakely shouted, and we all erupted in laughter. Just then the door chimed, pulling our attention to the woman standing in the doorway.

Susannah stood there with swollen eyes and tears streaming down her face, which looked unusually orange.

"Hi, Susannah. Is everything okay?" I asked, trying to hide the panic from my voice and making an effort to appear relaxed and not alarmed by her appearance.

"Look at me. It's the night before my wedding, and I have a zit in the center of my forehead," she said, pointing to her forehead. Violet and Blakely tucked their lips between their teeth, because clearly no one wanted to tell her that the zit was the least of her worries.

"It's all right. Don't worry at all. This stuff happens all the time. Come to my office—I've got just what you need." This had always been my area of expertise. Violet was a little more rough around the edges when it came to handling sensitive situations. Her strengths were negotiating contracts, marketing the business, and running the books.

I was all about the details.

Susannah followed me back to my office, and I motioned for her to sit in the pink velvet chair across from me. Blakely followed us inside, handing us each a bottle of sparkling water and setting down a small plate of cookies before hurrying out.

Getting married should be an experience.

The Blushing Bride always tried to provide that.

From happy moments to meltdowns, which always arrived somewhere between thirty-six hours and three hours before the ceremony.

So, we were right on time, coming in around twenty-eight hours until we'd be gathering at the Seaside Inn.

"You have your rehearsal dinner tonight, right?"

"Yes," she said, and the word broke on a sob. "And look at me. Jesse just sent me over the edge when I went to ask him if my zit was noticeable."

"What did he say?" I asked as I pushed the cookie plate toward her, and she reached for an oatmeal raisin and took a bite.

"He said that the pimple wasn't noticeable." She sniffed and swiped at her eyes.

I moved around my desk, grabbed the box of tissue, and took the seat beside her.

"He's right. It's barely noticeable. I can give you some ointment, and we'll get it dried up, and then it will be easy to cover with makeup by dinner tonight."

"But that wasn't all he said."

Was it typical for a groom to say the wrong thing the day before the wedding? Yes. It happened all the time.

"What did he say?"

"He asked if I was supposed to be orange!" she shouted in outrage before turning to me and breaking out in a fit of hysterics. "Am I orange?"

I sighed. I always told my brides to avoid spray tans the day before the wedding, but most of the time they ignored the tip and did it anyway. This wasn't unheard of.

"You look beautiful, but I think this spray was probably set a little too dark for your fair skin. But we can tone it right down and have you good to go by dinner tonight."

"Really?" she asked. "Damn, Brit told me she'd practiced with the new tanning gun she'd just bought for her business. But it did feel like it went on awfully thick."

Brit Hansen had recently opened a mobile spray-tan company, called the Spray & Stay. She ran the whole thing right out of her peach-colored VW Bus, and she traveled to her clients' homes with bronzing guns a-blazing. She'd caused me more stress on wedding days these last few months than feuding families of the bride and groom and unexpected food allergies from wedding guests.

"I've got everything you need, and it will just tone everything down a bit." I pushed to my feet, walked to the large antique cabinet that held all my worldly wedding planner secrets, and pulled the doors open. Premade bags for this exact situation sat on the shelf, and I reached for the pimple cream that I kept in a basket beside it. I made my way back over to her and bent down to meet her gaze. "Here's what I want you to do. You're going to head home and get in the shower. There's an exfoliating glove and exfoliator in this bag, and I want you to scrub down your entire body and face under hot water. Once you get out and dry off, you'll put this cream on that pimple, and it will dry it right up. It's a miracle worker."

She sniffed a few more times. "How will I know if I'm the right color?"

"Because I'll be over to your house in thirty minutes. I just need to stop by Blushing Blooms and check on the arrangements with

Charlotte. I'll meet you at your place, and we'll make sure you're looking perfect for tonight."

"Thank you." She pushed to her feet and hugged me tight. "I don't know what I'd do without you."

Well, you'd most likely be walking down the aisle the wrong shade of neon orange.

"You'd be the most beautiful bride in the world regardless. Now get going and stay under that hot water and scrub yourself down for several minutes. I'll see you soon."

"Thank you. Hey, I do have something else I wanted to talk to you about," she said.

"Sure. What is it?"

"I wanted to check with you and make sure you were okay about seeing Phillip and Angel at the wedding tomorrow."

I'd rather take a sharp stick to the eye.

"Of course I am. He's Jesse's best man; I knew he'd be there." I cleared my throat, dreading that I'd have to be face to face with him and his supermodel fiancée tomorrow while I'd be working the event. "We ended on friendly terms."

"Okay, that's good to know. I met Angel, and for the record, the man traded down. There's not a lot going on upstairs," she said, tapping her temple as she chuckled.

"Well, that's sweet of you to say, but I wish them nothing but the best," I forced myself to say before I led her out of my office.

Always the professional when it comes to my weddings.

She waved at the girls before making her way out the door.

"The Spray & Stay is going to be the death of us at this rate," Violet said over her laughter. "Perhaps she should have done some research when she switched professions."

"Well, she wasn't the best dental hygienist either," Blakely said. "Remember I had to use eye drops for days when she blasted me in the eye with that water gun? I think Brit has found her calling as a spray tanner; she just needs to learn how to adjust the strength."

We were all laughing now.

"I'm going to stop by the flower shop and then head over to make sure she's scrubbed enough layers off her body." I chuckled.

"I'll walk with you. I'm heading to the inn to check on the tent setup." Violet grabbed her purse and followed me outside.

It was almost game time, and we were both in work mode now.

Exactly the way I liked it.

CHAPTER TEN

Myles

I stepped out my front door the following day, already agitated that I'd been guilted into flying home for my parents' anniversary party tomorrow night. I'd tried making up an excuse that I was buried in work, and of course my father had reminded me that he and Samuel saved lives for a living and they were able to make it. I believe his exact words were, *"Some of us have patients who actually depend on us to continue living, yet we are going to be there. You can take a break from chasing your unfulfilled childhood LEGO-building dreams for one evening and show up for your family."*

If I had a nickel for every time the man threw my love for LEGOs in my face, I'd be a very rich man.

Well, I already am a very rich man, so fuck Dad and his snide comments.

I came to a stop when I noticed an unusually freaky creature standing on my porch, staring at me.

What the actual fuck is with this town?

I'd already had to deal with that giant fucking moose with balls the size of King Kong's walking around downtown like he was window-shopping; there'd also been a black bear on my back porch yesterday, and I swear the dude had winked at me before taking off for the trees. And now this odd-as-fuck thing that I was fairly certain was some sort of white porcupine was in a standoff with me.

My phone vibrated in my hand, and I cautiously put it to my ear when I saw it was Montana.

"Will Hall is here at the inn with me, and he said he was supposed to meet you about some supplies you'd had him look into," she said.

This was how it was every day. We'd speak for different reasons throughout the day about absolutely nothing most of the time.

"Listen to me carefully," I whispered. "There's a weird fucking rodent squaring his shoulders like he wants to take me out on my front porch."

Laughter filled my ears. "What does this weird rodent look like?"

"Montana. I'm not fucking around," I snarled as the animal moved closer, and I backed up until I was touching the door with my shoulders. "I think it wants to fight. It's white and prickly, looks like some kind of porcupine. He's looking me straight in the eye like a fucking mob boss. This dude is not backing down. Fuck."

"Take it down a notch, Moneybags." She chuckled. "That's Porky. He's my favorite."

Of course he is.

"Well, fucking Porky looks like he wants to bite me in the shin." I squared my shoulders and growled at him.

"You did not just growl. Myles. Stop. He's super sweet. Bend down and get lower."

"Fuck no. This thing will stab the shit out of me."

"Just trust me."

"My mother told me I should never trust a diamond dealer."

"And my good senses have told me never to trust a man who destroys historical real estate, but here we are," she said. "We're friends, remember? I'd never let you get hurt. Just bend down, and then say his name. Watch what his quills do."

"This is fucking madness. I don't even know what the hell I'm doing here," I griped before bending down and doing what she suggested.

"Are you down low?" she asked.

"Yep."

"Say his name."

Fuck me.

Fuck Blushing, Alaska.

Fuck my father, just for the sake of throwing him in there any chance I got.

"Porky," I grunted, and I'll be damned if the little dude's quills didn't go down instantly.

"Okay, he doesn't look pissed anymore," I whispered into the phone. "His quills are down."

"Yes. He flattened them for you. He wants you to stroke his back. He's super friendly and affectionate."

"For fuck's sake. First, I practically have to take a number to see you at your office because a well-endowed moose is standing on the sidewalk, and now I'm giving a porcupine a goddamn massage?"

"Welcome to Blushing, Moneybags. Give him a little love, and then get over here. I told Will to wait in the inn's office because I have a wedding to throw in two hours. So you best put some pep in your step."

"You sound a little amped up," I teased as I ran my hand over Porky's back and then pushed to stand.

"I'm in my type A, overachiever mode. I'm like a wedding ninja. A woman with only one focus. Prepare to be dazzled."

I rolled my eyes and carefully moved past the chunky little fucker as I made my way down the porch steps toward the inn.

"I can't wait," I said, oozing sarcasm, just as I heard someone shout her name, and she said she had to go and ended the call.

Montana Kingsley has become the most fascinating woman I've ever met.

I was looking forward to seeing her in her element. Her father had bragged on her when I'd been over there yesterday sampling more of his meals. The guy could hold his own with any chef I'd ever worked with back home.

Not only had Blushing, Alaska, proved to be a diamond in the rough, but so were a few of the people who lived here.

I turned the corner and walked the short distance to the inn, noting the commotion of people hustling in and out. Chairs were being carted inside, and three men stepped in front of me carrying boxes of floral arrangements.

Violet came around the corner with a can of hair spray and a box of Band-Aids in her hands.

"Hey," I said as she strode up the walkway with me.

"Have you seen our girl yet?" she asked.

Our girl.

"No. Just got here. Seems like a madhouse."

"You have no idea." She chuckled. "But thank you for offering her that piano, Myles. It means more than you know."

I knew it would, but I don't know why I care so much.

"Yeah, it's not a problem. I know she's attached to the place." We made our way into the entry, and I looked out through the glass doors to see Montana setting floral arrangements on each table as people moved around her like they were on a mission. "You think she'll be all right that this is the last wedding here for a while?"

She adjusted the bud in her ear, and it was the first time I noticed she was wearing some sort of headset. I'd attended plenty of weddings in my day, but I'd had no idea just how much went on behind the scenes until I'd watched this all go down over the last few days.

"Yeah. She'll be okay." She shrugged. "I think seeing her ex here with his new fiancée tonight will bring a bit more drama than we normally have at a wedding, but you know Monny—she'll play it off like she's fine and do her job."

"That prick is going to be here?" I asked. She hadn't mentioned it, and seeing as we spoke daily, that surprised me.

"'That prick' is the best man in this wedding. He'll be impossible to miss."

"Fuck him."

"My sentiments exactly." She winked as she spoke into the microphone resting at her chin. "I'm here, girl. Be right out."

I sighed. "Have a good wedding. I'm going to meet a guy in the back about some supplies."

She held her hand up and waved, and before I walked off, I stood there watching Montana outside a little longer. I liked to watch her when she didn't know I was there. Her intensity when she was working was something I related to. I could see the passion written on her face.

Her head tipped back with a laugh as she fixed the way the napkins were sitting on the plates, and Blakely threw her hands in the air like she knew Montana would be adjusting them.

She took pride in her work.

It was impossible to miss.

"There you are." Howard's voice pulled me from my daze. "You've got Will Hall waiting for you in the office."

"Thanks. I thought you were moving today."

"We did. But Lydia and I will be attending the wedding, so I came back a little early to see if Montana and Violet needed any help."

"That was nice of you," I said, clapping him on the shoulder. "Hey, I had a quick question for you."

"Hit me with it."

"There's a really intricate mural painted in the office on the back wall. It looks like you brought in some famous artist to do it. What's the story with that?" I'd noticed it a few times, and I'd been drawn to the detail.

He chuckled, and then he blinked a few times. "Montana painted that for me when she was home from college one summer."

My eyes widened. "Montana painted that mural? By freehand?"

"Yep. She spent hours doing it." He cleared his throat. "Lydia is a cancer survivor, but she went through a couple rough years, and I sank into a pretty dark place the summer my wife started chemo. But Montana came home that summer and found me sulking in the office, and she decided to force me to see the good. She wanted me to make one of her vision boards, and I refused. I was a bit of a stubborn ass back then, worrying about my wife night and day. She and Daniel kept this place going those first few months, and she spent hours every night painting those flowers and butterflies on the wall, because they're Lydia's favorite."

"Wow. I had no idea she was such a talented painter." I crossed my arms over my chest. "And I'm happy to see Lydia doing so well now."

"Yep. She's been cancer-free for two years, and we just take it one day at a time. And Montana has a huge heart, and there's nothing she won't do for the people she loves." He shook his head. "She took the sale of this place really hard, but what I keep trying to tell her is that it's not the inn that she'll miss. It's not the structure. She's attached to the memories that she made here. But those will live on whether or not this place is still standing. You can't buy someone's memories."

"Yep. That's the truth." I glanced up to see Will sitting in the office, staring out the window. "All right. I've left him waiting long enough. I'll see you when I'm done."

"I hope you're going to stick around for the wedding. Watch these girls work their magic. The whole town will be here."

"I'll stop by for sure." I held up my hand and made my way to the office.

"Hey, Will. Sorry I'm late. Thank you for waiting."

"Yeah, not a problem. I checked on the supplies you'd sent over, and we're good to go on everything."

"That's great news. Thank you for checking on that. I'll have my team get the orders placed immediately."

"Great. I'll be leading the crew next week for Charlie. He said you had some questions about salvaging a few pieces before we demo the place."

"Yep. There's a few things I'd like to keep if it's possible."

"Anything is possible if you're willing to pay for the time and manpower to do it."

"Well, money is no object when it comes to this, so let's walk the interior and I'll point them out to you."

We both moved to our feet. He had his iPad in hand to take photos, and we walked every inch of the inn.

After Will took off, I ducked into the kitchen when the guests started arriving. Music piped through the inn, and it appeared that everyone in town was coming out for this wedding.

"Hey, I didn't know you were still here," Montana said as she came walking into the kitchen. She reached for a carrot stick from one of the trays that had been offered to the guests when they'd first arrived.

"I'm here." I shrugged. "I thought I'd stick around and see you in action."

"Well, buckle up, Moneybags, because it's go time." She winked before speaking into her microphone. "I'm heading to the bride's suite to get the bridesmaids. You've got the groomsmen all lined up, Vi?"

And she turned and hurried out of the kitchen like she'd been shot out of a cannon.

Daniel chuckled as he moved to the oven, and the smell of garlic and butter wafted around the space. He had at least fifteen to twenty people working around him tonight; they'd need a lot of help getting this food out to the guests. It was impressive.

"She doesn't mess around," I said.

"Never. She takes her job very serious. Glad I taught my girl about having a work ethic."

I moved closer, keeping my voice low. "Let me ask you something, Daniel."

"Sure. What is it?"

"Violet mentioned that Montana's ex is going to be here with his fiancée tonight. Is that going to be a problem for her?"

His gaze filled with empathy. "You know, I don't really know. I never thought he was right for her back when they were together. She never seemed all that happy with the guy. I sure as hell never trusted him, and I thought he was up to something the last few months because he traveled all the time. But I'm sure that seeing him move on so fast has hurt her. But when it's Montana, she'll never let you know it."

"Why is that?"

"Because my daughter learned at a young age to guard her heart, unfortunately. She's tough, and she won't tell you if she's hurting even if she is. I probably did a shit job of teaching her that it's okay to tell someone you're sad or angry, but I've never been real good at it either. Montana likes to fix things, not the other way around."

I nodded. I understood it. "I think you've done a damn good job."

The music changed, and Daniel called out to Hank. "I'm going to go watch these kids get married. You hold down the fort?"

"Yes, sir. I've got it," his sous chef said.

"Come on, St. James. Let's go see my girl shine."

And I followed him out to the outdoor area, just in time to see Susannah walk down the aisle.

Montana was in full work mode, speaking quietly into her microphone at the end of the aisle, where she'd just sent the bride down.

I couldn't take my eyes off her. Her long dark hair was pulled back in a ponytail that swung down her back. She was wearing a floral sundress that hugged her curves on top with a flowy skirt that came down to her ankles. I noted the cowboy boots as she strode off to the side of the aisle, her eyes on Susannah.

My eyes on her.

But mine weren't the only eyes on her.

I looked up to see the man standing beside Jesse at the other end of the aisle.

The man she'd dated for years who was now engaged to another woman.

I didn't know if she was there, because if she was—he wasn't watching her.

His eyes weren't on his best friend, or the bride who'd just made her way down the aisle.

They were on the same woman I was watching.

My hands fisted at my side.

Protective and feral in a way I'd never experienced.

He must have felt it, because his head turned slowly, and his gaze locked with mine.

That's right, motherfucker. You're not the only one who wants her.

CHAPTER ELEVEN

Montana

Things had gone off without a hitch, unless you counted the fact that Susannah had snapped the heel on her shoe right after she walked back down the aisle with Jesse.

Luckily, we always kept unopened slippers nearby, and she was able to wear those while we repaired her heel with the E6000 glue I kept in my belt bag.

At the moment, the biggest issue was the maid of honor, Larsa, who was three sheets to Drunkville. Violet was trying to sober her up behind a tree, insisting she drink some water.

I'd enjoyed every minute of watching them say their vows at this particular location, because I knew all weddings moving forward would be different. It would be a new place, and a different vibe. I'd made peace with it.

I hadn't been bothered the few times I'd looked up to see Phillip watching me. Oddly enough, I'd been more flustered by the new owner of the inn, whose gaze had locked with mine multiple times during the ceremony.

Maybe it was because we'd formed a friendship.

Maybe it was because I still couldn't get the one night we'd spent together out of my mind. Even if we hadn't had intercourse, it was the most memorable sexual experience of my life to date.

It didn't matter, because for whatever reason, having him here comforted me in a way that I couldn't begin to explain.

The wedding party had been called over. I was standing on the perimeter of the tent, speaking to Violet in the mic, when I saw Phillip walking my way. Angel was beside him, and my shoulders tensed. I told Violet to hold off on appetizers until everyone had their first cocktail in hand and then turned my attention to the couple standing in front of me now.

"Hey, Montana. It's great to see you," Phillip said as he moved in for a hug, holding me a little longer than normal, which was very awkward with his fiancée standing there, staring at us.

"Hi, Phillip, it's nice to see you." I pulled back and turned toward the woman extending a hand. "You must be Angel. It's lovely to meet you."

"Nice to meet you, too, Montana. I've heard lots about you."

I sighed. I wasn't sure how to respond. "Thank you. Congrats on the engagement. It's very exciting."

I didn't feel sad. I didn't feel angry.

I just felt uncomfortable, if I was being honest.

Like when you walk in late to a party and everyone turns to look at you, and you just want to run out of the room.

That was how I felt.

I wanted to get away from them.

"Thank you. Did you hear how Phillip proposed?" she asked, and I startled at the question.

Why the hell would I want to know how he proposed?

Phillip appeared to find the question equally awkward, since he shot her a look that was impossible to miss.

It was one of those *What the fuck are you doing?* looks.

"Um, no. We haven't spoken, so I haven't heard anything." I cleared my throat.

"Well, let me tell you. This man remembered our first kiss last year on that very same day, and he took me to the exact place we'd been that night." She clapped her hands together and smiled as her gaze locked with mine.

Last year at this time, Phillip and I were very much together.

"Angel," he hissed, and the look she gave him caught me by surprise. This did not appear to be a couple who was happily engaged, at least not at the moment.

I was shifting on my heels, desperate to end this conversation, when a warm hand found my lower back. "Hey, baby. I've been looking for you."

Myles St. James showed up just when I needed him most.

"Hey," I said, turning in his arms. "I'm right here."

His hand moved to the side of my neck, and he leaned down and kissed me.

We're not talking about a casual peck on the lips; this was a full-on make-out session in front of my ex-boyfriend and the woman he'd clearly cheated on me with.

Tongue and all.

And I'm here for it.

When he pulled back, I just stared up at him with surprise.

"Yes, you are." His voice was deep and sexy.

"Um, er, and may I ask who this is?" Phillip asked, and his question pulled me from my daze.

"Of course you may." Myles chuckled and extended his hand. "I'm Montana's boyfriend, Myles St. James."

Phillip cleared his throat. "Oh, you hadn't mentioned that you were dating anyone."

"And who are you?" Myles asked, his hand finding mine as our fingers interlocked.

"I'm Phillip Moon. Montana's ex-boyfriend of many years."

Myles smirked and gave him a nod. "Ahhh . . . yes. Obviously, I knew she had an ex, but she's never mentioned your name, just that the split was amicable and she was happy to be moving forward. And I'm guessing she hasn't mentioned me because you two don't have reason to talk anymore, do you?"

Damn. He was so smooth.

"Correct," I said. "We haven't talked in months. And this guy keeps me pretty busy." I leaned my body into him as he wrapped his arms around me, and I rested his chin on my shoulder.

"Very busy, baby." He nipped at my earlobe, and I squealed.

Phillip's eyes were wide, and he looked stunned. Was it that hard for him to believe that I could have moved on as well?

Angel reached for a champagne flute when the server passed by with a tray, and she tipped her head back and drank the whole thing.

"All right, well, I need to get back to work. Enjoy the rest of the wedding," I said, but I refused to look at Phillip. I'd just found out that he'd been cheating on me when we were together, so I was not going to offer pleasantries or attempt to make this more comfortable for him.

I didn't want to be around him for one more second, and I reached for Myles's hand, hoping he'd take the hint and tug me away.

"Montana," Phillip said, just as we turned to walk in the other direction.

"Yes," I said, the word harsher than I meant it to come out, as I looked over my shoulder.

"I was hoping we could grab a coffee tomorrow and catch up," he said. "You know, for old times' sake. Just wanted to see how your dad is doing and fill you in on what's happening with me."

My gaze moved to his fiancée, who looked like she was ready to blow at any moment. Her face was bright red, arms folded across her chest, lips pursed.

But before I could answer, Myles kissed my forehead before speaking. "Phillip, I'm going to give you a little advice. Asking my woman out on a coffee date in front of your woman will not sit well with anyone. I suggest you make that your last mistake of the evening, and walk away from us right now."

Shots fired.

Phillip's eyes were wide before he took Angel's hand in his and walked away.

"The fucking balls on that asshole," Myles said against my ear. "You all right?"

I chuckled. "I am, actually. How did you know I needed you right then?"

"Violet had called me over to cause some interference just as we both overheard his fiancée explain the way that he'd proposed. Your best friend filled me in as to the fact that he'd clearly been cheating on you, and here I am."

"You're a real white knight, St. James." I sighed.

"I think the fact that he just tried to ask you out right in front of his fiancée says it all."

"I don't know about that. He knew I'd done the math and quickly figured out the timing of everything. He probably wants to explain." I shrugged.

"Hey." Violet came up behind me and kissed my cheek. "You okay?"

"I'm fine."

"I can't freaking stand that guy." She shook her head with disgust. "But listen, why don't you take off? Things are winding down. You don't need to see Phillip and Angel for another second. You've worked your magic, and the wedding was perfect. Blakely and I have got this."

I normally stayed until the end of an event, but she was right. It wasn't necessary for me to be there.

And I didn't want to be there any longer.

"All right. I'll take you up on that," I said, leaning forward and hugging her. She looked completely relieved that I'd actually agreed.

"Love you, Monny," she said, giving me the tightest squeeze.

"Love you too."

Myles caught me by surprise when he reached for my hand and led me out of the tent and through the yard. It was getting late, yet the sun was still out, because that's how we did it here in Blushing.

He came to a stop and dropped my hand before shoving his hands in his pockets. "I'm glad you're leaving. No sense sticking around to deal with that asshat. You're probably exhausted, huh?"

He shifted on his feet, gaze searching mine, and if I didn't know what a cocky bastard he was most of the time, I would've guessed that he was a little nervous.

I had no idea why.

"Actually, I'm not tired." I smiled up at him. "Are you tired?"

"Well, considering it feels like the middle of the day and not almost eight o'clock at night, I'm wide awake."

"Interesting." I chuckled. "Does that mean you want to hang out?"

He grinned. "Yeah, Honey Badger. I'd like to hang out."

"What do you have in mind?"

"We could go back to my place and take the boat out on the water. We could pretend to look at the stars, even if we may suffer blindness from making direct eye contact with the sun."

My head tipped back in laughter.

Myles St. James was the best distraction.

"Let's do it."

We stopped inside and said goodbye to my father, who was in the middle of the chaos. He gave me a quick hug goodbye before we turned and made our way outside.

We walked the short distance to Myles's house, and I wondered what I was doing by agreeing to go home with him.

We were friends. I enjoyed his company.

He made me laugh.

He made me mad.

He made me smile.

He made me frustrated.

But the truth was that I wasn't going home with him for any of those reasons. I hadn't forgotten our one night together. Hell, it was the last thing I thought about every night before I fell asleep.

And tonight, I wanted to feel something different. Something passionate.

I knew he wasn't staying in town forever. I knew it wouldn't go anywhere.

But look how things had turned out for me with Phillip. A man who'd grown up here. A man I'd known most of my life.

Maybe forever wasn't necessary anymore.

After all, everything was changing right now. The inn was being demolished, which meant my business was going through a lot of changes. My father was leaving a job that he'd been at my entire life. A year ago, I'd thought my whole future was mapped out, and literally so much had changed.

So maybe it was time for me to make some changes.

I wanted Myles St. James, and fighting it was exhausting.

I knew that I was playing with fire, but I couldn't seem to stop.

And that kiss a few minutes ago—it only added to the desire that was coursing through my veins.

We turned the corner and were making our way up the steps to his front porch when a movement had us both turning.

Myles startled. "Good Christ. That thing is still here?"

I laughed as I bent down, and he walked over to me. "Porky likes it here. He's clearly drawn to you."

Myles rolled his eyes and bent down on the porch beside me as we both stroked his back once his needles had flattened.

"Are you claiming we have a lot in common?" His voice was teasing, but I looked up to see his green eyes soften as he stroked the little guy.

"You're both a little prickly." I chuckled. "Sorry. Porcupine humor was a must. I couldn't help myself."

We pushed to stand, and Porky walked down the front porch to a bushy area on the side and disappeared into the lush landscape.

Once we were inside, we both washed our hands, and he moved to grab a bottle of wine. He led me out the back door and onto the dock, where we had the option of a motorboat or a canoe, and he told me to pick. I chose the canoe, because the idea of just floating out in the water right then sounded pretty nice.

The sky was finally starting to darken. This was always my favorite time of year, to catch those brief hours when the sun actually went down for the night.

Once we'd settled in the canoe, he used the oars to move us out to a quiet spot beneath some trees and dropped the oars inside the boat. He reached in his back pocket for a wine opener and shook it in front of me like he'd just done a magic trip.

"Very suave, Moneybags."

"What can I say? I'm a classy guy." He uncorked the bottle and handed it over to me to take the first swig.

I took a sip and handed it back to him. "You're going to watch the sky darken before your eyes."

"It's beautiful," he said as he took a pull from the bottle, but he wasn't looking up at the sky; his eyes were on me. "Was that tough for you tonight? Seeing your ex?"

I shook my head. "No. I don't feel anything for him anymore, but hearing the timeline, and the fact that he'd clearly kissed her a year ago, when we were still together—that really pisses me off."

He laughed. "Well, it's better to be mad than sad."

"I feel like I wasted a lot of time on him, you know? I wasn't all that happy, looking back, but I was loyal to him. And he was out there, going on dates and kissing other women." I shook my head and pointed up at the sky. "Here we go."

"I'm glad you left the wedding early. You shouldn't have to see them, or deal with it." He handed the bottle back to me.

"I was happy you showed up when you did."

"Yeah? He seemed pretty bothered, and I fucking loved it. You deserve better, Honey Badger."

"Thank you. I agree, actually. And that's my new motto: 'No settling.'"

"Good. You should never settle."

"Are you still planning to go home tomorrow?" I asked, because he'd mentioned it a few days ago, and he hadn't sounded thrilled about it.

"Yep. My parents' anniversary party. It'll be a lot of bullshit, and my father will make as many digs as he can get in over the few hours I'm with him. But I'll suck it up and do it." His eyes locked with mine, and I saw the sadness there.

"Is there anything I can do to help?"

"You want to help me, Montana?" He winked, and I squeezed my thighs together in response. The man was ridiculously sexy. Unfairly good looking.

"I do. You helped me tonight. You gave me a real mic drop moment. So how about you let me do the same for you. Name it, and I'll do it."

He sat forward and reached for the bottle. "Anything I want?"

"Well, within reason."

"Hmm . . ." He tapped his chin with his pointer finger. "A pre-home-visit blow job could be a nice way to relax."

I laughed and took another sip of wine. "Of course that's where you'd take it."

"Actually, as much as I would enjoy that, I think there's something that would be even better."

"Wow. Better than a blow job. Let's hear it."

"Come home with me." He tipped his head back to look at the darkening sky as if he hadn't just said something surprising.

"Come home with you? To New York?"

"Yep. I've got a plane. I fly out tomorrow. We'd be home Sunday night."

"Where would I stay?"

His gaze locked with mine, and he smirked. "I have a large apartment in the city. There's plenty of room for both of us."

"And what would I be required to do there?" I asked, my heart racing.

"Oh, for fuck's sake. I'm not hiring you to sleep with me." He laughed. "We'll go to New York, we'll eat good food, and you'll come to the world's most awkward dinner party that will be pretentious as fuck. You can pretend that you're crazy about me to distract my father and help me survive it."

"Myles St. James, are you asking me to pretend to be in love with you?"

"You can do whatever you want. I'd prefer to be distracted when I'm there. It'll make it easier."

"I thought you had ladies that you take out in the city. You don't have someone there that would like to go with you?"

"I have plenty of women I could ask, Montana." He took another pull from the bottle and then looked at me. "But I'm asking you. The woman I'd like to take with me."

"Fine. I'll be your doting girlfriend this weekend." I sighed. "And feel free to kiss me whenever you want. That was a fabulous kiss tonight."

He chuckled and put the cork back in the wine bottle and set it down on the floor of the canoe. "You liked that?"

"I did."

"Come here." His voice was gruff and commanding.

My eyes widened as I carefully maneuvered myself forward, and he tugged me onto his lap. I had one leg on each side as I straddled him. His hands were on my face, my neck, in my hair. "You're fucking gorgeous, Montana Kingsley. And you don't ever have to ask me if you want my lips on yours."

"What are you saying?" I teased. "I can kiss you anytime I want while you're here in Blushing?"

"Anytime you want."

I leaned forward, my mouth crashing into his.

Apparently, I wanted to kiss him right now.

CHAPTER TWELVE

Myles

We'd made out for so long on the canoe that I was certain my dick would need medical attention if we continued; it was hard as steel.

I'd carried her from the dock to my house.

I didn't know what the fuck I was doing, but I wanted this.

Wanted her.

Once we were inside, I set her on the kitchen counter and stepped back. "Fuck. What are you doing to me?"

Her gaze searched mine. "Does this mean you like kissing me as much as I like kissing you?"

I moved forward, taking her hand in mine and placing it over my throbbing erection. "Yeah. I definitely like kissing you. And that's saying a lot, because I've never been big on kissing. I usually get right down to business."

It was the truth.

But something was different with this girl.

Even from our first night, I'd been cautious with her.

Knowing immediately just how special she was.

"Maybe you like the fact that we're friends," she said as I moved to stand between her legs. "Friends who occasionally make out."

I nodded. I was fairly certain that wasn't the case. But I wouldn't say that, because I didn't want to scare her off by telling her how attracted to her I was.

"Sure. I think it should be our new friendship rule: 'We make out whenever we want to.'"

"I can get on board with that," she whispered as her fingers moved along the scruff of my jaw. "You're only here for a few more weeks, right?"

She was so focused on the timeline. I wasn't wired that way. But that was probably because I wasn't a guy who looked for long-term relationships. So, how long I was staying had never been a factor. I traveled a lot. It wasn't an issue for me.

"Correct." I nipped at her bottom lip.

"I should probably get going—we've got a flight to catch in the morning." Her gaze searched mine, and I saw the conflict there.

She wanted this.

But she was scared.

And all it did was make me want to comfort her.

"Don't go." I buried my face in her neck before pulling back. "No sex, I promise. Just stay with me. And I'll take you home in the morning to pack a bag. It'll be practice for our trip."

She smiled as she thought it over. "Friends have sleepovers. And I did sleep really well the one night I spent here."

"Because I gave you multiple orgasms, so you were relaxed."

"Good point. But we weren't friends then," she said. "You thought I was a diamond dealer from Chicago. We know more now."

I scooped her up, and her legs wrapped around my waist. "We definitely know more now."

I carried her down the hall to my room. She asked to borrow a tee and walked to the bathroom. When she came back, her hair was falling around her shoulders, and her small frame was drowning beneath my white cotton shirt. I didn't miss the way her hard peaks poked through the fabric, and I tried not to stare.

I'd been with women who wore ridiculously sexy lingerie, yet Montana Kingsley wearing my oversize shirt was the sexiest thing I'd ever seen.

She jogged over to the bed, and I chuckled as I made my way to the bathroom. I brushed my teeth and took off my clothes, stripping down to my black boxer briefs. I gripped the counter of the vanity and stared in the mirror.

What the fuck are you doing?

I flipped off the lights, made my way to the room, and slid into the bed beside her. Her body heat was impossible to miss, and I tugged her closer.

"You're a little hot tamale," I teased.

"Well, this bed is pretty cozy," she whispered. "Thank you for having my back tonight, Myles."

"I've got you." I wrapped my arms around her as her cheek settled against my chest.

"I know you do. And it means a lot to me."

Those words hit me hard. I wasn't used to my actions meaning anything to the people in my life. Sure, I loved my family, particularly my mother and my brother. I worked hard and was proud of the business I'd continued to build.

But this girl, she was big on the feelings. And hurting her wasn't an option.

So I kissed the top of her head and hugged her tighter.

And I let sleep take us both.

"It's such a bougie way to travel," Montana said early the next morning. "Wow. No worrying about your luggage being lost. No worrying about security finding a water bottle in your carry-on and getting tasered and dragged to airport prison." She held up her phone and took a selfie of us on the plane, just before we took off. "Vi and Blakely are going to die that I'm on this plane right now."

I chuckled as Whitney, our flight attendant, came by to let us know she'd be bringing breakfast as soon as we were up in the air.

"Do you get taken to airport prison often?" I raised a brow as Walker, our private pilot, came over the speaker and told us to prepare for takeoff. Montana turned her phone off and tucked it in her purse.

"Well, no. But you know, they're always shouting in that line. Reminding you that if you have a water bottle, or you don't pull out your laptop—there will be serious consequences."

I laughed. "Whitney won't be giving you any consequences. We've got a seven-hour flight, and you can relax."

"Did you always have money? Growing up I mean?"

I nodded. "Yep. Both of my parents came from very affluent families, and financially I wanted for nothing. But keep in mind, that doesn't mean that life is perfect."

"Well, I get that. But I imagine it's easier to deal with the hardships of life when you're not wondering where your next meal is coming from." Her voice was teasing, but I also didn't miss the way her gaze locked with mine.

"Did you worry about your next meal when you were growing up?" I didn't hide the concern from my voice. Thinking of a young Montana stressing over money at a young age didn't sit well with me.

"Oh, no. I feel very fortunate for the life I've had. But my father and I lived paycheck to paycheck most of my childhood; however, with him being a chef, he could make fabulous meals on a shoestring budget. We didn't go on fancy vacations or anything, but we always had fun. We'd play cards and board games and go out on the water in the kayak. We'd paint and read and just hang out together, you know? My childhood was a magical one."

Wow. Not many people can say that. Me included.

"That's pretty cool. I don't think my family has ever played a board game. We've played tennis and golf, and we get ridiculously competitive. My mom, Samuel, and I would watch movies together occasionally. But we had a large staff, and my brother and I spent a lot of time together."

"You and Samuel are close?"

"Very. My brother is the best. We've always been close. But he's been working hard since we were young, chasing this approval from my father. It's an exhausting task, but he's finally made it."

"He's a surgeon?"

"He is. And a brilliant one. Though I question if he's actually happy with the choices he's made. He and I discuss other options for him often." I paused when Whitney set our coffees down in front of us, along with a basket of muffins and a fruit platter.

"'Other options'?"

"Yes. He's working crazy hours, and after being so driven for so long to get here, I think he's questioning if it was worth it. If this is the life he actually wants. I'd just like him to know that he has options. I'm proud of him regardless of what he chooses."

"You're a good brother, Myles. I'm sure he's very proud of you."

"I actually think he is. He encouraged me to drop out of medical school when I'd shared how miserable I was. My brother is the reason I can't fully give up on my family. He desperately wants us to be united." It was the truth. I was more than ready to dip out from the madness many times, but Samuel would join our dad in pushing hard for these constant reunions of sorts. Holidays, anniversaries, birthdays, funerals.

"He wants your family to stay close," she said, tearing off a piece of the muffin and popping it in her mouth. "It seems doable, right?"

I chuckled at the honesty of the question.

"My father is a narcissist. He's judgmental, which is annoying enough, but then his actions are never held up to a mirror. And that is a hard pill for me to swallow."

"I get that. It's sort of like people who live in glass houses and continue to throw stones." She shrugged, and I had the sudden urge to kiss her. I'd slept with her in my arms for a second time, and I'd liked it. And here we were on this small plane, and I was taking her home with me.

We weren't dating.

We'd never had sex.

I wasn't even sure what the fuck this was.

Yet, I want her here.

"Yes. And everyone allows him to get away with it. Because he's brilliant and rich and people fear him a little bit."

"Do you fear him?"

"I think I did as a kid. Feared what would happen if I made my own decisions. But it's deeper than that."

"How so?" she asked, completely invested in the conversation. I ran my hand over the back of my neck. I didn't like sharing this much.

"I don't know. And this is a very boring conversation. Let's talk about that asshole ex of yours."

Her gaze narrowed. "Don't do that."

"Do what?"

"Jump out of the conversation the minute it goes deep. Tell me something that he did to stop you from making your own decisions. We're friends—you can trust me." Her words were so earnest they caught me off guard.

"Friends who make out." I chuckled. "Listen, no one wants to hear about the rich dude's baggage. I've had a good life. I'm not going to sit here and complain."

"Myles, just because you have money doesn't mean that your father can't be an asshole. Now tell me something, because I shared my horror story about my mother with you."

I rolled my eyes and took a sip of my coffee. "All right. When I was thirteen years old, I came home early from school because I was sick. My mom was away on a vacation with her sister, and Daniel, our driver back then, picked me up. I got home and went to my room to lie down, but I found my father there instead. He was in my bedroom with our housekeeper, Wendy. The man missed sporting events and graduations because he was so fucking important in the medical world, but here he was on a random Tuesday, fucking the housekeeper in my bed."

"You're serious?" Her mouth gaped open, and I shrugged.

"I told you we shouldn't talk about it."

"Just because it's shocking doesn't mean we shouldn't talk about it. I told you that my mother told my father he could put me up for adoption when I was four years old." She sighed. "But yes, him having an affair and you witnessing it had to be traumatic. Was he horrified that you'd caught him?"

"That's a hard no, HB." I cleared my throat at the memory. "It was the first of many, actually. I'm fairly certain Wendy's son, Caleb, is my half brother. She lives in the guesthouse on our property, and he was raised there. Like this is a perfectly normal thing to do. Keep your mistress living on the property and working at your home. This is the kind of shit I'm talking about."

"What did they do when you caught them?" she asked, completely innocent to the twisted narcissist that is my father.

"Um, they continued doing it in that moment. He shouted at me to get out of the room. He then came out after and told me if I mentioned it to my mother, I would be very sorry."

"What? What does that even mean?"

"Over the years, I learned that he was referencing a very hefty inheritance, which had very little to do with him, since it came from grandparents on both sides. But he was protecting himself, because if my mother were to have left him, it would have been a costly divorce. So he made sure I knew that somehow I'd suffer if I told. He also said I'd be responsible for destroying our family, which was clearly already destroyed, though I didn't understand all that at the time."

"You were just a kid. So what did you do?" she asked, moving closer and reaching for my hand.

"I caught them a few more times, because apparently once I was aware, it was impossible to miss. And he continued to threaten me. The weight of lying to my mother was a heavy one, and for years I struggled with what to do." I cleared my throat, unsure why I was even telling her all of this. "And I told her on my sixteenth birthday. I couldn't hold it in anymore. It was a huge relief once I actually said the words. Once I stopped carrying his secret."

"What happened?" she whispered.

"She wasn't surprised. She knew about it. She said that no marriage was perfect, and she cried because she knew the toll that keeping that secret must have had on me. My mother is an amazing woman, and I just don't know why she'd settle for it, you know?"

The next thing I knew, she was unbuckling her seat belt and pushing up the armrest between us before climbing onto my lap and wrapping her arms around my neck.

"I'm sorry, Myles. That was a shitty thing to go through." She pulled back. "And living in a mansion and having private planes and all the things that money can buy doesn't change that."

There was a goddamn tear coming down her cheek.

She was taking on my pain.

Pain that I didn't even feel anymore. Maybe I'd been sad when I was a kid, but now all that sadness had turned into anger.

As an adult who'd gone through a few good years of therapy, the one thing that had surprised me was my pursuit of going to medical school. It hadn't been something I'd dreamed of or even been drawn to. But my disdain for my father was complicated. And for a long time, I still craved his approval, which was why I had taken that path originally. But the day I walked away from medicine was a turning point for me and my father. I no longer cared what he thought of me, nor did I seek his approval. In fact, I welcomed his disappointment most of the time. And he couldn't stand that. So in turn, he became meaner. Angrier. More hostile every time we were together. And I felt nothing for him at this point in my life.

I used the pad of my thumb to swipe away her tear and shook my head. "Don't apologize for something you didn't do."

"I'm glad I'm coming with you. If there's anything that I can do to make things better, you just say the word."

"Is making the mile-high club an option?" I asked. She pinched me on the shoulder before sliding back onto her seat.

"I'm serious, Myles."

"I am too." I winked and her cheeks pinked. "We're already friends who make out. Why not up the stakes? We can be friends who have sex in airplane bathrooms?"

Truth be told, I'd be willing to spend a whole week with my father if it meant I could spend twenty minutes in the airplane bathroom with Montana Kingsley.

CHAPTER THIRTEEN

Montana

We'd arrived in New York a few hours ago, and a car waited on the runway for us. Myles St. James sure knew how to travel in style. I'd been flustered the entire flight because the man teased me relentlessly about joining the mile-high club.

I'd always laughed at the concept. I had a memory of a flight that Phillip and I were on a year and a half ago, when we flew to Hawaii for a wedding for one of his fraternity brothers. He'd gone on and on about how his friend Carl had made the mile-high club with his then fiancée. Phillip thought it was ludicrous to cram into the small space with your partner. He'd made the comment that he would be more content with just himself and his hand.

I should've been offended.

But the truth was, I had no desire to cram into a small space with Phillip Moon as he panted in my ear and chased his own pleasure.

In that moment, I remember thinking that my middle seat in coach and my bag of nuts were way more appealing.

But I'd be willing to cram into a small space and stand barefoot on a floor covered in up-facing nails if it meant I could have sex with Myles St. James.

That's how attracted to him I was.

And it also terrified me, because I liked him.

I liked him a lot.

Every time I thought about him leaving Blushing, my chest squeezed.

I was getting attached to a man whom I'd probably see once a year, when he popped into our small town to check on his gargantuan hotel.

I pushed the thought away as I applied eye shadow to my lids. He'd given me my own room at his stunning penthouse apartment in the middle of Manhattan, but he'd followed the offer by telling me he liked sleeping with me last night, and he'd be pleased if I slept in his bed again.

No strings attached.

But my internal heartstrings were attaching like jellyfish tentacles to a human foot.

All needy and desperate.

I sighed before putting on a coat of mascara. I was meeting Myles's family tonight, and he'd basically prepared me for the worst possible experience one could conjure up.

I took one last look in the mirror and ran my hands down my black cocktail dress, turning to see the way it hugged my ass perfectly. I slipped on a pair of red Manolo Blahniks, my big splurge when the Blushing Bride was mentioned in *Cosmopolitan* magazine last year.

My hair fell in loose waves over my shoulders, and I slipped on a few gold bracelets and grabbed my gold sparkly clutch before stepping out of the guest bedroom.

There was classical music playing in the living room, and Myles stood behind the bar as his eyes scanned me from head to toe. I didn't squirm or call him out, because I liked it.

I liked when his eyes were on me.

And they usually were when we were in the same room.

"Wow. You look stunning."

"Thank you. You don't look too bad yourself, Moneybags." I sauntered over to the bar and took the glass of chardonnay that he held out for me. He wore a black suit with a black dress shirt, and he looked like he belonged on the cover of a magazine.

The views from his apartment were magnificent.

I moved to stand in front of the floor-to-ceiling windows that lined the wall in his living room, taking in all the people moving quickly up and down the street below. Cars honked, and a siren blasted in the distance.

"It's different here, huh?" he asked as he stood beside me and sipped his wine.

"Yeah. You're definitely not going to run into a moose or a porcupine."

He laughed. "Yeah. It's high energy, and there's always shit going on around you."

"Do you like living in the city?" I asked him, putting the glass to my lips and then groaning as the fruity flavors flooded my senses.

"I do most of the time. It's all I know, though, because I grew up here. But I'm not going to lie—I've enjoyed being away. I haven't missed it, which has surprised me. I get a lot of work done in Blushing because it's always fucking daytime, so my inner achiever enjoys the longer hours." He chuckled.

"Yep. All of my weddings take place during the summer months, and during the winter, wedding season is pretty slow."

"You don't say? People don't want to get hitched when it's pitch black outside?"

"Nope. But that's when I find new ideas and focus on the marketing and all the business stuff that I can't deal with when we're busy."

"That makes sense." His phone vibrated, and he glanced at it. "All right, the car is downstairs. Let's go."

The drive to the restaurant was brief, and Myles reminded me several times not to be offended by his father.

"Relax. I'm fine. I'm here to support you. Don't worry about me."

The look he gave me had my chest squeezing.

I do worry about you.

Once we arrived, Myles hurried out of the car and opened my door. His parents had rented out a super-swanky restaurant in the city, and they were having all their closest friends join them in this celebration.

When we stepped inside, I gasped. Crystal chandeliers hung above throughout the grand space. The lighting was dim and romantic, and there were white floral arrangements on every table. There had to be over a hundred people here, and I guess I hadn't expected this intimate dinner to be this large.

Jazz music piped through the surround sound, and candles were lit on every table.

Myles's hand found mine as our fingers interlocked. I smiled up at him, and he winked.

The man had more swagger than any one person should be allowed.

"Myles, it's about fucking time." A man who resembled him pulled him in for a hug before turning to me. "Hey, you must be Montana. I'm Samuel, this guy's brother."

I was surprised he knew I was coming, as it was a very last-minute trip.

I reached for his hand and shook. "It's lovely to meet you, Samuel. I've heard lots about you."

He raised a brow, pausing when a server came over with a tray covered in champagne flutes, and he helped himself to a glass as Myles took one for each of us.

"Wow. Talking about the family, is he? Lucky for me, I'm his favorite." Samuel chuckled. "I've heard a lot about you as well. You started your own business, and you're dominating the wedding industry in Alaska, from what I've heard."

Myles had told his brother about me?

My heart raced at the fact that Myles had even mentioned my existence.

"He's being a bit generous. I'm only in Blushing. But thank you." I sipped my champagne, and this definitely wasn't the kind of cheap bubbly that I once threw up from in college when Violet and I drank a whole bottle on our own. This was delicious.

"Where is Brianna?" Myles asked.

"She's, er, not coming tonight. Long story. I'll fill you in later."

Myles had told me that his brother had a longtime girlfriend, and they were ridiculously in love. I was surprised that she wasn't here.

"I hope she's all right." Myles paused and studied his brother, who made it clear he wasn't going to say more at this time. "How's it going here so far?"

"I mean, it's a celebration, right?" Samuel smirked. "Dad invited Wendy and Caleb, and Mom seems fine with it. She invited Gino, so I guess that's payback."

Myles turned to look at me, keeping his voice low. "Gino is my mother's trainer, and Samuel insists they are having a . . ." He paused and waited for his brother to chime in.

"They're having an 'emotional affair.' They're together every day, but my mother is too much of a rule follower to do anything about it while she's married." Samuel sighed and shook his head.

My eyes widened, but I tried to act unaffected, which made them both laugh.

"You're wondering why they would throw an elaborate anniversary party, and then bring their own dates?" Samuel asked over his laughter.

I shrugged as if it didn't matter. "Hey. Not my place to judge. I'm just happy to be here."

Samuel studied me before turning to his brother. "Shall we get this part over with?"

Myles kept his hand in mine as we made our way through the elaborate space. He paused and introduced me to several people, bragging about my wedding planner business and singing my praises.

It was a bit ridiculous.

I was a small-town wedding planner. It wasn't that I thought the Blushing Bride wasn't fabulous, but I certainly wasn't known outside of Blushing, Alaska. This man was a freaking real estate tycoon all over the country. His father and brother were brain surgeons.

Nevertheless, he was making an effort to make me feel comfortable, and it was sweet. Because I'd come here to support him.

He'd saved me last night during a very uncomfortable situation with Phillip, and I wanted to offer him the same in return.

His grip tightened around my hand as we approached a man and a woman who were staring at us. Samuel strode up beside us, and I assumed he was sticking close to his brother for moral support.

"Look who made it," the man said. He was tall, but Myles had about an inch on him. His salt-and-pepper hair worked for him, giving him that stately, handsome appearance. "I figured you'd be off playing with LEGOs and miss the party."

"Ignore your father," the gorgeous woman beside him said. I assumed she was his mother. She had the same green eyes as Myles, and her dark hair was pulled back into a sleek chignon. She wore a peach-covered satin gown that flowed to the floor. "He just likes to give you a hard time. I'm Myles's and Samuel's mother, Sophia. You must be Montana. You're absolutely stunning."

She startled me when she pulled me in for a hug.

"It's so lovely to meet you. Thank you for letting me join in on the celebration."

She squeezed my hands and smiled before stepping back.

"Montana, is it?" Myles's father turned his attention to me, and there was something very condescending in his gaze. I immediately stiffened as he sneered in my direction. "That's an interesting name. I'm Dr. Winston St. James."

I nodded, taking his hand briefly and giving it a curt shake.

This man was giving off *devil in an Armani suit* vibes.

"Nice to meet you, Dr. St. James."

"So, Montana," Sophia said, "my son tells me you have this booming wedding business. I can only imagine how fun it must be to plan the most special day in the lives of your clients for a living." She sipped her champagne. "I wish my boys would consider walking down the aisle. I'd like to have some grandkids one day."

Samuel smiled. "I'm working on it."

Myles rolled his eyes, but it was Winston who caught my attention.

"Kids aren't easy," he said. "You give them every opportunity, you offer them the best education, and they still throw it all away."

Wow. Myles wasn't kidding. I assumed that since it was a party, the topic wouldn't come up. But he'd barely waited five minutes before he'd sunk his teeth into his son.

"Nice segue, Dad." Myles cleared his throat. "I do have a degree, and I do use it daily. Just because I'm not staring inside someone's skull does not mean I'm not doing good work."

"It absolutely means that. How is building a hotel in some hokey little town with ignorant, uneducated fools and a population of a hundred doing good work?"

No. He. Didn't.

I was fine biting my lip most of the time. But this was not one of those times.

Sophia hissed at her husband just as the words left my mouth.

"Obviously you've never been to Blushing, because we have a population of nine thousand two hundred and seventy-seven people who live there. The majority of the kids who have grown up there do go away for college, but they return because they love the people and the beauty that surrounds us. I've never had anyone refer to the people that live there as 'ignorant' or 'uneducated,' so I'm not quite sure where you're doing your research, but you might want to do some fact-checking before you make a statement like that."

Samuel laughed, and Myles stepped closer to me, wrapping an arm around my shoulder, almost as if he was attempting to shield me.

But I didn't need shielding from this small-minded asshole.

His words didn't hurt me. They angered me.

And my chest squeezed at the thought of Myles growing up with this man.

"Are you fucking drunk?" Myles snarled. "How dare you insult my date. Pull your shit together, Dad. People are watching."

"Your date? Well, buckle up, Myles, because Gigi Wellington is making her way over here, and I think she thought she'd be your date this evening."

"Why the fuck is Gigi here?" Myles spewed, glancing over his shoulder and making no effort to hide his irritation.

"I just found out that your father invited her a few minutes ago," Sophia said, giving her son an apologetic look.

"I can run interference with Gigi," Samuel said, clapping Myles on the shoulder. "She's a gold-digging narcissist, so you definitely owe me one."

Myles didn't take his eyes from his father. "You're an asshole."

"Yes. We've established that many times." He smirked. "Ahhh . . . here she is. Gigi, so nice of you to join us tonight."

I turned to see a tall blond woman wearing a red body-hugging dress with cutouts everywhere I looked. There was very little left to the imagination, but she had a rocking body, and she owned it. Her breasts were barely contained, and she moved toward Myles as his arm left my shoulder and he gave her a quick hug.

"I was hoping you'd be here," she purred, and I just stared at her, waiting to be acknowledged, as he placed his arm around my waist and tugged me close.

"I was not expecting to see you here, Gigi."

"Well, your father called this morning, and he said you'd be here and that he was certain you'd want to see me."

I wasn't sure what the hell was going on, but it was definitely awkward.

I had no claim over Myles St. James, but this woman was coming on strong, and it was pissing me off that she wouldn't acknowledge me as I stood beside him.

. "Gigi Wellington, this is Montana Kingsley," Myles said, taking my hand in his and smiling at me.

I extended my free hand, and she sneered at me. "Montana? That's your name? Someone actually put that on a birth certificate?"

Montana was actually not an uncommon name. Her name was less common than mine.

Glass houses, Gigi.

"Yes. Someone did put it on my birth certificate. My mother actually chose it before she ran off and abandoned me to be with her new family." I tilted my head to the side and chuckled. "But I'm okay, because I've got the hottest date in the room on my arm. Don't you agree, Gigi?"

A wide grin spread across Samuel's face, and Winston and Gigi both gaped at me. Sophia just smiled as if we were discussing the weather.

But it was Myles who caught me by surprise. He was looking down at me with so much adoration it nearly took my breath away.

"I don't know about that, Honey Badger. I'm certain that I have the hottest date in the room."

And then he leaned down and did the most unexpected thing.

He kissed me.

CHAPTER FOURTEEN

Myles

This was quite possibly the best time I'd ever had at a family event.

Even my father couldn't get under my skin, because I was too enamored with my date.

She'd been completely unaffected by my father or Gigi.

And here I was slow dancing with her, where I'd normally be brooding over an old-fashioned . . . or fourteen.

"How are you so good at this?" she asked, tipping her head back to look at me.

"I've been attending black-tie events since I was in kindergarten. I can cut a rug on command. How about you? Have you spent a lot of time dancing with moose and porcupines?"

She rolled her eyes, but her lips turned up in the corners as a wide smile spread across her face. "I'm a wedding planner. I can't very well help my clients if I don't know everything about weddings. So I took dance lessons. I could probably hold my own in a ballroom dancing competition. I had Bella, my amazing hair girl, teach me how to fix a fallen braid or attach some loose extensions. I know how to fix broken heels, broken nails, and broken hearts."

"You're the fucking CEO of romance, aren't you?" I chuckled.

"The 'CEO of romance.' That's the best title ever."

"Thanks for being here tonight. You're making this tolerable, and I'm grateful." My hand found the side of her cheek, my thumb stroking her jaw.

"You made last night tolerable, and I'm grateful."

"And you handled my father and Gigi like they were a mild inconvenience."

"And that surprises you?" she asked, her hips swaying with mine as I moved one hand down to the small of her back.

Wanting her closer.

Needing her closer.

"Yes. My father and Gigi probably eat kittens for breakfast without blinking an eye."

"Yet you dated her, right?" she asked.

"I wouldn't call what we did 'dating.' We're old family friends, and we've attended some events together over the years, among other things."

"Ahhh . . . 'among other things.' So you've had sex with her," she said as her tongue swiped out and ran along her bottom lip. It wasn't a question; it was more of a statement.

"I have, yes. But it's been over six months since anything's happened between us. She wanted more, and I wasn't interested in pursuing a relationship with her, so I cut things off. I'd always been honest about what I had to offer. And that was a sign that we weren't on the same page."

"I told you, 'sex' and 'casual' don't always go together." She chuckled. "And she doesn't seem over it."

"How can you tell?"

"Because she keeps looking at me like she wants to scratch my eyes out," she said. "She has no idea who she's messing with. I could totally take her."

Now it was my turn to bellow out in laughter. Had I ever laughed this much?

"I wouldn't let her put a hand on you," I said, leaning down close to her ear. "The only hands I want on you are mine."

I could feel her heart pounding against my chest.

I wanted her so bad I didn't know how to handle it.

She pulled back and looked up at me. "Sometimes I want your hands on me too."

I didn't see that coming. Pun intended.

"All you have to do is ask," I said.

"Good to know."

We were interrupted when the music stopped and Samuel came to get us. Our mother wanted the photographer to take a family photo.

We did this at every event.

We had years of photos of the four of us, dressed to the nines and looking like the perfect family.

It was all a facade. But my mother enjoyed it, so for her, I wouldn't say no.

Some of the guests were leaving; others were indulging in their cocktails and eating dessert. I led Montana across the room, to an area where they'd set up a backdrop for photos. Her hand was in mine, and Samuel groaned as we got closer.

"I hate taking these bullshit photos," he said.

"You and me both, but Mom likes them, so it's the least we can do. She's married to an asshole. Let her have the goddamn photos."

Samuel and Montana both chuckled.

"Fine."

"Where's Gigi? I thought you were handling that situation."

"Um . . . did you want to give me a heads-up that she comes on a bit strong?" My brother glared at me.

"I thought that was kind of obvious. You've known her since we were teenagers."

"Dude." He turned to Montana. "And woman."

"'Dude and woman'?" I said over my laughter.

"Yeah. She's not a dude, she's a woman. Anyway, Gigi grabbed my package under the table. And it wasn't gentle. It was—fucking terrifying. She also knows I'm in a very serious relationship. The woman has no boundaries."

I shook my head with disbelief. "Jesus. The woman is out of control. What did you do?"

"I grabbed her wrist and stopped her. This is my parents' anniversary party, for God's sakes, not to mention that she's obsessed with my brother, and I'm in love with my girlfriend, even if she's not speaking to me at the moment."

I was worried about Samuel and Brianna. She was good for him. She loved him to his core. But she wanted him to be around more, and he worked ridiculous hours. It wasn't very conducive for the life of a family man. My father being the perfect example of that.

Montana used her hand to cover her mouth to quiet her laughter. "What did you tell her?"

"I called a car for her and told her to go home. I wasn't looking to be a pawn in her sick, twisted game."

"Speaking of sick and twisted, please turn around and take a look at this," I said, keeping my voice low.

My father was deep in conversation with Wendy and Caleb, his other family that no one spoke of. He'd invited them to his anniversary party, because he was a twisted bastard. I didn't expect to see Caleb here.

My mother was walking our way with her trainer beside her. "Boys, you remember Gino?"

"Yes, Mom. He's been training you at our family home since we were in middle school. It's safe to say that we remember him," I said with a laugh as I shook his hand. "Gino, this is my date, Montana Kingsley."

Gino shook her hand and said hello. He couldn't be more opposite to my father. He was kind and gentle, and he genuinely seemed to care for my mother.

The photographer stepped toward us and asked if we were ready, and I didn't miss the way his eyes traveled down Montana's body. He made no attempt to hide his blatant perusal.

Hell, every guy in the room had noticed her. I was a man who paid attention, and I wasn't oblivious to the fact that I had the most beautiful woman in the room on my arm.

Normally I didn't give a shit.

But with Montana, I gave all the shits.

I narrowed my gaze at the photographer.

Back the fuck off, asshole.

He nodded as my father strode into the room with Caleb beside him.

Samuel and I were convinced he was our half brother, since he looked like us and he also put up with my father, so we figured he knew the truth. We'd always just been told that Wendy had a long-distance boyfriend. But I saw the expression on Caleb's face when he looked at my father.

This desperate need for approval.

Hell, I related to it. At least I had at one point in my life.

"Look who just showed up to pick up his mom." My father laughed this boisterous sound that irritated the fuck out of me. "Apparently Wendy has had too much to drink tonight. She's been indulging a bit too much."

"I wonder why," I said, my voice completely flat.

My father glared at me, and I puffed my chest up because I loved getting under his skin. But a sharp pain hit me when I noted the way Caleb tensed at my words.

That was his mother.

I was being a dick.

"Caleb, are you looking forward to starting school?" I asked, because he was leaving for college soon. I actually liked the kid.

"I'm ready to go, Myles. I'm hoping you were serious about that summer internship you mentioned for next summer. I'd really like to come work with you."

"Pfft," my father huffed. "You want to play construction now too?"

Caleb's eyes widened, and he swallowed. "Um. Yeah. I think what Myles does is pretty cool."

"I do too," Montana said. "You should see the drawings for the hotel he's building in Blushing. It's really something."

"Oh man, I'd love to come see it as it gets built," Caleb said.

"I thought you were going to take the premed path," my father said.

"Um, no. I don't like science all that much. I'm actually looking into being an architect."

My father stared at me. Anger flared, and I just smiled.

He turned to Gino and handed him his empty glass with a few ice cubes left in it. "I'll take a whiskey on the rocks."

Gino narrowed his gaze. "I'm a trainer, not a bartender."

"But you're on my payroll, are you not?" He shook his glass in front of him, and Gino took it. "And we're about to take family photos, so you have no business being back here."

"Oh, Winston. Can we just have a good night, please?" my mother said, and I couldn't wait to get the hell out of there.

"I'll see you later. I'm going to get my mom home." Caleb held a hand up, and my father completely ignored him as he turned to speak to the photographer.

Montana looked up at me, and I knew what she was thinking.

"Hey, Caleb," I said as he turned back around to look at me. "If you want me to fly you out in a few months to see the hotel as it goes up, I'd be happy to show you."

"Really? I'd love to go to Alaska. I'd appreciate it, Myles."

I nodded, and my brother smirked at me.

"Caleb, I'd invite you into surgery, but it's not nearly as cool as building a hotel in Blushing," Samuel said.

"I agree. And surgery makes me queasy." Caleb chuckled. "Thanks, guys. I'll see you soon."

We spent the next twenty-five painful minutes taking photos. My brother insisted that Montana and I take a few photos together, and I didn't even fight it.

I wanted to remember this night.

I'd wanted to kiss her in the car on our drive home. I'd wanted to kiss her when we returned to my apartment.

But I was putting the ball in her court.

When we got home, I let her know that I was going to take a shower, and she informed me that she wanted to take a bath.

She didn't offer it up as an invitation, so I didn't push it.

I wasn't sure if she would go to bed after, or if she'd come out when she was done.

I'd never been this in my head about a woman before.

I was wound fucking tight.

I wrapped my hand around my dick and stroked it a few times as my forehead rested against the wall.

Relief. I just needed some fucking relief.

I hadn't had sex in a while, and I was fucking frustrated.

I closed my eyes, and I could feel her lips against mine.

A knock on the door pulled me from my thoughts, and I dropped my hard-as-steel cock from my grip. I opened the glass door to make sure I wasn't hearing things.

"Hello?"

"Myles?"

"Yes."

"Can I come in?"

"Of course," I said, my head still poking out of the shower door as she stepped inside wearing nothing but a white towel that was pinched in place between her perfect tits.

"Hey," she said as she moved closer. Her eyes scanned down my body through the glass and zeroed in on my dick before snapping back up to meet my gaze. "I wanted to talk to you."

"Interesting timing." I ran a hand down my face to push the water away. "What's up?"

"I've had sex with two men in my life, and both were uneventful. Both were serious relationships that went nowhere. So, I'm thinking it's time to mix things up."

My dick hardened at her words. "'Mix things up'?"

"Yes. I know you're leaving in a few weeks, but so what. Maybe we just do this one time, and never speak of it. Maybe we do it over and over until you leave because we like it. No strings. No expectations. Just two people who have fun together."

"You want to have sex?" I asked, surprised by her words. "You think that's a good idea?"

"I actually think it's a great idea. I know who you are, and I'm not going to try to change you. But I'm attracted to you, and I want to be with you." Her cheeks pinked, which was fucking adorable.

Montana rarely showed me her vulnerable side. She was putting herself out there.

I wanted this too. I'd been clear about what I had to offer.

She was agreeing. So why was my chest pounding? Why was I second-guessing myself?

I shook it off. My desire for this woman was not something I'd ever experienced.

I wanted her. She wanted me. That was all that mattered.

"I want to be with you too. How about you join me in the shower?" My voice was gruff.

She sucked in a breath and walked toward me. "Okay. We're doing this."

I pushed the door open, and I reached for where her towel was gathered and tugged at it.

It fell to the ground in a heap, and I just took her in.

Scanning every stunning inch of her.

Fucking gorgeous.

My mouth watered at the sight.

I offered her a hand, and she stepped inside. Her hair was tied up in a knot on top of her head, and she was makeup-free.

"I may not be a forever guy, but I know how to make a woman feel good. And I'm going to make you feel so good, you won't even remember the names of those two selfish fuckers you were with before," I whispered against her ear.

Her hands were on my shoulders before moving to my hair. She tugged me down, and my mouth crashed into hers. My dick throbbed between us as hot water pounded at my back. I pulled away, water droplets running down her neck and chest, and I dropped to my knees, burying my face at the apex of her thighs before spreading her legs farther apart. "I'm going to make you come on my lips, and then my cock."

Her breaths were coming hard and fast as her fingers tangled in my hair. "I'm good with that."

Her words were breathy and needy.

My hands gripped her peach-shaped ass as my tongue swiped along her slit. I sucked and licked, teasing and taunting her.

And then I dipped in, sliding in and out, slowly at first.

Her little noises were pure ecstasy, and I'd never wanted to please a woman more.

She ground against my face, desperate for release. I took her right to the edge before pulling back, over and over. It was the hottest thing I'd ever experienced.

"Myles, please," she begged.

I glanced up and nearly came at the sight of her.

Her eyes were wild with need, lips parted, cheeks flushed.

My thumb moved to her clit as my tongue drove in and out of her.

Faster.

Needier.

Her hands tugged at my hair as her thighs tightened around me.

I moved my mouth to her clit and sucked hard, just as I slipped a finger inside her.

And then another.

Working them in and out as I licked and sucked and took her right over the edge.

My name left her lips on a cry.

I stayed right there as she rode out every last bit of pleasure.

And damn if it wasn't the sexiest thing I'd ever seen.

CHAPTER FIFTEEN

Montana

I was wrapped in a towel and lying on Myles's bed before I'd even come down from the world's greatest orgasm. I'd never experienced a shower orgasm, and I was here to say that they were my new favorite thing.

This sexy, naked man down on his knees and giving me the best orgasm of my life.

Um, yes, please.

I'd attempted to return the favor, but he'd stopped me. He said that he couldn't wait another second to be inside me.

Has anyone ever made me feel so wanted?

I pushed up on my elbows as he reached in the nightstand for a condom, and a wicked grin spread across his face. "You're so fucking sexy."

"So are you."

And he was. He stood there completely bare, golden skin glistening, and his dick was hard and long and thick. He covered himself in the latex and then used his finger and thumb to flick my towel open. He just stared down at me like he wanted to memorize every single inch of me.

I will not make this more than it is. We are just two friends having a good time.

No strings.

No expectations.

No romanticizing.

Sex. I wanted sex. I wanted to feel something. Do something just for me. Something that I wanted.

Something that probably wasn't very responsible or wise—but it would feel amazing, and I'd deal with the consequences later.

His fingers moved gently down my cheek, and then my neck, before tweaking my nipples and causing me to gasp.

"You have perfect tits, do you know that?" His tongue followed the path of his fingers as he licked my neck and nipped at my ear.

"Thank you. I've never thought that they were all that noteworthy," I whispered, and he chuckled against my skin before lifting his head to look at me.

"I get off to your tits all the time. All the fucking time. Hell, I was just about to get off to you when you knocked on the door."

My eyes widened. "Really?"

"Really. You literally caught me with my dick in my hand." His fingers trailed down my body as his gaze locked with mine. He stopped between my legs. "Jesus. You're already so wet again."

"I was thinking about you too," I admitted, shocking myself as the words left my mouth.

"Yeah? Do you get off to me, too, Montana?"

I nodded, feeling my cheeks blaze. "Yes."

"Tell me what I'm doing to you when you touch yourself?" he asked as a finger slipped inside me, and a whoosh of air left my lungs.

"I think about kissing you. About touching you. About you touching me."

He smiled as he slipped another finger inside. "Have you been thinking about it since the first night I touched you?"

My back arched as he pumped in and out of me, his thumb flicking my clit.

"Yes," I groaned.

"Tell me what you want."

"I want you inside me now." My voice did not waver, and I wasn't even embarrassed about it. I'd been thinking about having sex with this man for weeks. Months, actually. I was done waiting. Done being teased.

Before I could even process what was happening, he was beneath me and pulling me on top of him, one leg falling on each side of him as I straddled his hips. His erection was standing straight up between us, and I ground up against it.

"Fuuuuccckkk. I want you to take control. Set the pace. Use my cock any way you want to, beautiful."

My God. He had a filthy mouth.

And I'm here for it.

I pushed up, adjusting myself just above his tip, as my teeth sank into my bottom lip, and I slowly slid down.

I gasped as I took him in. He was large and thick, and I paused to let my body adjust to the intrusion.

"Hey." His gruff voice pulled me from my thoughts. I looked down at those sage green eyes. "Breathe, beautiful. There's no rush."

I hadn't even realized I was holding my breath as I released the air from my lungs. I moved down another inch.

Slow.

Steady.

Breathing with each movement, my gaze never leaving his.

"Look at you taking me all the way in, beautiful. Gripping me like a fucking vise." His words were strained as he watched me.

I shifted once more and groaned as I took him all the way in, and I stayed perfectly still as I adjusted to him.

His hands reached for my face and pulled me down as he kissed me hard. Our lips locked, our bodies joined, and I started to move.

Over and over as we found our rhythm.

I'd never been so lost in the moment. So lost in a man. He kissed me until my lips ached.

My body tingled, and I arched my back as my hands settled on the tops of his thighs.

I moved faster.

Myles leaned forward, and his lips covered my breast. Moving from one to the other.

The sensation so overwhelming I groaned.

As if he knew just what I needed, his hand moved between us, and he found my clit.

Rubbing little circles as my entire body started to shake.

Lights exploded behind my eyelids, and I cried out his name as the most intense orgasm ripped through my body.

I looked down to find his eyes trained on me.

He thrust into me once.

Twice.

And a guttural sound left his throat.

My name a desperate plea on his lips.

We rode out every last bit of pleasure, his arms wrapped around me, keeping me close.

I buried my face in his neck as he fell back against the mattress, taking me with him.

Our breaths the only audible sound in the room.

When our breathing finally slowed, the room grew quiet.

He pushed the hair back from my face as I looked at him.

"What was that?" I whispered.

"That was fucking amazing," he said as he rolled us onto our sides before pulling out and moving to his feet. He walked to the bathroom, and I assumed he was getting rid of the condom.

When he slipped back into bed, he pulled me against him.

I wouldn't have guessed Myles St. James to be a cuddler.

But this man was full of surprises.

Violet: Your boyfriend doesn't mess around. They must have 25 guys working at the Seaside Inn again today. This structure will be built before we know it.

Blakely: She's going to insist he's not her boyfriend. Three. Two. One.

Me: He's not my boyfriend.

Me: Jinx.

Blakely: I knew it.

Me: He's not my boyfriend. He's leaving in a few weeks. It's a fling. But might I say, I have been missing out on this whole fling thing. It's the best relationship I've ever had—because it isn't going anywhere. LOL.

Violet: Oh yes. It's a fling that you insisted was a one and done in New York. It's been three weeks since you've returned and you're with the guy every night.

Me: Turns out I like sex with no strings attached. We've agreed to hang out until he leaves. That's it. It's over. Squashed. Donezo. Nada.

Blakely: And you don't think that will be tough for you? You spend an awful lot of time together.

Violet: Agreed. You didn't spend this much time with Phillip the dickhead and you dated him for years.

Me: In an exciting turn of events, I've learned that Phillip wasn't good in the sack. I always thought that I just didn't like sex all that much. But apparently, I was just with the wrong guy. Apparently, Phillip was the problem.

Violet: Of course he was. And speaking of dickheads . . . has Phillip reached out again?

Blakely: The nerve of this guy. He's engaged, and he's texting his ex-girlfriend. I wonder what Devil would think of that.

Me: Her name is Angel, and I doubt she'd be happy about it. He hasn't messaged again, but I didn't respond to the first two texts that he sent, so maybe he's realized I don't want to talk to him.

Violet: Oh my. Look who's here . . . <screenshot of Clifford Wellhung staring in the window of the Blushing Bride>

Me: I guess he walked through the jobsite yesterday at the inn and everyone had to take a break because he just decided to lay down and hang out for 20 minutes. Charlie didn't know what to do so he had everyone pause until Clifford moseyed on.

Violet: Charlie is so grumpy. He's always scowling. Obviously he's hot at the same time. And I'm not going to lie, it's kind of sexy that he raises a kid on his own.

Me: He's a great dad.

Blakely: He is really grumpy though. I find him kind of intimidating.

Violet: Moody guys don't intimidate me. I'm sure he's good in the sack, all grumpy and irritated. He's probably very dominant in the bedroom.

Me: That was a lot of information. Are we interested in Charlie?

Violet: Hells to the no. Just pointing out the obvious. He's not my type. I'm not a fan of small children and we all know that I prefer to be in charge, so I don't need a man who wants to be in control.

Blakely: Because you want to be in control?

Violet: Damn straight. I like to call the shots in and out of the bedroom. 😄

Me: TMI. I've got to go. Moneybags is taking me somewhere and won't tell me where. He just pulled up at my house.

Violet: This might be the weirdest fling of all time. You see him every day. He drops off lunch randomly when he knows you're working long hours. He's sent you flowers twice. He's flown you to a family event. He's taken you to his office in New York to show you off to his coworkers. And now he's taking you to a surprise location. I've got news for you, bestie . . . nothing about this is casual.

Blakely: Agreed. And also, I need to find me a billionaire and have a fling.

Me: We're just enjoying the time we have together and then we'll go our separate ways. For all I know, he might be ending things tonight. He was very cryptic in his text.

It had been three weeks since our night together in New York, and we'd been together every day since. I knew the lines were blurring for me, but I was giving this gift to myself. I'd never been happier, and I wasn't going to spoil it by focusing on the fact that it would be ending soon.

My new life mantra is: Live in the moment.

Don't think about tomorrow. Or next week.

I knew it would hurt like hell when he left, but I'd deal with it then. I'd always had the ability to rebound and pull myself up by the bootstraps.

Once I slipped into his car, he drove a few blocks away from town to one of my favorite areas on the river.

"You're being awfully quiet," I said, and I didn't miss the tic in his jaw.

He was tense. Maybe even nervous.

Myles St. James doesn't get nervous.

Oh God. Was this really it? Was he tired of this arrangement and taking me somewhere private to break it to me gently?

I knew there was the possibility that things would end before he left town.

The man didn't do relationships. He'd been honest about that. Yet we spent every night together. Of course he was over it.

This was too much for him.

This is definitely too much for him.

He cleared his throat. "I want to talk to you about something, and I'm not sure how you're going to react."

"You know that I'm not oblivious to how this all ends, right? You don't have to drive me out to the middle of nowhere and do a formal breakup." I shrugged. "It's a fling, Myles. I'm not going to fall apart because you're ready to move on. I've been preparing for it all along."

He pulled in front of the Murphy Ranch, which had been abandoned for years. It was one of the most beautiful pieces of property in Blushing. But it had been tied up in probate for years—a family inheritance dispute that had left this gorgeous home empty.

"You're serious?" he said as he put the car in park. He turned to look at me. "You think I drove you out here to tell you that I don't want to see you anymore?"

"Listen, this is all new for you. And you've really embraced the whole 'ongoing fling' thing well. And honestly, it's surpassed my expectations. But I know it's got an expiration date, and I'm not going to fall apart if it ends before you leave. I'm sure this is overwhelming for you."

"I'm not overwhelmed, Montana. I told you that I wanted to see you until I head back to New York. I didn't just make that up. If I didn't want to see you anymore, I would be honest with you," he said. "I don't do what I don't want to do, Montana. We have a few more weeks together, and I plan to fuck you every which way I can for twenty-one more days. I'm not leaving you just yet, Honey Badger. Even though you seem convinced that I'm going to call this done every other day."

So maybe I'd expected him to end it a week ago, when he'd set out a very romantic picnic on the boat for me.

Or the day we'd returned from New York, when he'd invited me over for dinner.

I was a girl who'd had the rug pulled out from beneath her feet a few times before. I didn't want to be caught off guard.

This was why I used a gratitude journal and vision boards. It was an effort to stop myself from expecting people to let me down.

"Fine. This isn't doomsday. I'm just letting you know that when that day comes, I'm going to be fine."

"So you keep telling me. Now get your ass out of the car so I can show you something."

"This place is abandoned. We could get arrested for trespassing."

"Just get out of the damn car, woman."

He came around to the passenger side of his rented Tesla just as I pushed my door open. "Why do you seem so nervous, then?"

He huffed out a breath and whipped around, and my chest slammed into his. "Maybe because this is new for me. Has that ever dawned on you?"

My eyes widened. "What's new for you? A fling that lasts a few weeks?"

"I see you every single day. You're in my bed every single night. It's a bit more than a fucking fling, yeah?"

Why is he so angry? He's the one who made the rules. I just agreed to them.

"Fine. I misspoke. It's a relationship that ends in three weeks. When you move away, and we don't see one another anymore."

He shook his head and cursed under his breath. "Can you just stop analyzing it, and let me give you a goddamn surprise?"

"You're so touchy today." I chuckled and then tried to catch up to him as he stormed toward the old farmhouse.

"You don't make surprising you very easy." He paused when we walked up the few steps to the front porch. "Now close your eyes and prepare to be dazzled."

I squeezed my eyes shut. "Fine. Dazzle me, Moneybags."

He took my hand and walked me forward a few steps. "Open your eyes."

CHAPTER SIXTEEN

Myles

This was not the norm for me. I didn't do romantic gestures.

I based business decisions on the bottom line.

Always.

But when this opportunity came up, I didn't hesitate. I knew that this would solve all of Montana's business issues while they waited for the hotel to be built, as well as give her the opportunity to invest further in her business and herself.

Maybe it was seeing the way my father had cut Caleb down.

Hell, he'd cut Samuel and me down the same way, more times than I could count.

Maybe I didn't want to be anything like him.

Or maybe it was just that I saw something in her. Something special.

I'd taken her by my office when we were in New York, and I was surprised how interested she was in what I did. I showed her a few projects we were working on, and she was fascinated. She met my assistant, Connor, who of course made it a big fucking deal that I'd brought a woman to my place of work.

It was a first.

All of these things were firsts for me.

It didn't change anything. This had obviously just turned into an extended fling—but at the end of the day, I didn't live here, and she did. So there was no sense wondering if it could go anywhere.

We had two completely different lives.

We were just enjoying our time together while our paths crossed.

I stared at her, waiting for her to open her eyes. "Did you hear me? You can open now."

"Well, now I'm nervous. What if you're a kidnapper and you've brought me here to be your sex slave?" She smiled. "It's the perfect setup. A mile out of town. An abandoned old house where no one would look for me. Are there ties and whips?"

"For fuck's sake," I said, reaching for her wrists and pulling her hands away.

She opened her eyes and glanced around. "How did you even get in here?"

"I've got my ways."

"It's been abandoned for a very long time. But I'm shocked that it's so clean and well kept."

"It wasn't. It was a fucking disaster. I had it cleaned up before I showed it to you."

"You had it cleaned up? Why?"

"Well, that's what I wanted to talk to you about. It's on a pretty magnificent piece of property. It has decent bones and wouldn't take a ton of work to get it open for business."

She shook her head, as if she was confused. "'Open for business'? What do you mean?"

"I bought it. Charlie said he could get a small crew out here and get it renovated in a couple weeks. I thought it might be the perfect location for you to throw your events. It's on a huge piece of land, so there's a ton of potential."

She blinked up at me as if she wasn't processing what I was saying. "I would throw events here?"

"You'd be a partner and make it your own. Your dad could run his catering business out of the kitchen, and you would be a partial owner."

"I don't understand. I can't afford this place."

"Correct. But I can. And you would make monthly payments that you could afford, and you'd have a stake in the place."

"Myles." Her eyes watered and she swallowed. I moved closer and put my hand beneath her chin.

"What? You don't like it?"

"This place had to cost a few million dollars. How can I have a stake in a place like this? I don't have that kind of money."

"I do this for a living, remember? I know what I'm doing. I want to invest in you. In your business. Obviously not in the Blushing Bride, because you've built that on your own. But in this venue, which you could make your own, I'd like to invest in that. In you."

"So, Violet and I would make payments every month to have a stake in the property?" Her voice shook.

"Yes. The Blushing Bride would be a partner in this property. I'd put the financial investment up, and you could do whatever you want with the place. You could turn it into a boutique hotel, or just use it for events. The land on its own is valuable, so we can do whatever we want with it."

We.

That was a foreign concept for me.

Sure, I'd invested in friends before, but this was definitely different. I wanted her to have this. Wanted her to achieve her dreams.

"I don't know what to say."

"All you need to say is that you want to do it," I said with a chuckle.

She flung herself into my arms and hugged me. "I used to come out here when I was a teenager. I'd ride my bike on the trail that led down to the river in front of the Murphy Ranch. There's an actual beach down by the water, with all these gorgeous trees. I used to sit down there and write in my journal. It's so peaceful and beautiful. How did you even pull this off? I heard they were locked up in a court battle."

"They were. But I made them an offer they couldn't refuse. In a way, it allowed them closure, because they'd been fighting for so long, and everyone was exhausted. This way, they all got a nice payout, and they can finally move on."

I'd overpaid for the place. That wasn't something I normally did.

But I'd come out to see the property after Connor had mentioned it, and I knew that it would be perfect for her.

Sometimes you found something that was worth overpaying for.

Something priceless.

I was in for the long game on this investment, so it would only increase in value once we renovated it a bit and got it up and running.

"Are you sure we can afford to invest in it? I mean, this is way over anything we could afford, Myles."

"Yes. I'm not worried about it. Hell, if you want to just put sweat equity in and oversee the renovations, that's fine with me." I put my hands up to stop her when she started to argue. "I knew that wouldn't be what you wanted, so we'll work out a reasonable payment plan. My attorney will draft something up this week. I just wanted to show you around and make sure this would work for you. How about we go walk the place and talk it through?"

She nodded. We took our time going from room to room as her creative juices flowed. This home was much larger than the Seaside Inn; it had twelve bedrooms, a library, and a parlor. She talked about having a suite where the bride and her bridesmaids could get ready. And a room set aside for the groom downstairs, where he and the groomsmen could smoke cigars and relax before the ceremony. She liked the idea of a boutique hotel, and they could book the rooms out for guests flying in for weddings, as well as having rooms available for tourists when it wasn't wedding season.

This was the reason I'd wanted to invest in this woman.

Not because she had a magnificent pussy and the most perfect tits on the planet.

Not because she made me laugh harder than anyone ever had.

Not because I liked having her in my bed when I went to sleep at night and when I woke up in the morning.

Not because, somehow, she'd become the best friend I'd ever had in a matter of a few months.

It was because I knew a diamond in the rough when I saw one.

And Montana Kingsley was exactly that.

She had an eye and a talent, and she worked her ass off at everything she did.

I knew she'd turn this into a gold mine.

"I like all of that. And we've got a generous budget to renovate and make some updates, and I'd like you to work with Charlie to choose the finishes you'd like. This is your baby, and you'll be the day-to-day person overseeing things. I want you to make this what you want it to be. Obviously if we're turning it into a full hotel, we'll need to hire employees, and I'll have you work directly with Connor to get everything going. He'll be the one handling the budget, and he's set up many businesses for me, so he's a pro."

She nodded, eyes wet with emotion, but I saw something pass for a brief moment that I couldn't place.

Maybe a little bit of sadness behind all that joy she was feeling.

Because I'd be moving on to the next project. Sure, I'd fly in and check on the Seaside Inn and this place occasionally, but once they were up and running, my expertise would no longer be needed.

I was the visionary. I saw what something could be and helped get it there. Once it was going—I passed the project off and looked for the next.

"That sounds like a plan. I can't wait to show Vi. She's going to freak out."

"Good. I'm glad you're excited about it. Let's go outside and walk the property," I said, reaching for her hand out of habit.

I'd never been a fan of affection. But when it came to Montana, I couldn't keep my hands off her.

What the fuck does that even mean?

"Oh my gosh, Myles. Picture long tables in the grass over here," she said, pointing to a large green area with tons of growth surrounding it. The mountains sat in the distance, and the gorgeous river was just a stone's throw away. "We could have a long aisle leading down to the water for ceremonies. It's quite possibly the dreamiest backdrop you could find. And then the reception over there, under all those trees. We could have lanterns hanging everywhere and bring in beautiful flowering bushes and landscape. We can create a magical oasis out here."

I smiled. Watching the way her eyes danced with excitement as she talked faster than usual because she was bursting with ideas.

"I think it sounds perfect."

"I can't believe you did this," she said, reaching for my hand. "I cannot believe I waited this long to have a fling."

I laughed and tugged her closer. "Do you forgive me for tearing down the inn now?"

"I suppose I forgive you." She pushed up on her tiptoes and kissed me.

I lifted her off the ground, and her legs wrapped around my waist. It was getting cooler out now that we were heading into fall, and I carried her back toward the house.

I set her back on her feet once we were in the kitchen. "Glad you forgive me. How about we seal our business arrangement by christening this place, one room at a time."

"You want me," she teased as she pushed me backward toward the single chair sitting beside a little bistro table that had been left behind. "I do."

"Well, it's your lucky day. Because I want you too."

I sat down on the chair as she stood above me, one leg on each side of my thighs. She reached down for the button on my jeans, and I lifted enough for her to shove them down, along with my briefs. I was hard as steel already, and she licked her lips as she stepped back and unzipped her skirt, letting it fall in a puddle on the floor.

She wore a champagne-colored sweater that was falling off one of her shoulders, her lacy white panties, and her white cowboy boots.

Dark hair fell all around her shoulders, and golden skin covered her lean legs.

"I told you I'm on the pill now. You said you've never been with anyone without a condom, right? And neither have I."

I reached for her, tugging her closer. "I want to fuck you bare, baby. I want to feel every inch of you."

Her teeth sank into her juicy bottom lip, and she smiled. "Me too."

I reached for the side of her panties and tore them right from her body.

"That's the second pair you've ruined," she said with a raised brow, a sexy smirk on her face.

"I'll buy you your own lingerie store to make up for it."

She positioned herself above my tip, and I teased her entrance. I'd never been so hard in my life. I'd never wanted anyone the way I wanted her right now.

She slowly slid down my throbbing cock, and my head fell back at the feel of her warm heat gripping me so tight I had to fight the urge to come right there.

Right now.

She moaned as she took her time taking me in, inch by inch.

My fingers tangled in her hair as I tugged her forward, my mouth needing to be on hers.

My tongue slipped inside, and I kissed her hard.

Her body rocked up and down, slowly at first.

I trailed my lips down her jaw and her neck as my hands moved up her back and unsnapped her bra. I cupped her perfect breasts before tugging her sweater all the way down and exposing her tits so I could lick and taste them.

We found our rhythm, our breaths filling the space around us.

I flicked each one of her hard peaks before sucking them between my lips as my hands gripped her ass.

Her head fell back, and I knew she was close.

I found her clit with my thumb, knowing just what she needed.

"Come for me, beautiful," I commanded against her ear.

Her body quaked, tits bouncing, lips parted, as I drove into her over and over.

She shattered around me, and I could feel every inch of her.

I went right over the edge with her as a guttural sound escaped my lips.

"So fucking good," I groaned.

And we rode out every last bit of pleasure.

Once we'd both calmed our breathing and slowed our movements, we just stared at one another.

No words were said.

But the message was clear.

How will we ever say goodbye?

CHAPTER SEVENTEEN

Montana

"Are you kidding me right now?" Violet said as she and I walked through every room in the Murphy Ranch. I'd stayed up most of the night tossing and turning and daydreaming about the best way to turn this into a boutique hotel and wedding venue.

So, when Myles and I weren't rolling around naked in the sheets, I was updating my Pinterest board. Because apparently, I had a two-track mind now.

Sex and interior design.

"It's spectacular, right?"

She came to a stop in the kitchen and turned to look at me. "My God, Monny. When you overcame the vajabbies, you just went all in."

I shook my head and chuckled. "What are you talking about?"

"Well, you met the man when you were spiraling in your life. You decided to have the fling of all flings, and then the man made you a part owner of this mansion? When life gives my bestie lemons, she makes some big-dick lemonade."

Now we were both laughing hysterically.

"First of all, I am not part owner. *We* are part owners. And it has nothing to do with sex. He doesn't live here, and he wants a partner. He saw an opportunity."

She smirked. "He sure did."

"Well, don't make it sound so dirty." I stared out the window, my stomach fluttering with excitement over everything that we could do with this place.

"'Dirty' isn't so bad. Maybe you should give it a try." She pushed the back door open and stepped outside. "I like all of your ideas. You know I'm more of a numbers girl, so the creative stuff is more your wheelhouse. But with the budget he's set aside, I don't see why we can't do everything you want to do. So when do we start?"

"Well, he just bought the place. We've got to agree upon the terms and then sign contracts. He said Charlie has a small crew that will be working out here, so it shouldn't take that long. Vi, we could be up and going over here in six to eight weeks. I don't want to bring clients out here yet, until it's all official, but this will solve a lot of our challenges for the upcoming year."

She studied me. "Are you going to be okay when this guy leaves? I've never seen you so happy. Hell, you never seemed this upbeat in all the years you dated the douchebag."

"I knew what this was when we started. So, I'll be fine. Completely fine. Of course I will be. It's a fling. Nothing more. We're friends, of course, and sure, we complicated it with sex, but I'm fine. Totally fine."

"Wow. That was very convincing." I didn't miss the look of concern in her gaze.

"Stop worrying. I'll throw myself into work. You know me, I'm very resilient."

She nodded. "Yeah, but that doesn't mean it won't hurt. Do you think you'll keep in touch with him?"

"I don't think that would be wise. I mean, you don't become pen pals with your fling when they leave town, right? He helped me move forward with my life, and I'm grateful. I'll start dating again after he leaves."

She nodded, but I could tell she knew I was full of shit. I was crazy about the man. It was going to hurt like hell. But I already knew that, and I wasn't doing anything to stop it at this point. It was my choice. I'd deal with the consequences after.

"All right. And he'll probably be back in town occasionally to check on his businesses, right?"

"I'm sure once in a blue moon he'll fly in, but Connor will handle everything for us out here. Myles has a big project that he's starting in Manhattan next month. And then apparently, he just bought a city block in Chicago that he's going to build on. The man has big plans, and they aren't here in Blushing." I cleared my throat and walked back inside.

"Wow. The man has some serious big-dick energy. Do you think he takes on lovers when he goes to different cities?" she asked, and for whatever reason the question hit me right in the center of my chest.

He'd told me he'd never been friends with a woman or spent time with anyone the way he did with me. But I'd met Gigi back in New York. They clearly had some sort of . . . entanglement.

"I don't know, Vi. I really don't want to think about that." We stepped back inside, and I turned all the lights off.

"Oh man, you're in deeper than I thought you were."

"I'm fine." I shook it off and locked the house up. "Come on, let's get back to the office. I have a meeting with Tracy and Bryan, and I need to focus, because she's going to be a handful."

Violet laughed. "That girl is outrageous. She might take the term 'bridezilla' to a whole new level."

Tracy Levett was probably the most high-maintenance bride I'd ever encountered, but I was up for the task. Violet was already over her, and I would definitely be handling most of the interactions moving forward.

We walked past the Seaside Inn, and it was still difficult for me to see that the structure had been taken down to the studs. They'd already started framing, and things were moving quickly. There were trucks parked right on the property with supplies and materials. Several of the crew commuted from Anchorage every day, and they had a lot of people working on this. My eyes scanned the area, and I quickly found him.

Myles St. James.

He was wearing dark jeans, cowboy boots, and a white tee. I knew he dressed differently when he was in the city, but I was partial to this look. He wore it well.

He was deep in conversation with a few of the guys, and I came to a stop and took a minute to just take him in. I rarely got to watch the man without him noticing. His shoulders strained against his tee as he pointed to one side of the property, and the men listened intently.

"Damn. Is he that commanding in the bedroom?" Violet whispered.

I almost forgot she was there. I turned and started walking. "A woman never shares her secrets."

"Please. We share all our secrets." She laughed as we paused when we turned the corner and saw Clifford lying under the large tree across the street from the Blushing Bride.

"He sure likes it over here."

"I think Clifford probably wants a woman, and he'd be the marrying type for sure," she said as she pulled the door open.

"Great. Now we're planning weddings for the local moose." I chuckled.

Blakely's eyes were wide, as if she was trying to tell us something without saying it aloud. "Tracy and Bryan arrived early, and they're in the conference room waiting for you, Monny."

"Well, good luck with that," Violet said under her breath.

I made my way to the conference room and pushed the door open. "Hi there. Nice to see you both."

"I hope you're taking this wedding seriously, Montana. We've been here for ten minutes," Tracy snipped as Bryan stared down at his phone, completely disengaged.

"You arrived thirty minutes early, Tracy. I had another appointment. I'm still twenty minutes ahead of schedule. I assure you, I am on top of everything with the wedding."

"Well, aside from moving the venue," she griped.

"Again, that wasn't my doing. The property sold, and I thought you were happy with the new venue." I took the seat across from them, where Blakely had left their file for me.

"We are. It holds more people, which I'm happy about. I'm just—I'm stressed out with this wedding coming up so soon, and I need to make a few small tweaks."

I need to make a few small tweaks.

This was her favorite saying. And the tweaks were never small. She'd already changed her wedding colors, guest list size, and menu. Luckily, my father was the caterer, and he was flexible, as long as he had time to make the adjustments.

"We're really close to the big day, Tracy, so making tweaks at this point is not going to be possible."

"Well, too bad, so sad. It's happening. I'm changing the wedding party. Bethany is out."

"Bethany Wilson? Your maid of honor?" I asked, not hiding my surprise.

"Yes. She cut her hair. She cut her freaking hair before my wedding day, without checking with me!" she shouted.

Like my bestie had stated, this woman was bringing the "bridezilla" concept to a whole new level.

I glanced over at Bryan, still completely disengaged.

"Tracy, I think the wedding nerves are just getting to you. I'm sure Bethany's hair is fine. We have a fabulous stylist who's going to be doing everyone's hair on the big day. She will be able to work with whatever length she needs to."

"She cut off an inch. An inch!" she shrieked. "I'm sure her bun will be completely fucked now!"

Days like this made me question my career choice. I questioned if being a therapist would have been a more fitting route to take.

"So it's basically a trim?" I said, keeping my tone completely even. "Her hair is long; an inch is not going to be a big deal."

"No offense, Montana, but if you were in my wedding, I'd insist you wore hair extensions because your hair is just past your shoulders. Sure, it's thick and lovely, but it's not as long as what I prefer. That length just doesn't make for a nice bun. And Bethany's hair is already thin, and now her bun will look like shit."

No offense, Tracy, but being in your wedding is not on my list of life goals.

She was not someone I would have the patience to be friends with.

But she was a client, and I was a professional, so I'd keep my mouth closed.

I let out a breath, making an effort to keep my tone even. "Everyone will be looking at you. So I wouldn't worry about it."

"They will, won't they? I mean, look at me." She shrugged. "I was meant to be a bride. I've got the hair. The face. The body."

The ego.

Quite possibly the most annoying personality on the planet.

"Yes. You're stunning." I glanced over at her groom, and I suddenly felt annoyed that I had to deal with her while he got to stare at his phone. "I'm sure Bryan agrees."

His head popped up. "Yes, baby. You're the most beautiful woman in the world. And Bethany's bun is fucking tragic."

I wanted to roll my eyes at how well trained he was.

The man would say anything to avoid her wrath.

I'd witnessed her lose her shit on him more than once, and he was clearly doing whatever it took to keep the peace.

"And this is why we're together. You just get me, baby," she purred.

I shot him a look. I needed him to get on board.

Throw me a bone.

Help me out.

Because once Tracy started spiraling, there was no bringing her back to baseline.

"I was just saying that I thought everyone would be looking at Tracy, so we should not be cutting Bethany from the wedding party. And no one will be looking at her bun when your beautiful bride walks down the aisle, because all eyes will be on the bride."

He nodded quickly. "I agree. And you have been best friends with her since kindergarten."

"Fine. She can be my maid of honor. But I want to talk about the table seating plan that we had."

She spent the next forty minutes changing the seating chart, because she now wanted all of her ex-boyfriends to be seated at one table.

So they could share stories about what a loss it was for them that they didn't marry her.

Her words, not mine.

I couldn't make this shit up.

I agreed to the changes, and hoped this meeting would end now.

"Okay. We're good. You'll need to fix things with Bethany, though. I told her that she was out of the wedding party last night." She pushed to her feet. "She's working at the Brown Bear Diner today if you want to go over and let her know she's back in the wedding. I've got too much to deal with today to take that on."

Sure. Let me go patch things up with your best friend because you're a complete asshole.

"Yep. I've got it. I'll take care of it."

"Okay, we need to go. I'm getting a hot oil treatment on my hair today. Wedding prep has started." She pulled the door open and then snapped her fingers when she realized Bryan was still sitting and staring at his phone.

He jumped to his feet like a trained puppy and followed her out the door.

Violet had just come out from her office as we walked out, and she raised a brow as she took me in. "Everything good?"

"Yes. Everything is great. Montana has some drama to clean up, but she's great at that, right?" Tracy chuckled, and Violet's face hardened. She had never been good at hiding her feelings with her facial expressions.

"She's the best. You're lucky to have her planning this wedding for you," Violet said before clearing her throat.

"Yes. I'm glad *you all* work for us. It gives me peace of mind knowing you will take care of everything. Because it's all about the bride in your business, right?"

I ushered her to the door and forced a smile. "Yes. Have a great hot oil treatment. I'll text you after I speak to Bethany."

Bryan gave me an apologetic look, and I forced a smile, even though he'd been very little help today.

And he was the damn groom.

Once the door closed, I turned around to see Violet and Blakely waiting for an update. I filled them in on the table seating and Bethany's haircut.

"Um, I had breakfast at the Brown Bear Diner this morning, and Bethany looks exactly the same. Her hair looked just as long," Blakely said over her laughter. "How is she even friends with Tracy? Bethany is so nice."

"Well, let's hope she's nice when I go there to convince her to continue as maid of honor after this whole mess. Otherwise, one of you will be her stand-in at the wedding, because apparently my hair would not make a perfect wedding day bun for Tracy either."

"This girl is out of her spray-tanned, bleach-blond, self-centered mind," Violet said. "And having a table with her ex-boyfriends—who, by the way, are not allowed to bring their plus-ones? I mean, this is reality TV type of drama. And for the record, you couldn't pay me to stand up in her wedding. I'd happily shave all my hair off before I'd tolerate her bullshit. But I wouldn't mind a seat at the ex-boyfriend table! I could get all the dirt on her."

Blakely laughed. "Yeah. I'm guessing that will be the best table at the party."

I sighed and tugged my purse up on my shoulder. "All right, I'll be back soon."

"Where are you off to?" Violet asked. "Are you going to stare at the hot billionaire who you claim you aren't dating again?"

"I'm going to the Brown Bear Diner to try to patch things up with Bethany. I have no intention of seeing the hot billionaire." I smirked before pulling the door open.

My phone vibrated when I stepped outside, and I glanced down to see a message from Myles.

Moneybags: Hey. I'm hungry. You want to grab lunch?

Me: Meet me at the Brown Bear Diner. I'm heading there now.

So maybe I had every intention of seeing him.
But I'd keep that to myself.

CHAPTER EIGHTEEN

Myles

I walked into the Moose Brew that evening, and Charlie waved me over. He was sitting at the bar talking to Benji. I'd become friends with these two over the last few months; Charlie and I had met there to discuss plans for the inn several times.

"There he is. I ordered us a couple of steaks. Though I did wonder if you were going to ditch me and go hang out with Montana." Charlie took a pull from his beer, and Benji set my old-fashioned down in front of me.

"Please. Have I ever canceled on you?"

"No. But you do seem to hang out with her a lot for a dude who doesn't do relationships." Charlie smirked.

We'd talked. He was a single guy, raising his daughter on his own. Benji was single, too, so we'd all been open about it.

"We work together. We're friends. It's not serious."

Benji laughed. "I stopped by the Brown Bear Diner today to get a milkshake to go, and you two were sitting so close, people were staring. Just admit you like the girl."

"I'm not denying it. She's great. Of course I like her. But I'm leaving soon. She knows that. We're just having fun right now."

I didn't miss the look they shared, but I shook it off.

I knew what I was doing was selfish, but I couldn't stop it.

While I was there in Blushing, I wanted to spend time with her. I'd never felt that way before, and I wasn't going to second-guess it. I'd be gone soon, and I'd go back to normal. We'd discussed things, and we'd both agreed that we wanted to spend these last few weeks together.

"'Having fun' together?" Charlie said with a chuckle. "Dude, you just bought the Murphy Ranch for her."

Benji laughed like the asshole that he was. "You bought that for Montana? Damn, dude. For a noncommittal guy, you sure go all out."

"You can both just fuck off." I rolled my eyes and took a sip of my drink. "It was a business decision. She's a business partner."

"With an unlimited budget to renovate the space and make it her own?" Charlie raised a brow.

"With a reasonable budget to get it where she wants it. I don't fucking live here, remember? She's going to run the place. So, she should be the one to make the decisions." I shot them both a warning look.

"Man, I'm just trying to remember the last time I bought a mansion for the woman I was casually seeing," Benji said, tapping his chin.

Charlie covered his mouth to keep from laughing. "Yep. I think I bought my last hookup breakfast, and that felt a little too intimate for me."

"Well, we've established that you're both dickheads, so there you go." I shook my glass for a refill because I needed another drink. "And for the record, I've never bought anyone I was dating anything before, outside of a meal and a ticket to a Broadway show."

That only invoked more laughter.

"That's our point, asshole. This is different. Just own it." Benji set my drink down.

"How about we just enjoy our drinks and stop talking about this bullshit? She and I are friends. I meet you two dickheads for dinner, and no one is questioning my motives."

"I'd be willing to put out if you bought me a hotel." Charlie smirked, and I flipped him the bird.

"Let me go grab your steaks. I'll be back." Benji tapped his knuckles on the bar top twice before walking away.

"So when you leave, I'll be dealing with Connor regarding the construction at both locations, right?"

"Yep. He'll fly in every other week and keep me updated on the progress. The dude is almost as good as I am," I said with a laugh. "And he'll keep me abreast of how things are going. I may come back out in a few months."

"You like the initial part of the project, huh? Then you pass the baton to Connor?" he asked.

"I do. I like coming up with a plan, and the vision for the project. And then I usually stick around for demolition and make sure things are rolling, and Connor takes it from there so I can move on to the next project."

Charlie nodded. "That's cool. I like the daily grind. Seeing things come together over a few weeks or months, depending on the size of the project."

"Yeah. You need someone for every stage, right? It takes a fucking village, dude." I paused when Benji set our food down and said he'd be back. The bar was getting busy.

"It does." He cut into his steak.

"Where's Harper tonight?" I asked, as he didn't like leaving his little girl on school nights often.

"She's with my babysitter, Abigail. She's the older woman who lives next door, and she loves spending time with Harper. But I'll get home in time to put her down. God forbid I don't read her *Pinkalicious* before bed. She won't let anyone else read it to her."

I smiled as I thought about how my mom would read to Samuel and me when we were young. It was one of my favorite memories from my childhood.

"Did you always know that you wanted to be a dad?"

"Fuck no." He answered so fast it made me laugh. "Never thought I'd be a dad, if I'm being honest. I had a fucked-up childhood myself, in and out of foster care, pending my mom getting her shit together every few years. I didn't see a need to repeat that pattern, you know?"

"Yet, here you are, running home to read *Pinkalicious*?"

He scrubbed a hand down his face. "That little girl fucking owns me, man. She's just pure sweetness. So I have no regrets. But it wasn't planned, that's for sure. So I'm going to do whatever I can to give her the best life possible. I'm sure I'm messing up every day. Raising her on my own isn't ideal, and I'm sure she wishes she had a mama. But I can't change that, so I just do what I can to show up, you know?"

"Trust me, you're doing a great fucking job, Charlie."

"And you know that because . . ." He smirked as he popped a french fry in his mouth.

"Because I grew up with a father who was a tyrant. He wasn't present all that much, and when he was, it wasn't pleasant. It was not a home where I was waiting for my dad to come read me a book. So, trust me . . . the fact that your little girl only wants you to read her that book before bed—that says it all."

He thought it over. "Well, thank you. I question myself all the time. Worried I'm fucking up or not giving her everything she needs."

"The fact that you worry about it means you're already winning."

"How do you figure?" he asked.

"Because you give a shit, Charlie. That's what matters most. You're invested. You want her to have a good life."

"Damn. You're so much less of an asshole than I thought you were the first time we met," he said over his laughter. "I'm kidding. And I appreciate what you said."

When I'd first met Charlie, we didn't have a whole lot to say to one another, but we'd grown friendly, and he definitely felt comfortable enough to give me shit now. And vice versa.

"Of course. And I'll still be calling you to check on progress occasionally," I said, even though Connor would handle most of the day-to-day. I considered Charlie a friend now, so I'd make an effort to check in with him.

I knew he'd tell me how Montana was doing without making me ask him.

"Of course you will." He laughed. "Do you normally spend this much time in one place when you're doing a new project?"

"A lot of the large projects I've taken on have been in New York, so that makes it easy. I've done a few in other cities, but they weren't quite this magnitude, where we bulldozed the entire building and rebuilt the structure from the ground up. So I'm usually in and out in a shorter amount of time. But I can't say I've minded it this time. It's peaceful here, you know? Different. And I've been able to work remotely, so it's been okay. But things will be busy when I get home."

"Your brother still thinking of coming on board?"

I'd told him about Samuel the last time we'd grabbed a drink together. "Yep. I think he's pretty serious about it. He's just working out the timeline and all of that."

"That'll take some pressure off of you," he said, reaching for his beer and taking a pull. "And he's trying to win his girl back?"

"Yeah. She'll take him back. She's great. They're great together. He just works too damn much."

Samuel had opened up to me that Brianna had threatened to leave him if things didn't change. She was tired of being lonely because her partner was never around. My brother took a hard look at his life. Of course my father picked a time when he knew my brother was vulnerable to turn up the pressure at work. My father was the chief of staff, and Samuel was a surgical resident. Dad had all the power, and he was pushing him harder than he pushed anyone else, according to my brother.

And I didn't doubt it for one minute.

"So how come your brother can have a relationship when he grew up in the same house that you did?"

At the end of the day, we both had parents who had caused a lot of turmoil in our lives.

"I think growing up in our home, we each had different perspectives. He just always wanted this perfect life, you know? Or at least what he thinks is perfect. A wife that he loves. A family that is happy and healthy. He wants kids, and he'll be an amazing dad. He used to point it out in movies that we'd watch. You know the ones where everyone in the family is supporting one another, and having a good time. But me, I never longed for that. I wanted to get out of the house. I never longed for a family, because I don't want to risk fucking up these small humans that are so affected by my decisions. I don't want to be in a relationship that's destructive and unhealthy, and that's all I've really known. My mother spent a lot of years loving a man who treated her shitty. I don't want to fuck anyone up like that, you know?" I took a sip of my drink and waited patiently for him to continue. "So, Samuel was always determined to have this storybook family. But I was different."

"How so?"

"For the longest time, I thought being a better surgeon than my father would be my way of sticking it to him. But I figured out that doing something that I wasn't passionate about was only punishing me."

"So you found something that you were passionate about," he said.

"Yes. I found my calling, and I fucking love building things. That's all I need." I chuckled, trying to make light of it, but nothing about it was light, actually.

"I get that. I felt the same way about being a parent. My dad bailed before I was even born, and my mom was a teenager when she had me, and she couldn't stay clean long enough to take care of herself, let alone a baby. So, being bounced around in foster care wasn't easy. And pulling myself out of it took a lot of work. But then Harper came into my life, and my whole perspective changed."

"How so?" I asked as I sipped my cocktail.

"I've learned that it doesn't matter what you've lived through, brother. Everyone has their own shit. Hell, you grew up in a mansion, and I grew up in the system, yet we're both fucked up in different ways." He cleared his throat. "So at the end of the day, it's up to you to decide who you want to be. I'm not my mother and I'm not my father. I'm determined to break that pattern, and that's up to me to do that."

"You're a good man, Charlie Huxley. But if you tell anyone I said that, I'll deny it."

He smirked as Benji walked over to see how we were doing. We both said that we were heading out soon, and they gave me shit that I was probably going to run to Montana's house.

"Nah. That's where you're wrong. We're doing our own thing tonight. She's going out with friends, and I'm going to go home and catch up on some work."

We'd talked about it, and we'd agreed that a night apart might be a good thing. We were spending a ridiculous amount of time together.

And now I was regretting that decision because I was ready to leave, and I didn't want to be alone.

I wanted to hang out with her.

"Well, look who the cat dragged in." Benji laughed as he motioned to the patio, where live music was playing, and I spotted her.

Montana, Violet, and Blakely were all dancing together, and I didn't miss the way every fucking dude out there had eyes on Montana.

"All right, we've stayed later than I planned. I need to go relieve Abigail and put Harper to sleep. You want to head out?" Charlie asked, arching a brow.

"No. I think I'll have one more drink," I said, and he and Benji both chuckled.

Assholes.

Charlie clapped me on the shoulder. "I'll bet you will. I'll see you tomorrow."

Benji grabbed me another drink, and I kept my gaze trained on the patio, until hers found mine.

She smiled and then walked into the bar, making her way over to me.

"Hey, I didn't expect to see you here." Her words slurred a bit, and I knew she'd had a few drinks.

"Have we met?" I said, my voice low and laced with humor.

Her eyes locked with mine, and she smiled devilishly. "I don't believe so. My name is Dominique Venezuela."

"What a great name. What do you do for a living, Dominique?"

"I'm a diamond dealer. I do a lot of importing and exporting." She chuckled as she sat down on the barstool that Charlie had just abandoned.

"Ahhh . . . that makes sense."

"Why is that?"

"Because I'm the king of finding a diamond in the rough."

She roared a full-bodied laugh, and it was my favorite fucking sound.

"That was smooth, Moneybags."

"I haven't told you what I do for a living. How do you know I'm not jobless?"

"I wouldn't care," she said, her hand moving over mine as it landed on her thigh.

"No? You're not after my money, Dominique?"

"Nope. It's your body I'm after." She chuckled.

"Check, please," I said as I held my hand up, and she and I both laughed.

And we were out the door within a matter of seconds.

CHAPTER NINETEEN

Montana

We were sitting on the floor in the living room at his rental home, and I was thrilled that he'd agreed to spend the evening making his first vision board. I'd insisted he try it, and I'd brought over two large canvases, a big bottle of Mod Podge, and a stack of magazines.

Country music crooned through the surround sound, and we had the fire going, with the temperatures continuing to drop outside. I'd made my favorite fondue to eat while we worked on our boards, and even though he'd complained relentlessly about doing this, I could tell he was enjoying himself. I popped a piece of sourdough bread smothered in cheese in my mouth as I glanced over at his board. He'd just cut out a giant lion, and he was gluing it in the center.

"Admit it. You like this," I said as I used my glue-covered paintbrush to attach a photo of a porch swing to my board. I didn't have a large enough front porch for a swing yet, but I knew that was something I wanted someday.

"It's fine. I don't think I'll be making a vision board back in Manhattan, but I understand the concept. I think I've always had a vision board in my head."

"It doesn't matter where it is, whether it hangs on your wall or is permanently imprinted in your brain. It's all about going after what you want, and not focusing on what can go wrong. That's why I started doing these, because I had a lot of fear for a long time."

He set his brush down and reached for a piece of broccoli and dipped it in the cheese, groaning when he popped it in his mouth. "What kind of fears?"

"Well, I used to worry about everything. Something happening to my dad, and me being left alone. Then I worried about my grades in college, and about paying for tuition, about my father being alone back in Blushing, about marrying the wrong man. You name it. I worried about it."

"Damn. That's a lot to carry."

I chuckled. "You aren't a big worrier, are you?"

"No. But I did almost derail myself by choosing a profession that I didn't love. So I understand the need to stay focused on what you want. You don't have to be a worrier to derail yourself."

I nodded. "I'm impressed that you stood up to your father. I'm sure it wasn't easy."

"I don't really give a shit anymore what he thinks of me; I just know that I don't want to be like him. He's an empty shell of a man, really. He just needs his ego stroked, but he doesn't have much in life that truly makes him happy."

"What makes you happy, Myles?"

"Creating things. Building things."

"Well, that's what makes you happy professionally. But what makes you happy personally?" I asked as I cut out a photo of a gorgeous wedding dress.

He was quiet for a beat, and I looked up at him to make sure he'd heard me. I realized he was processing. That's one of the things I loved about Myles. He wasn't a bullshitter. He was a straight shooter, and he answered questions with thought and honesty.

Not everyone was that way.

I respected it.

"I don't fully know how to separate personal from business, if I'm being honest. But I can tell you that it makes me happy when my brother is doing well. It makes me happy when my mother is not worrying about my father's bullshit and living her life. And it made me happy when you got teary eyed that we were going to partner up on the Murphy Ranch."

My heart pounded at his words.

I still couldn't wrap my head around the fact that we were going to be partial owners of the place. We were still working on the specifics. He wanted to go fifty-fifty on our partnership, and that felt completely unfair and ridiculous. He was putting all the money up, so why would the Blushing Bride have that large of a percentage in the business?

Hearing that it made him happy to see me happy—I didn't know how to process it.

I knew I was head over heels in love with Myles St. James.

I knew that I'd never loved anyone the way that I loved him, and I'd had two very serious relationships over the years, so that was saying a lot.

But I also knew that loving someone was not always enough.

He had a big, bad world that he wanted to conquer.

And he preferred to conquer things on his own.

He was the lion that he'd just glued onto his board.

And I was the girl who wanted to grow old with her partner, sitting out on a porch swing together.

We wanted different things, and that was a hard pill to swallow.

"Oh, also, it makes me super fucking happy I get to fuck you with no condom and feel you come all over my cock. That's my personal favorite. In fact, I need a photo of that for my vision board."

I gasped. "You have the filthiest mouth."

"I speak the truth."

"But you're also much sweeter than you let on."

"Only for you, Honey Badger."

He focused on the photo of the porcupine he was cutting out, and I used my hand to cover my mouth to keep from laughing. "Are you putting Porky on your board?"

"That fucker has grown on me."

"You don't say." I raised a brow. "I guess I shouldn't be surprised. You bought him a crate, and you feed him every day."

"Those are table scraps."

"It's okay to say you like him. To say you like it here." I reached for my glass of wine and took a sip, watching him over the rim.

"I like you. That's all I'm admitting to."

"I like you too." I cleared my throat, trying to push the large lump that had settled there away.

"What makes you happy, Montana Kingsley?"

"Family. Friends. Nature and animals. Good food. Painting. Weddings. Books. Writing. Music. All the things."

"Wow. Your answer is so much better than mine." He shrugged. "Do you want to get married and have a family someday?"

We'd never talked about the future, because we'd known we didn't have one.

But then he'd bought this business, which I guess was very much something that affected my future, so it was only natural to discuss these things at this point.

We'd grown to be more than a fling, and we both knew it.

"I do. I want to get married and have a family. I always wished for a sibling when I was growing up, so I'd like to have at least two kids. And I didn't grow up with a mama, so I'd like to be one. I spent so many years when I was young dreaming about what it would be like to have a mom, you know? Like all the other kids in my class. And I guess it made me realize that just because I didn't experience it as a child, I could still experience those feelings as a mother."

His gaze locked with mine, soft and full of empathy. "You'll be a great mom. And from my experience, sometimes it's better not to have someone in your life if they aren't going to show up. My father was a shitty dad, and having him around did not enrich my life. Sure, he provided for me. I'm not taking away from that. But he was verbally abusive and dominant and disrespectful to my mother. So, maybe him being absent would have been better. I would have found a way to make money whether I was born into it or not."

"I never thought about it that way. I was lucky to have the best dad, you know? He stepped up and did the job of two parents, and I never felt like I wasn't loved a day in my life."

"Then you were already winning," he said, holding up his board to look at the porcupine and the lion and the sports car and the mountains and the photo of downtown New York.

"I think so."

"So I'm curious now—seeing as you're a wedding planner, do you want to have an enormous wedding when you find your fairy-tale prince on a white horse?"

Forget the prince on a white horse.

I'd take the broody billionaire in a Tesla if it were up to me.

"Actually, no. I already have my entire wedding planned out. And I'm not looking for a prince on a white horse, which you probably know, considering you met my narcissistic ex-boyfriend." I chuckled. "I want to get married on the river with the mountains behind us, and just my groom and me. I don't want a show; I want a marriage. A life. A happy life. With a family that I love, and that's enough for me. Throw in a porch swing, and I'm a happy girl."

Is it weird that we're talking about this?

"You must have a song, though. What's your wedding song?"

"You know how everyone picks these traditional wedding songs about this perfect life or finding your soulmate, and though I like those songs, they just aren't what I'd want to represent my wedding. I'd go with something more raw. Something that spoke to me."

"You know you've already picked it. What is it?" He smiled as if this was a riveting conversation.

"Well, I'd go with 'I Remember Everything,' by Zach Bryan." I pulled the song up on his phone so it would connect to his speaker. "Listen to these lyrics."

The soulful sound of Zach's voice was raw, and Myles listened intently. "It doesn't sound like they're together."

"Maybe they are, or maybe they're not. Maybe they break up and get back together because they can't live without one another, who knows? But it's the lyrics and his voice that speak to me. The man singing this song can't live without the woman he's singing about. He doesn't want to remember every detail about her—in fact he wishes that he didn't—but he does. And then she sings about her pain, too, right? They beg each other to stay, because they don't want their time together to end. It's that kind of love that destroys you and puts you back together. I think they're true soulmates. And I've never experienced that kind of intensity, and I think when I promise myself to someone for the rest of my life—I'll feel this way."

He just listened to the lyrics and nodded. "I like it. There's no bullshit in your wedding song, Honey Badger. It's raw and emotional. Good for you. You know what you want."

I smiled and shook my head. I'd never shared this with anyone, and I loved that he didn't judge me for what I wanted. Just like I wouldn't judge him either.

"Thank you. I'm glad you agree."

He played the song on repeat, and we continued listening to it.

"So what about a catchy wedding phrase for your big day? Your very own hashtag?" He thought it was hilarious that we used our big whiteboard in the office to brainstorm wedding slogans and hashtags for our couples.

I came across a photo of New York City, and I cut it out. I'd only been there once, and it was short and sweet, but I'd loved the energy of the city. And Myles lived there, so maybe I wanted a piece of him on my vision board.

"Nope. I think I've had to come up with too many to ever want to do it for myself. And since I don't plan to have an actual wedding, and it would just be me and my sexy groom, we wouldn't really need a slogan. But I do have my hashtag picked out, just for shits and giggles."

"'Shits and giggles,' huh?" He smirked before studying my board. "Tell me what it is."

"It would be bad luck to tell anyone their wedding hashtag before telling my groom what it is."

He looked up at me, his eyes moving to where I'd just glued a photo of NYC on my vision board. He had the mountains and the water on his, so I had a feeling he liked Blushing more than he let on, just like I'd enjoyed New York more than I'd expected to.

"Come on, Montana. You've got to tell me." He took a sip of wine. "We aren't going to speak after I leave, so it's not like I'm going to tell anyone."

"Fine. You get three guesses. If you can get one of the words, I'll tell you what it is. Even though you might be jinxing my future nuptials by making me tell you."

"Hmm . . . let me dive into that overthinking head of yours. You're overly positive about everything that doesn't involve me, so it will be filled with all the sappy mojo. It must not involve names, because you don't know the name of your groom yet." He tapped his chin and thought it over.

"Wow. Shots fired. I had this hashtag when I was dating Phillip, by the way. But I still didn't use names."

"Because deep down you knew he was a douchefucker, and you were never going to marry him."

"Maybe. So let's hear your guesses, ole wise one."

"'Happily ever after.'" He raised a brow in question.

"Nope. It's cute but it's overdone. Two more guesses."

"'Love never dies.'"

My head tipped back in a fit of laughter. "You don't want to put 'death' and 'dying' in your wedding slogan."

"Hmm . . . one more guess." He cleared his throat. "'Forever with you.'"

"Damn you, St. James. You got one word."

"Tell me."

I sighed. "I don't know why you even want to know."

I suddenly felt self-conscious that I had a wedding song and wedding hashtag and no groom. How desperate was that? I'd picked both of them out a while ago, and it just felt like they fit the marriage I'd want to have someday.

And I'm a wedding planner, for God's sake. This is what we do.

"Are you seriously going to weasel out of a bet? I thought you were a woman of your word."

"I told you my name was 'Dominique Venezuela' when I met you," I reminded him.

"Say it."

"Why do you care?" I groaned.

"Montana, don't make me force it out of you." Before I could say another word, he had tipped me back on the floor and tickled me.

I hated being tickled.

I squirmed and laughed and shrieked. "Fine! I'll tell you!"

He pulled back and reached for my hand, helping me sit forward. "That was ridiculous, by the way." He added, "I'm waiting."

"'You, me, and forever.'" I tipped my chin up. It was a damn good saying, and one I wanted to embody in my future marriage with a man I'd never met.

"It's better than I expected. A little corny, but I guess if you're marrying someone, you'd be feeling corny."

"Unless it was you, and then you'd be feeling horny." I chuckled.

"Well played, Honey Badger."

"So do you plan to be a bachelor for the rest of your life?" I asked, because there wasn't anything we didn't talk about anymore, and I wanted to know.

"Yes." He set his brush down and leaned his back against the couch. "I had a horrible example, and statistically speaking, marriage is a bit of a crock."

"You literally just insulted my entire livelihood."

"I didn't say weddings were a crock. I said marriage was."

"Myles, that's an ignorant statement." I glared at him. "And you just invested in a wedding business."

"Exactly. There's a lot of money to be made there. Some people have two and three weddings. I'm investing in a booming business. People want to believe in fairy tales. I'm not investing in the success of the marriage. I'm investing in the fact that they'll spend a shit ton of money on this one special day—regardless of the outcome, the math makes sense."

"That's not fair. Your parents are not the norm, Myles. In fact, I don't know anyone who would remain married, knowing their spouse was having a long-term affair. That's rare."

"Well, your parents aren't together. And your longtime boyfriend was unfaithful. So how can you even argue this?"

"Because I like the idea of people finding happiness. Myself included. And I'm not in the business that I'm in because I want to make money. I'm a wedding planner because I believe in love and marriage and happily ever after." I pushed to my feet.

Why am I so angry now?

I carried the fondue to the kitchen and went to find my coat.

"What are you doing?" He was standing now.

"I'm going home. I don't want to be here anymore." I tugged the sleeves of my coat over my arms and zipped it.

"You're fucking kidding me. I made the goddamn vision board. I'm sorry that I didn't grow up wanting some fucked-up version of 'You, me, and fucking forever.' And because I don't believe in some bullshit fairy tale, I'm the asshole?"

"No, you're an asshole for just tearing apart my profession as a whole." I stormed toward the door, and he followed. "And you're an asshole for asking me to partner up with you when you don't even believe in what I do for a living. I don't have any desire to build a hotel, but I still support your passion for it. I would never say that it was bullshit."

I didn't have a car here, so I'd have to walk, which wasn't a big deal, considering it was still light outside. But he followed me out the door anyway, cursing under his breath.

"Get in the damn car. I'll give you a ride."

"I'm walking." I turned onto the sidewalk and headed toward my house. It was only a few blocks.

"You're so fucking stubborn, Montana."

"Well, add that to the list of things you don't like about me," I huffed.

"I liked the song. Don't I get credit for that?"

"It's not about credit, Myles. Everyone likes that song. It's Zach freaking Bryan. But it's what the song actually means to me that I care about. So no, you don't get a trophy for liking the same music as me."

"This is insane," he called out from behind me, and I ignored him.

I continued walking to my house, and after I'd made my way up the porch steps and put the key in the door, I glanced over my shoulder to see him standing there at the end of the walkway.

He'd made sure I got home safe.

But I didn't care right now.

I pushed my way inside and slammed the door.

As far as I was concerned, Myles St. James could kiss my ass.

Well, I might actually like that.

So he could kiss Clifford Wellhung's ass instead.

CHAPTER TWENTY

Myles

I hadn't spoken to Montana since she'd stormed out of my house last night.

And this was why I didn't do relationships.

I'd pissed her off. Personally I thought she was being absolutely ridiculous.

So the fuck what if I don't believe in happily ever after. I never claimed I did. This was not something that we agreed on, and now I was suddenly the bad guy for not believing what she believed?

Hell, she brings up the fact that this is a fling every goddamn day.

Why was this suddenly a surprise?

We'd talked about this, and she'd said she understood my perspective. And now she appeared appalled by me.

How was that possible?

She knew I wasn't a man who bought into the whole happily ever after fairy-tale bullshit. She knew how fucked up my family was.

So why was I the bad guy now?

My phone rang, and I saw my brother's name flash across the screen.

"Hey. You're not in surgery this morning?"

"No. Everyone's brains are intact today, apparently. I'm sipping a latte in the hospital cafeteria."

"Such a glamorous life," I said with a laugh. "What's up?"

"Well, Mom has been trying to reach you, and you're too busy playing house in small-town Alaska to return her call. Although, it's fair that you're ignoring everyone while you're distracted with Montana. I don't know how you convinced her to hang out with you. She's far too cool for you."

I rolled my eyes. He'd already told me she was out of my league several times since he'd met her. "Yeah, I think she figured it out too. She's not speaking to me at the moment. Shocker, right? So what's up with Mom? Everything okay?"

"Mom is filing for divorce."

My eyes widened. "They just had an anniversary party."

"Yep. Well, she said she felt like Dad was disrespectful to Gino, and she's done."

"You're fucking with me."

"I'm a brain surgeon, Myles. We don't really fuck with people."

"Let me get this straight. He has an affair with our housekeeper, and they have a love child that we all know about, and he's a complete asshole every single day of his life—but he asked Gino to get him a cocktail, and that's her breaking point?"

"I can't make this shit up, brother."

"Damn. That's a call I wish I'd taken. I'll get back to her after we hang up. Does Dad know?" I asked.

"Yes. She said he's moved out of the house. He's staying at a hotel."

"Damn. It took her long enough, but I'm happy she finally got there."

"Yeah. Me too. I wanted to talk to you about something else," he said, and I didn't miss the change in tone. It sounded serious.

Obviously, our parents' pending divorce should have been serious, but considering it came about two decades later than it should have, it only felt like a relief. For my mother at least.

"What's going on?"

"I've been thinking a lot about what we've been talking about." He cleared his throat. "About changing professions. And I'm thinking of doing it sooner rather than later."

Being a brain surgeon was a whole different level of stress. My brother was the best guy I knew. He wanted to make a difference in the world, but he also wanted a life. And right now, his entire life was his work. It was costing him his relationship, one that I knew was very important to him.

"You want to come play with LEGOs, Samuel?" My voice was laced with humor.

"I think about it. I look at my attending, and he's on his third marriage; he has no relationship with his kids. I look at Dad, and I certainly don't want to follow those footsteps. I don't know, man. I'm starting to wonder if there's more to life. Brianna wants to start our life together, and I can't even find a weekend to sneak off to the courthouse to marry her. She deserves better. We have trust funds that we'll never be able to spend, so it's not like I'm in this for the money. I do like helping people, but I just don't know at what cost."

My brother deserved the fucking moon. He was nice as hell and had a heart of gold.

"Listen to me, Samuel. You are the smartest dude I know. If you're ready to jump, I'm ready for you to land at St. James Corp. We're growing, and having two of us at the helm just means that the sky is the limit. But I know it's a tough decision, and I admire that you aren't quite as impulsive as I am." I chuckled.

I'd literally talked to my grandfather on the phone after taking an exam while in medical school and then caught a plane home and never looked back. I withdrew from school and started my life that day.

One that I was proud of.

"Fuck. I'll never hear the end of it from Dad."

"Who gives a shit? He's not a good guy, Samuel. I don't know why the fuck we wanted his approval so badly. Maybe because he was a verbally abusive dickhead when we were growing up, and he made us feel like we needed it to be successful."

"Goddamn, brother. That is some good money spent on therapy right there."

"It sure is. Listen to me. I know how much you love Brianna, and it sounds like she's at the end of her rope. Not coming to Mom and Dad's party was a statement. You need to take her seriously."

"I know. I'm working on it. And you know how she is. She broke down last night and said she doesn't want to change me, but she can't keep living this way either. I just need some time to figure out how to do this. I'm going to finish this rotation and really think about it." He cleared his throat.

"Don't waste your life thinking. Trust your gut, okay?"

"Yeah. I wish I had your gut sometimes. I've never been as sure about things as you are."

"You're sure about the shit that matters. Trust yourself."

"All right. I can do that. But back to more pressing issues. Why isn't Montana speaking to you?"

"Hmm . . . great question. I said something about marriage in general being a joke, and seeing as it's her livelihood, she got offended. I tried to fix it by telling her that I understand why she wants to be a wedding planner, because come on, there's a shit ton of money in this business. Everyone wants to throw a big party and celebrate some bullshit fairy tale, which will inevitably implode. But kudos to her for cashing in."

"Good Christ, asshole. Did you seriously say that to her?"

"Oh, I forgot that I'm talking to a guy who wants to get married." I chuckled. "You and Brianna would be the exception. But statistically speaking, the success rate isn't super impressive."

"Damn. We're so fucked up." He sighed. "I've been dating a girl for more than a decade and I haven't proposed, even though I know she's my person. I love her so fucking much, and I'm messing it up because I'm terrified of ending up like our parents. And you can't seem to hold a relationship for more than a hot second, although you've been awfully clingy to Montana, and don't think I haven't noticed."

"Is there a point here?"

"What the fuck are we doing, Myles? We have everything we could want as far as stuff goes. Big homes and private planes and Grandpa's yacht. But all we do is work. We aren't really living. We're just putting on a show. So, in the end, we aren't really any different than Mom and Dad. We're going through the motions."

His words hit me hard, but I shook them off. "That's a bunch of bullshit. We aren't pretending to play house. We aren't fucking up innocent children."

"But what if we could have it all, Myles? An actual healthy relationship and a family where our kids actually like us?"

I laughed. "You really are in a deep self-reflection phase, aren't you?"

"Brianna left me."

I startled at his words. "What? When?"

"Right after the anniversary party. She said she was done waiting for me to figure out what was important in life. And she's right, you know?"

"Holy shit. Are you still living together?"

"She moved out. She's staying with her sister."

"Fuck. You should have led with this."

"I guess I didn't even want to say the words aloud. I'm still processing it. And do you know what I've concluded?"

"What?" I knew how much he must be hurting, and he'd waited all this time to tell me.

"Dad may have affected our lives up until now—but we're adults. We can do whatever the fuck we want to do now. We don't need his approval. We don't need to please anyone else. So what the fuck are we doing?"

"Sounds like you've already made your decision about work," I said.

"Yeah. I think I made it before she left, but I was too scared to do anything about it. And it doesn't have anything to do with Dad at this point, if I'm being honest."

"What is your hesitation?"

"I made it, you know? It's one of the most brutal career paths, and I just don't want to let anyone down. People will think I'm insane. Who suffers this long through medical school and residency, only to quit and go play with LEGOs?" He chuckled.

"Samuel fucking St. James. That's who. Who gives a shit what anyone thinks? It's about what you want out of your life. Come build things with me, brother. And go get your girl back."

"Working on it. Just wanted to make sure you were ready for me. I'll be in touch soon."

"Sounds like a plan." I paused. "Hey, Samuel."

"Yep."

"If you need me, I'm here. You know that, right?"

"I've always known it, Myles. Your heart's much bigger than you think it is. You're the guy I've always leaned on. Best big brother I could ask for."

My fucking chest squeezed.

"Right back at you."

"All right, my pager is going off. I've got a patient. Talk soon."

He ended the call, and I mulled over his words as a text message came through. I was disappointed that it wasn't Montana, but I opened the text from my assistant.

Connor: Montana sent the contract back unsigned.

Me: What? Why didn't she sign it?

Connor: She sent a counter offer.

Me: How the fuck do you send a counter offer when it isn't a negotiation? We offered her company 50 percent ownership of the venue with a payment of $1 a month and sweat equity. It doesn't get any sweeter than that.

Connor: Well, she doesn't like the offer. She asked for 25 percent ownership of the venue and land and $1000 a month payment. You offended her by making the payment too low.

Me: Because we don't need her money. It was a formality that she was contributing, but we don't need a financial contribution. She'd be investing her time and energy.

Connor: She attached a personal note to you. Would you like me to give you the message?

Me: I can't wait to hear it. ☺

Connor: Thanks for the generous offer, Moneybags. But if you want a partner, then I suggest you treat me like one. And if we invest in this business, you will need to get on board with what we're selling, or I'll have to pass on the partnership.

Me: I offer her the deal of a lifetime and she counters with this bullshit?

Connor: I kind of love it. You found the only woman on the planet who doesn't give a shit how rich you are, Moneybags.

Me: Call me that again and I'm canceling your bonus. . 👍

Connor: I'm guessing you two are in a fight of sorts seeing as she didn't send this counter to you? This is saying a lot for you, considering you don't usually stick around long enough for the first lover's quarrel.

Me: It's not a lover's quarrel, asshole. She's always pissed at me, but this time she seems a little angrier than usual. Probably for the better. I'm out of here in a week, so there's no sense dragging it out. The demo at the inn is nearly done. I'll be heading home when they start construction in the city.

Connor: You brought her home and exposed her to the madness of your father. And then you brought her to the office. I think you like this girl, Myles. Don't be a stubborn ass. You must have done something to piss her off.

Me: And you just assume that I'm the one who fucked up?

Connor: Not a doubt in my mind. I know you well. 😌 And Samuel told me she put your father in his place. I like this girl.

Me: Keep this on the down low, but Samuel might be joining us sooner than we thought.

Connor: Fuck yeah. And that would mean you could work a little bit less if you had a partner.

Me: Stop thinking like a sappy bastard and think like a businessman. This means we can grow quicker than we planned.

Connor: Stop thinking like an asshole and start thinking like a human. Maybe you could actually have a life, which would mean I could have one. Samuel needs his own assistant. I can't handle two St. James. 😄

Me: We'll work it out. I'm heading over to the inn now to check on the progress. Jackson said all the drawings were approved and permits are in place. We're ready to roll.

Connor: Now go fix things with the girl. At least you can enjoy your last week with her there. You know you want to spend the last few days with her. Stop being a stubborn ass and go fix things with her.

Me: Thank you, Dr. Phil. Now get to work. We don't have time for all the theatrics.

Connor: Myles?

Me: Yes.

Connor: Be the man Clifford thinks you are.

Me: Who the fuck is Clifford?

Connor: The town moose, dickhead.

Me: How the fuck do you know his name? And it's Clifford Wellhung by the way.

Connor: Because Montana told me all about him. She's a much better friend than you are. And if you two break up, I'm keeping her.

Me: We aren't together, dickfuck. You can't break up with someone you aren't technically dating.

Connor: Keep telling yourself that, Moneybags.

I didn't respond. Instead, I dropped my phone in my back pocket and made my way outside. Porky must have been out foraging, because he wasn't on the porch. I made my way to the inn, where Charlie and the crew were hard at work.

"You guys got this down quicker than expected."

"This is our best season to work," he said. "It's still light for a good portion of the day, and these guys like the overtime."

"Were you able to salvage the things we discussed?"

"Yep. I'll get everything transported when we start renovations at the Murphy Ranch soon."

"Those shouldn't take too long, huh?"

"Nah. It'll be quick. Just waiting for you to give me the go-ahead over there."

"Yeah. Montana will head up all the decisions on that site, but we're still working out the details on the contract. So we can't move forward until she signs it."

He gave me a puzzled look. "You two are always together—I would have thought that would be the easy part."

"Nah. She's got an issue with the partnership. I offered her a great deal, and she's arguing for less. I can't fucking figure her out sometimes."

He laughed. "She's just a very proud person. Always has been. So you've got to make her feel like she earned that piece of the pie and it's not a handout."

"How the fuck do I do that?"

"You're a resourceful dude, Myles. I'm guessing you can figure it out. She's not someone you can throw money at. I'm sure you know that by now. So, try speaking her language instead of yours. But hey, feel free to throw all the money at me anytime you want."

"Well, this was completely not helpful, but I'll figure something out."

"I'm sure you will." He chuckled.

I shook my head at the shit show this morning had turned into.

And I knew that I needed to fix this before I left town.

I would make Montana Kingsley sign that contract if it was the last thing I did.

CHAPTER TWENTY-ONE

Montana

I'd just taken a bath and slipped into my robe with my hair tied in a knot on top of my head when the knock on the door pulled me from my thoughts. It was late, and the sun was going down earlier and earlier these days. I looked through the peephole and was surprised to see Myles there.

I hadn't talked to him in a few days, and part of me thought it was probably for the best. He was leaving soon, and to say that I'd grown attached was an understatement.

I hated sleeping alone now. I hadn't minded having my bed to myself when I was dating Phillip. I actually looked forward to the nights we didn't spend together. It gave me time to read and watch the shows I liked.

But I crave Myles in a way I've never experienced.

Even if he'd acted like a pompous ass and completely diminished what I did for a living.

I pulled the door open. He stood there in a pair of dark jeans and a black sweater. He smiled when my eyes locked with his, and that little dimple on his cheek was showing.

That's when I knew the smile was genuine.

"Hey, Honey Badger," he said as he held a large square object, wrapped in brown paper, in his hand. "I have something for you."

"It's going to take more than a gift to get me to speak to you again," I said.

"I know. But the gift comes with an explanation."

I stepped back and motioned for him to come inside, and he moved across the room to sit on the couch. My place was much smaller than his rental house, but it was cozy and charming, and I loved it. I'd worked hard to buy my first home, and I'd hired Charlie to help me make it everything I wanted it to be.

The original wood floors creaked as I made my way over to the couch beside him.

"I shouldn't have said what I said to you."

"Agreed."

"I may not believe in that whole 'happily ever after' bullshit—er, fairy tale," he corrected himself. "But that doesn't mean that I should diminish what you believe in. Hell, one of the things I admire most about you is your ability to see the positive in everything. It's why your business is so successful."

"Thank you for saying that."

"I understand you have an issue with the contract."

"I do. It's too much. And I know you were coming from a good place, Myles, but the payment plan was offensive. How can we be partners if we're paying twelve dollars a year? I know we can't contribute what you've contributed, but we can contribute much more than you're asking for, and we want to. We want to invest in this. But we don't want a handout; we want it to be fair."

"Life's not always fair, Montana. So what if once in a while someone comes along and gives you a break? Why not just take it? You've been dealt unfair hands before, so if an opportunity arises that's good—why not just accept it? You've earned it, just by breathing. By existing. By being the amazing fucking woman that you are. And I don't say that lightly, because I dislike most people."

My jaw was hanging open, and I shook my head. "That is very sweet of you to say. I just want it to be fair, Myles. You've also been dealt unfair hands before, and I don't want to be another person who takes from you."

He smiled. "I made you something. I wanted to show you what you're contributing to this partnership."

He handed me a large square-shaped object that looked like it was maybe a piece of art. I unwrapped it, and my eyes widened as I took in the vision board he'd made. At the top of the board were letters cut out that said THE BLUSHING BRIDE. And then photos of couples wearing wedding attire and hugging and dancing were plastered all over it. It had photos of the ocean surrounded by mountains, and wedding cakes and flowers. There were words cut out and glued onto the board that said "I do" and "Happily ever after." The left side of the board had letters running down the length of it that spelled out I BELIEVE IN LOVE.

"What is this?"

"This is why I want to be partners with you. I may not be a believer in the whole concept of marriage and love, but I told you that I have a gift for spotting diamonds in the rough. And you, Montana Kingsley, are the rarest I've ever met. Determined and strong. Creative and talented. Everything you touch is better for it. Me included. I am a better man for knowing you." He cleared his throat, and I sat there gaping at him. Myles wasn't a man who liked to be vulnerable. So when he gave you a compliment, you knew that he meant it. "I have more money than I know what to do with. This is not a big-budget project for me. But what I know *will* make it successful is bringing you into it. You will make it everything that wedding dreams are made of. I can't bring that to the table. I can put the money up front. I can see a piece of land and a building that will go there—but I can't see this." He held up the canvas. "This is all you."

A tear ran down my cheek, and I swiped it away. I moved to sit on his lap, one leg falling on each side so I was straddling him. I stroked his cheek. "Thank you. I'm a better person for knowing you too. And

I know that we'll be going our separate ways, but just know that you have changed me for the better. And when you leave, you'll be taking a piece of this with you." I placed his hand on my heart as his beautiful green gaze searched mine.

"If I had a heart to give you, I would give you mine." He ran his fingers over my cheek.

"You do. You're the only one who doesn't know it."

"So does this mean I'm forgiven?"

"You're forgiven. I won't ever be mad at you for being honest with me. But what you said the other night was bitter and jaded. And I understand why you feel the way you do, but it's important to me that you know who I am. I'm not someone who would be doing what I'm doing if I didn't believe in it."

"I know. And I've been miserable these last two nights without you."

I sighed. "I have too. But it's been a reminder of what's to come. You're leaving, Myles. We probably won't even talk once you're gone. You'll go back to world domination, and I'll be here living my best life." I forced a smile, because the reality of it all was sad.

"What if I come in town and see you every few months? Or you could come visit me in New York sometime. You did put it on your vision board, so you must not hate it." He smiled.

I shook my head. "I can't see you a couple times a year. I can't be a part-time girlfriend to you. I couldn't stand the thought of sharing you. I know myself too well. And there are things that I want in this life that you can't give me. And that's okay. I respect your choices, but I respect mine too. So I can't be halfway in with you." Another tear ran down my cheek. I wanted to tell him that I loved him, right here. Right now. But what was the point? That would probably scare the hell out of him. He'd feel guilty that he couldn't say it back.

"Fuck. How did this get so complicated?" he asked.

"Who'd have thought that night we met that it would turn into so much more? You've become my best friend, Myles. And you annoy the hell out of me most of the time, but I'm sad when you're not around. And that scares me because you're leaving in a few days."

"I've never known a woman like you." He shrugged. "I didn't expect that. I didn't expect to feel all of these things, and it's fucking with my head."

I placed a hand on each side of his face. "I wouldn't change it, you know?"

"What do you mean?"

"If I'd known that night we met that it was going to feel like this—that I was going to completely fall for the arrogant, broody guy at the bar, and that he'd leave a few months later, and it would hurt like hell—I'd still do it. Because you're worth it."

He squeezed his eyes closed and found my hand and brought it to his lips. "So what does this mean?"

"It means that my gut tells me we should call this done right now. But my heart wants these last few days with you. So, which one should I listen to?"

His eyes were pleading. "Please give me these last few days, Montana. And if when I leave, you ask me to leave you alone, I'll respect it. If you can't have me in your life part time, I'll fucking respect it. But it'll kill me. Because I'll want to know how you're doing. I'll want to know that you're okay."

"I'll always be okay, Myles. I'm tougher than I look. I deal diamonds for a living, after all. Those imports and exports are very challenging."

"All the ports," he whispered. "Tell me what to do. If you want me to leave, I'll leave."

"Let's enjoy these last few days, and then we'll agree to part ways. Because I won't move on if you're checking in on me every few weeks. I'm not built that way. I-I-I just feel too much, you know? And I'm trying, Myles, I'm trying really hard to keep things light. I need you to understand that when you leave, I can't do halfway with you. So, let's call this . . . 'You, me, and right now.'"

"'You, me, and right now.'" He nodded. "Yeah. I like the sound of that."

"Thank you for taking the time to make that vision board. I know it wasn't your favorite thing, and I'll save it and hang it out at the ranch as the reason you swayed me to partner up with you."

"So you'll sign the contract?"

I sighed. "If you adjust the payment to what I asked for, I'll sign the contract."

"Great. We're fifty-fifty partners. I'll have Connor make those changes and send it back to you. Charlie will meet with you and Violet and go over the renovations. There's a healthy budget, so make it everything you want it to be."

My heart ached at his words. I knew that this was Myles's way of showing love. He wanted me to have this, because he loved me in his own way.

He didn't know how to say it.

How to trust himself with it.

But I felt it every time he looked at me.

Myles St. James loved me. But his fear was too overpowering to let himself go there.

"And I'll deal with Connor on all the business stuff?" I asked.

"Yep. But just know that if you need anything, all you ever have to do is pick up the phone." His gaze was earnest, and I felt it deep in my soul.

I need him. Nothing more.

"If we're going to spend these last few days together, let's not start talking about the end just yet, okay? It's 'You, me, and right now.'"

He nodded. "I have something to tell you."

"What is it?"

"My mom is filing for divorce from my father."

He wasn't big on sharing, so this caught me off guard. "What? When did that happen?"

"Samuel told me recently. I'd missed her calls, but I sure as shit had not expected that. And I've talked to her a few times since, and she seems happy about it. Like it's something she's wanted to do for a long time, but just didn't know how to do it."

"I get that. She's been in a loveless marriage for so long, it's all she knows."

He nodded. "My dad is pretty stunned. His world is unraveling, because Samuel has decided to leave medicine and come work with me."

Now I was gaping at him. "What? We went a few days without speaking, and your brother is no longer going to be a brain surgeon and your mother is leaving your father?"

"Yep. And I've wanted to call you a dozen times. I've never been like that before, you know?"

"Like what?"

"Where I find something out and I want to tell someone. But I wanted to tell you, Honey Badger." He scrubbed a hand down his face like it was torture that he wanted to share things with me.

"It's not a bad thing to confide in people, Myles. To share things that affect you. You are not made of steel. You actually have a working heart. I can feel it," I teased as my hand moved to his chest and rested there.

"Whoever ends up with you is going to be the luckiest fucking guy on the planet," he said, shaking his head. "And I already fucking hate him."

I chuckled. "I feel the same about you."

His gaze searched mine. "If I were capable of those things, it would be you, Montana. You know that, right?"

I did, actually.

"Yes. And that's the reason I'm going to let us just enjoy these last few days."

"You don't have a wedding this weekend, do you?"

"Nope. We've got this next week off, and then we have three weddings back to back."

"Tell me their hashtags," he said as he ran his thumb over my bottom lip.

"You know the first one. It's the bridezilla from hell. Tracy and Bryan Wright. Hashtag 'marrying Mr. Wright.' Although I don't know that this is the right thing for poor Bryan." I chuckled.

"She's a piece of work. Who's next?"

"We have Crystal and Jalen Berry. So obviously, hashtag 'Berry fond of you.'" I chuckled again as he just smiled at me like I was the most entertaining person he'd ever met. "And then we have Sarah and Wesley Aster, so we went with hashtag 'happily ever Aster.'"

"Damn, you're good at these."

"I've had a few years to practice." I shrugged.

He looked deep in thought. "So let's enjoy these last few days. We've both been working a lot. How about this weekend, you let me take you away somewhere special?"

"Fine. I'm all yours for the next week."

You, me, and right now.

CHAPTER TWENTY-TWO

Myles

"You aren't going to tell me where you're taking me?" she asked as we settled on the plane.

I studied her for a few beats. "You aren't used to surprises, are you?"

"I've never really been surprised." She chuckled. "I mean, my whole life is pretty planned out."

"You never had a surprise party growing up?" I asked, tucking her hair behind her ear.

"No. My dad is a pretty logical guy, and he'd always worry about doing things right, because he was on his own. So we would talk things through. He'd ask if I wanted a birthday party or if I'd like he and I to do something special. So we'd plan things out. And I guess I've just always been that way."

"I get that. I'm a planner. I live by a schedule and a calendar. I don't like to be surprised. And I don't normally surprise people, but I like the idea of surprising you," I admitted.

Her gaze narrowed, and she smiled. "Why?"

"I don't have a fucking clue, Honey Badger. But I wanted to take you somewhere special. You've been working long hours, and I thought it might be nice to take a break."

"I just threw a bunch of different things in my bag, so I don't even know if I have what I need."

"You have what you need," I said, because I'd already called ahead and made sure the house was stocked with everything she'd need. "Stop worrying. When was the last time you had a vacation?"

She thought it over. "I don't really know. I mean, I'm twenty-seven years old. I don't really take vacations. When was the last time you had a vacation?"

"I travel for work often. So I mix work and pleasure, because I'll explore when I'm in different places, but I wouldn't say it's a vacation per se. But we've got three days, so we'll call this a weekend getaway."

"I've definitely never had a weekend getaway, unless you count my girls' trip with Violet and a few of our friends from college to Cabo. But I needed a weekend getaway after that weekend getaway. It was like spring break gone wild." She laughed.

"Did you go wild, Montana?" I asked, not hiding my curiosity.

"No. It's not really my thing. And my friend Alana drank way too much and couldn't stop vomiting on night one, so I was busy trying to hold her head up over the toilet all night. And then night two was spent with Violet insisting we do karaoke night and making fools of ourselves singing, until some guy came up onstage and got touchy, and Violet hit him over the head with a barstool, so we spent the night in jail. Night three, I stayed in the hotel alone and had room service."

I laughed.

That's my girl.

"You're an old soul, Montana Kingsley."

"I think I was born a fifty-year-old woman. I was making to-do lists for my dad in kindergarten."

"I admire how close you are with your dad. The way he talks about you—it's the way a parent should talk about their kid, you know?"

"How does he talk about me?" she asked as she popped a piece of blueberry muffin in her mouth.

"Like you set the sun. He's so proud of you. You can feel how much he loves you just by the way he speaks. That's rare. I notice the same with Charlie when he talks about Harper."

"Yeah. They are both really great dads." She cleared her throat, peeking up at me through long dark lashes. "Have you talked to your mom?"

"Yep. Apparently, Samuel was right. She and Gino have had an emotional relationship for many years. He's her best friend, and she has feelings for him. She won't consider dating him until her divorce is final." I shook my head with a laugh. "She has this sense of loyalty to a man who has another child with a woman who works in our home. It's insane to me that she would stick by him all these years, and feel the need to honor her marriage until a piece of paper tells her that it's okay to move on. And do you know what she said to me?"

"What?" She was watching me intently, as if this was the most important conversation she'd ever had.

"She said that she stayed with him all these years for me and Samuel. She wanted to give us the perfect family," I said, still trying to process those words.

"She thought she was doing the right thing. Sometimes when you're in something, you can't see your way out. I was in a relationship for years that was a dead end. There was no passion. It was just—comfortable, I guess. But sometimes when you've invested so much time into someone, you just don't want to start over. It's a cop-out and it doesn't logically make sense, but it's easier to see that when you're on the other side of it. She was in this for so long that she probably justified it. She thought she was doing the right thing by you and Samuel. The right thing for her family."

"I guess so. I just don't get it. They fought all the time, because she knew the shit he was doing. And she knew that I knew about it years ago. How could she think that was a good environment for us? It only showed me what I didn't want."

"Sometimes that's exactly what you need to see, Myles." She shrugged. "Knowing what you don't want can show you what you do want."

"That sounds like some Freudian shit right there." I laughed.

"I'm serious. You saw a very broken marriage growing up. You saw a dad who was a bit of a bully to his kids. And you knew that wasn't for you."

"And what did you see?"

"Well, I didn't see any kind of relationship because my dad never dated anyone seriously when I was growing up. I mean, he'd go on dates occasionally, but never anything long term. But I saw a really good father. I know what it means to be that person for a child. I also know what it means to have a parent who wasn't there, and I'd never want to be that. So I had to kind of find my own footing in relationships, because I had nothing to go off of. But I know what kind of parent I'll be. And I also know what kind of relationship I want. And honestly, Myles . . ." She paused and interlaced her fingers with mine. "You've taught me that just in the time we've spent together."

My heart pounded in my chest at her words. I was the last guy who should be influencing a relationship. Hell, I hadn't had a serious relationship. Ever.

"How so?"

"Don't panic. I'm not saying I expect that with you, but you showed me how good things could be. Even if for just a short time. It was never like this with Phillip, or with my boyfriend in college. It was sort of . . . meh. You know? There wasn't passion and excitement. You and I have only known one another for a few months, but we laugh, and we fight, and we have a friendship at the core of all of it. And not every relationship needs to last forever to be impactful. Ours is one I will carry with me forever, though. Because you showed me what it means to feel treasured and cared for. And even if we never speak again after you leave, you'll still be with me, Myles. It's a connection, you know? And maybe we were meant to meet, and we've healed one another in a way."

Her words hit me hard. I didn't expect that. "You think I need to be healed?"

She smiled up at me. "Yes, Moneybags. We all do. Because deep inside, there's still a little boy who carried a secret for his dad and felt the pressure to choose a career to please his father. So yes, I think we all need to be healed sometimes."

"I'm content with my life, Montana," I said, my voice hard. I wasn't looking to be fixed. Or saved. I'd worked hard to get where I was.

"You can be content and wounded all at the same time. Both can be true."

"You sound more like a therapist than a wedding planner," I said, my voice lighter now. Because I knew she was right.

"Most of the time I'm both. I swear, I'm dreading doing Tracy and Bryan's wedding. I don't know why people tolerate her." She shook her head and shrugged.

I thought about my father because I'd wondered the same thing about him many times. Yet I hadn't completely cut him out of my life either. "I think sometimes you have a history with someone, and you feel an obligation, you know?"

"Well, you know the saying, 'You can love someone, but that doesn't mean you have to like them.'"

"I haven't heard that, but I get it." I did not like my father, but I suppose deep down I loved the asshole. Even though I didn't want to.

"Stick with me, Moneybags. I'll teach you all the things," she said with a laugh.

Walker's voice came over the speaker to let us know that it was time to prepare for landing. Montana stared out the window.

I had a home in Banff, Canada, that I'd bought a year ago because I'd gone to Calgary to check out a business opportunity that I ended up passing on, but I'd enjoyed the small town of Banff. So I'd found a home there and made it a place I used whenever I needed to work without distraction. It had become an escape for me, and it was my favorite place to spend a few days to decompress.

I'd never taken a woman here with me. My brother and Brianna had stayed at the house one weekend when he took off work, but I'd never brought anyone there with me personally.

But I wanted to do something special for Montana before I left.

Enjoy this last bit of time we had together.

And then we'd go our separate ways.

I'd never thought so much about an ending the way I thought about this one.

This dark looming cloud that kept reminding me that this would end.

I didn't know why it was such a thing this time around.

But everything about Montana Kingsley was different.

"Okay, where are we?" she asked once the plane had dropped its wheels and landed safely on the ground.

"Such an impatient little Honey Badger." I smirked. "Come on, let's go."

Whitney and Walker both said they'd meet us back here in three days, and we said our goodbyes. My car was waiting for me at the airport, since I didn't use a driver when I came here.

I kept a car here to make it easier.

It was usually just me.

But I was looking forward to sharing this place with her.

We climbed in the car, and I turned toward her. "We're in Banff, Canada."

"Banff. I've always wanted to go to Banff. I've heard it's beautiful."

I drove the short distance to my house, and she stared out the window at the surrounding mountains.

"It's so pretty here."

"Yeah. They've got a charming downtown area that's similar to Blushing, but it's a pretty peaceful place." I pulled into the long circular driveway, and she gaped at the house.

I'd fallen in love with the architecture. Rich woods and stone covered the exterior, with large black-paned windows from floor to ceiling; two peaks on each side of the home were covered in stone.

"Wow. Myles. Did you design this place?"

"No. But if I were to design a home, this would be it. I knew the minute it hit the market that I wanted it." I put the car in park and moved around to help her out. I grabbed our bags, and we made our way up the two steps to the tall front door. Once we stepped inside, she came to an abrupt stop, turning slowly and taking it in. The back wall of the home was floor-to-ceiling glass doors that were opened to the mountains.

"This is spectacular."

"Yeah. It's the perfect indoor-outdoor living. Come on, I'll show you around."

She chuckled. "How are the doors already opened and the fire is going in the fireplace?"

"Sistine is a woman who takes care of the property for me. She stocks the house before I arrive and comes and makes sure the heat is on and gets the fire going and leaves groceries in the refrigerator."

Her eyes were wide. "That sure makes it easy when you get here."

We spent the next few minutes going from room to room as she admired every single feature from the claw-foot tub to the stone fireplace in the primary bedroom and bathroom.

"Are you hungry?" I asked, taking her hand and leading her toward the kitchen.

"Starving."

"Good. Let's see what she brought us."

The kitchen cabinetry was black, with a huge copper hood over the oven. The island was a dark wood, and all the counters were white marble with gray veining.

I opened the refrigerator and pulled out a few to-go containers. Montana jumped up to sit on the counter, and I turned around to find her watching me.

"What?"

"Do you bring a lot of women here?" she asked as I pulled out two plates and set them on the counter.

"No. I've only come here alone. It's a place I like to decompress."

"Thank you for bringing me here, Myles. I'm excited to decompress with you," she teased.

I moved to stand between her legs and wrapped my arms around her neck. "I plan to do lots of decompressing after we eat."

"I can get on board with that."

CHAPTER TWENTY-THREE

Montana

I'd dated Phillip Moon all through high school and then again after I'd graduated from college. I'd dated Brad Smith during college for a few years. Those were the two steady relationships that I'd had to date.

And I'd been having what I could only define as a long-lasting fling with Myles St. James over the last few months.

I'd had two long-term relationships in my life.

And I'd had one fling.

I didn't differentiate between the two types of relationships based on feelings or intensity. I defined them strictly by the basic guidelines I'd always followed. A relationship was when two people were dating and had hopes of lasting forever.

Yet neither of my previous relationships had gone the distance.

A fling was when two people enjoyed one another's company, or could also just enjoy some sexy time together, with no intention of it going anywhere.

This fling had been a complete surprise.

And what I hadn't expected was for the fling to be the most intimate relationship I'd had to date.

I'd never felt this strongly about another person in my life.

This comfortable. This connected. This cherished.

It was confusing, and I didn't understand what was happening between us, but I was terrified to question it.

The fire roared in front of us as I straddled him on the couch and my favorite Noah Kahan song played through the surround sound speakers. His eyes never left mine as I rode him slowly. We weren't speaking or laughing or teasing one another. His hands were interlaced with mine, and I wanted to memorize every inch of his handsome face.

I arched my back and slid up. Over and over again.

My body so tuned to his it moved of its own volition.

I love you.

I wanted to say the words, but I was afraid to say them aloud.

Myles St. James was not supposed to be the love of my life.

Yet I'd never loved anyone more.

And loving a man I knew would never reciprocate those feelings felt like a cruel joke the universe was playing on me.

"You're so fucking beautiful," he said, his voice gruff. "I love watching the way you take me all the way in, Montana. Like you were fucking made to ride my cock."

I was.

His hand moved between us, knowing just what I needed.

My body responded immediately.

His eyes telling me exactly how he felt about me.

I moved faster.

I started to shake as a groan escaped my lips.

He tangled his hand in my hair and tugged me down, kissing me hard as I went right over the edge.

I cried out his name just as a guttural sound left his throat.

"I love fucking you, Montana Kingsley," he whispered against my ear.

I love you, too, Myles St. James.

He thrust one more time, and that's all it took as he followed me into oblivion.

And in a perfect world, we'd stay here forever.

"Do you not cook often?" I asked as I held a hand beneath the spoon when he wanted to sample the sauce I was making.

"Not really. I have a chef at home who prepares my meals for me. I grew up with a chef at our home. And I never guessed this to be enjoyable." He leaned down and tasted the sauce. "Damn, that's good. You make being in the kitchen much better than I thought possible."

I reached up and used the pad of my thumb to swipe the sauce from his cheek. "Cooking is relaxing to me." I stirred the sauce one more time before setting the spoon down and turning back toward the island, where we'd pulled everything out of the refrigerator to make a salad.

Country music swooned in the background, and Myles looked adorably handsome the way he stood there watching me, like I was performing life-saving surgery instead of making penne pasta with tomato sauce.

"I'm feeling relaxed too." He handed me a glass of wine. "So now we make the salad?"

I chuckled. "Now we make the salad."

I had already cleaned all the veggies, and I handed him a knife and told him to start chopping the tomatoes and the cucumbers.

He took his job very seriously, meticulously cutting them into tiny cubes.

I tore apart the lettuce before placing it in the bowl, and he scooped up his pile of vegetables and tossed them in as well.

I was about to make a quick vinaigrette dressing when he startled me by pulling me against his chest, wrapping one hand around my waist and one around my neck. We swayed to the sweet sounds of Noah

Kahan, and it was surprisingly romantic. The fire crackled in the family room, and we just moved to the beat of the music.

It was simple. It was intimate. It was romantic.

I breathed him in, wishing this trip would never come to an end. Wishing my time with him would never come to an end.

When the song changed, I pulled back and smiled up at him. "I'll make the dressing; you check on the garlic bread."

It was our last night in Banff, and we'd spent another day exploring this gorgeous place, having lots of sex, and eating the best food. We window-shopped, walked through an art gallery, and caught the tail end of a local band playing downtown while we sipped a glass of wine.

This was my new favorite kind of vacation.

We took our time chatting as we ate dinner, and I was trying hard not to focus on the fact that we were heading home tomorrow. Which meant this was almost over.

We were almost over.

We cleaned up our dinner dishes and decided to go soak in the hot tub. Myles chuckled when he came walking back in the house after getting the fire going outside. "Why are you wearing a bathing suit?"

"I thought you said we were going in the hot tub?"

"We are. But no one is out here, so I'm not wearing a bathing suit."

I raised a brow, strutting past him in my white bikini and his oversize white robe. "Well, maybe I'll let you take it off once we're outside."

"Such a tease. Go get in the water, and I'll grab us each a glass of wine."

The outdoor fire was beautiful against the dark sky. It looked so pretty with the mountains in the distance and the moon overhead.

I set the robe down and slipped one leg at a time into the hot water. I tipped my head up to look at the stars. It was so peaceful out here. The tall trees swayed in the breeze as I sank into the hot water and groaned.

"I see you're still wearing your bathing suit." His voice was sultry and smooth as I turned to look at him.

Myles St. James was stark naked, holding two glasses of wine in his hands.

He was muscular and toned, and my eyes trailed down his distinct six-pack to see his erection standing straight up, per usual. He strode toward me with so much confidence as his long legs and thick thighs closed the distance between us.

"Wow. Are you always this . . . excited, or are you just happy to see me?" My eyes zoomed in on his erection.

"It's all you, baby. Just the thought of you out here in the hot tub has me hard as a fucking rock." He handed me the glass, and I set it on the patio beside us next to his.

"I can see that."

He slipped into the water, making all sorts of ridiculous noises about it being too hot, until he was submerged with me. I stayed on the other side across from him. I reached for my wine and took a sip as my gaze locked with his.

"Are you going to stay over there and play hard to get?" he asked.

"I never seem to be able to stay over here if you're over there, do I?"

He reached for his glass, taking a sip of chardonnay before setting it back down. His eyes never left mine.

"It's been that way with us from the first day we met, hasn't it?" he asked.

"I think you're right." I pushed to stand, my body only submerged from the waist down now. I reached for the tie on my bikini top at the back of my neck and pulled it slowly as it came apart. And then I reached behind my back and untied the other bow, tossing the top to the side.

His tongue swiped out along his bottom lip as he watched me. "Goddamn, you're beautiful."

"You think so?" I whispered teasingly as I reached for my glass and walked toward him slowly.

His eyes were on my breasts when I stopped in front of him. He ran his hands down my back gently, and his touch had me arching toward him. He took the glass from my hand, and he caught me off guard when he tipped it forward, drizzling the white wine down my chest. He leaned down and licked a path over where the wine had just dripped. And then he did it to the other breast. My fingers were in his hair as my breaths came fast.

"Look at me." His voice was deep and gruff.

I lifted my head, and he held the glass to my lips, and I took a sip of wine before he did the same.

He set the glass down, and his hands moved to my hips, where he untied both of the bows of my bathing suit before he pulled the bottoms away and tossed them on the patio.

He tugged my mouth down to his and kissed me. I thought he'd position me above him, but he didn't. Instead he cradled me against his body and just kissed me. For the longest time.

I could feel his desire thick and hard against my hip, but he still didn't make a move to have sex.

When he finally pulled back, he wrapped his arms around me, settling his chin on my shoulder and hugging me tight.

"I thought you wanted hot tub sex," I said with a laugh as I tipped my head back.

"So did I. But I just want to hold you right now."

My breath caught in my throat.

We sat in silence.

Emotion thick and impossible to miss.

"I never expected things to go this far, Montana," he whispered.

I processed his words. "Well, it was my first fling. So I probably messed it up for us."

He chuckled against my ear, kissing my cheek. "You messed it up by simply existing. By just being you. You're impossible to stay away from."

"Thank you."

"I'm sorry if I've made things hard for you."

I turned in his arms to face him, one leg falling on each side of his thighs as I straddled him. "I wouldn't do anything differently if I could go back. And yes, it's going to hurt when you leave. But we'll be okay, right? I think I read in a magazine once that it takes twice as long to get over someone as the time you spent with them. So, by my calculations, I won't even be thinking about you in six months."

"Six months?" he asked. "That's half a fucking year."

"I don't know if it's true. I mean, I don't ever think about Phillip, and I dated him for years. So, by the same calculations, I should be in my late forties before I forget him, and that is definitely not happening." I laughed.

"So what happens after I leave? You seriously don't want to just see one another a few times a year? I don't understand why we can't keep in touch."

I rolled my eyes. "Myles, that makes no sense. I don't date for the sake of dating. And how can I have a meaningful relationship with another man if I keep a side fling going long distance with you? I'm not built that way. I can't fly into New York to attend a fancy party with you and spend a weekend in your bed and come back and return to my normal life."

"Why? That sounds like a fan-fucking-tastic weekend to me."

A lump formed in my throat, but I forced a smile. I'd made a deal with myself that I would not fall apart in front of him. I'd save my tears for when I was alone after he left. "We want different things. I won't move on and meet someone else if I'm talking to you. Because the truth is, no one compares to you, Myles St. James."

"So let me get this straight. In order to be fair to your future loser boyfriend, you can't talk to me because he would suck in comparison?"

"I mean, if you want to put it that way, you're probably right," I said. "But I'm hoping there's someone out there that is as dazzling as you and also wants to be with me."

His face startled at my words. "It's not about me not wanting you, Montana. You know that, right?"

"I mean, at the end of the day, it kind of is."

"I don't live in Blushing, Alaska," he said, his tone hard. "If I did, things would be different."

But I didn't believe that to be true, because he'd never suggested that I move to New York. Or that we try to figure something out. It was just known that it would end. That he'd given me more than he'd expected to give. More than he'd probably ever given another woman.

But he'd never considered asking me to come with him.

It wouldn't be something I'd take lightly, as I had a business and a life in Blushing.

But I was in love with Myles, and if he asked me to move, I'd consider it.

I'd at least try to come up with a solution.

But all he was offering was a booty call once or twice a year.

And that would never be enough for me, even if it sounded tempting in the moment.

I wanted more.

"Myles, it's okay that we're different. You were honest from the start. You don't want the same things that I do. You aren't looking for a partner. You're looking for a good time." I shrugged. "And we've had a really good time."

"You're a lot more than just a good time." His green gaze looked wounded.

I sighed. "So are you."

"I don't understand why we can't continue to be friends at the very least," he pressed.

Another lump formed in my throat so thick it made it difficult to swallow.

Just say it. Tell him the truth. What do you have to lose?

I looked up, placing one hand on each side of his face. My eyes were wet with emotion as I blinked a few times, trying to push the tears away.

"Because I love you, Myles St. James. I can't be your friend, because it would never be enough for me. And it will hurt me too much to see you and not be with you. Because I love you." My voice trembled as the words left my lips.

The look in his eyes caused the dam to break on my tears as they rolled down my cheeks. Because my words had clearly caused him pain.

He didn't want me to love him.

It wasn't what he wanted to hear, and he had no argument now that I'd confessed how I really felt.

"Baby," he whispered, burying his face in my neck. "You deserve so much more than me."

I pulled back to look at him. "You don't have to say that. You don't have to say anything. I just need you to understand why I can't do this halfway with you. Do you understand now?" My words broke on a full sob, and he searched my gaze as he swiped at the falling tears.

He wrapped his arms around me, holding me close again. He didn't say a word.

He was deep in thought, and I could feel it.

This internal battle that lived inside him.

And we just sat there under the stars and the moon, wrapped around one another, wishing things could be different.

CHAPTER TWENTY-FOUR

Myles

"You fly out tonight?" Charlie asked at the construction site.

"Yep. In a few hours. I just wanted to make sure things were still rolling over here."

"Mm-hmm. I talked to Connor, and he said this is the longest you've ever stayed anywhere. And you've done larger projects than the Seaside Inn." He smirked.

"Is there a fucking point to this?" I grumped. I'd been off all day after Montana and I had returned from Banff.

I'd lain awake all night last night, watching her sleep.

Her words an echo in my mind. Permanently etched there forever.

I love you, Myles St. James.

How did I let it go this far? I wasn't the man she wanted. The man she needed.

The man she fucking deserves.

She was caught up in this romantic fantasy we'd been living.

It wasn't real life.

It was temporary.

The thought of hurting her killed me. It was the reason that I normally didn't allow myself to go this deep. Because I wasn't capable of the kind of love that she deserved. Not long term.

I'd fail her. I'd hurt her. I would not be that man.

I will not be my father.

Taking her away was a fucking mistake. Spending three days wrapped around one another.

What the fuck was I thinking?

"My point is—you could have left three weeks ago, once the foundation was poured. I think you stayed for a different reason."

"I thought you were a man of few words. Since when are you so fucking chatty?"

"Just saying. Do you normally do romantic weekend getaways when you're on a jobsite?" Charlie arched a brow.

"I hope Harper makes you read *Pinkalicious* to her every single day for the rest of your life."

He laughed. "Hey, man, if you can't take the truth, just say so."

"I can take the truth, asshole. I know what this is. She knows what this is. It was just a little getaway to say goodbye. It's been great, and now—it's over."

"I know you like to keep things casual, dude. But is this your idea of casual? Hell, I like casual. That usually entails dinner, a cocktail, a little small talk, and maybe good sex if things are going well. That's it. I don't typically hang out with my casual hookups for months on end and then travel together. That's just not normal. But maybe it's a big-city thing." He smirked, knowing that it wasn't a big-city thing.

I'd fucked up.

Made this harder for her.

Made it harder for myself, if I was being honest.

I didn't know, because I'd never done this before.

I wasn't used to doing the simple things with someone the way I did with Montana. Cooking dinner together. Window-shopping and running errands. Grabbing lunch most days. Drinking our coffee together in bed. Making vision boards and watching movies and slow dancing in the kitchen.

How the fuck had I let things get this complicated?

"Listen, we've had a great time." I cleared my throat.

"And you really don't think you'll keep in touch? I don't know, man. You seem kind of attached."

"Shut the fuck up. I'm a busy man. I offered to keep in touch, and she turned me down. She doesn't want a guy that she sees twice a year and talks to occasionally. She wants to go cold turkey, or she doesn't think she'll move on if we don't cut things off."

I love you, Myles St. James.

She wasn't the first woman to say those words to me. Hell, there had been a few over the years. But they hadn't hit me like this. They'd come out of nowhere. They'd just felt like words being thrown out for a reaction.

Montana's words felt real.

They caused her pain to admit, because she knew I couldn't say the words back.

"Well, I get that. And she's the kind of girl that's going to get snatched right up. Hell, half the guys in this town have had their eye on her since she and Phillip broke up. She didn't seem to jump back into the dating pool after he left, but maybe you were the perfect rebound guy to help her to move forward." He clapped me on the shoulder. "Maybe you did some lucky bastard a big favor."

"Fuck you, Charlie," I said.

I didn't want to think about some dirty fucker touching her.

I couldn't fucking handle the thought.

He laughed. "Yeah. That's what I thought. Good luck with that, Myles. I'll be here when you want to cry in your fucking old-fashioned about what an idiot you were to walk away."

"Hey," I said, crossing my arms over my chest. "I'm the one who wanted to stay in touch. She turned me down."

He chuckled again. The dude had never laughed this much in all the months I'd known him, and it was pissing me the hell off. "Let me get this straight. You hang out with the girl every day for months. You take her to meet your family. You take her on a romantic weekend getaway right before you leave. And you think offering to talk on the phone every couple of weeks or months, and fly in for a booty call twice a year, is a fabulous offer? I can't imagine why she turned you down."

I shrugged. "It's the first time I've ever offered it. I don't usually push to stay in touch, Charlie. But she's different."

"No shit, Sherlock. And I think you actually like that she isn't agreeing to your offer, because I think even you know that she deserves better."

"I don't doubt that she deserves better. But I'm a selfish man, Charlie. I want to know how she's doing. I want to see her when I can. I'm a busy man—that's the best I can do."

"Bullshit. We're all busy, Myles. You've got more money than you know what to do with. You could have made her a much better offer than that."

"Says the guy who doesn't date. Glass fucking houses, asshole."

"Correct. I don't date. Been there. Done that. I've got a little girl to answer to at home. That is my priority. But if I found someone that I couldn't get enough of, you bet your ass I'd do something about it. I'm sure as hell not looking, but I'm also not a dumb shit, and if I found it, I wouldn't insult the woman with a lame-ass offer."

I narrowed my gaze. "It was not a lame-ass offer."

"Well, you may be used to women who are cool with just going to dinner with you, or getting wined and dined, and that's enough for them because they like the money. What you're offering works for them. Montana isn't that girl, and you know it. And I think that's why you're drawn to her. She's different. She's real. She's genuine."

"What the fuck, Charlie. Sounds like you want to date her."

"And if I did?" he said with a smirk.

"I'd tell you to dig a hole out by the lake before I beat you senseless and buried your fucking body there."

He laughed hard. "Relax, buddy. Montana's more like family. I'm not looking to date her. But that response is real interesting for such a casual guy."

"Hey, I'm not denying that I care about her." I blew out a strained breath. "How about you help me out and keep me posted on how she's doing?"

He rolled his eyes. "Don't hold your breath. I'm hardly one who pays attention to town gossip."

"Fine. I don't know what the fuck is wrong with me. The plan was always to leave. It'll blow over. I'll head back to the city, and I'll be buried with work. I won't have time to think of anyone once I start this next project." It was the truth. And it was the way I liked it.

"You're a smart dude. I think you'll figure it out."

"Exactly. I'm not worried about it. This is the way I live my life. That didn't change after spending a few months here. Plus, I'm over that fucking moose and the porcupine. I'm ready for the chaos of the city. Horns blasting, people flipping one another the bird when they get in their way, the world's best coffee."

"I don't know, Myles. Once you've been here, it's tough to leave."

"Says the dude who has lived here his entire life."

"Like I said, it's hard to leave."

"Myles," someone called, and I turned around to see Daniel Kingsley walking my way. "You got a minute?"

Charlie leaned in and whistled near my ear. "I'm guessing your future father-in-law is coming to kick your ass."

"Of course. I'll be right there," I called out as he stopped to say hello to a few guys on the crew. I turned back to Charlie. "I'll be in touch. Thanks for everything, Charlie."

He clapped me on the shoulder and pulled me in for one of those half bro hugs that guys do. "Fine. I'll keep you posted on your girl, you big pussy. It's been nice hanging with you, brother."

"Don't get sappy. I told you I want you to come to New York. You can bring Harper with you. I've got plenty of room at my place. You're always welcome."

I didn't make offers like that lightly. I kept my circle small for a reason. But Charlie Huxley had become someone that I considered a friend.

"Count on it. Once we get this hotel up and running, we'll take a trip out your way. She'll like that."

I nodded before turning to walk toward Daniel.

"Hey, Daniel. I was going to come say goodbye to you before I head out of town tonight."

"I appreciate it. Just wanted to catch you and see if we could talk for a minute," he said before clearing his throat and glancing around as if he was looking for a place to sit.

"Why don't we grab a quick bite at the Brown Bear Diner," I said. I was anxious to get over to Montana's house before I left in a few hours, but I respected her father, and if he wanted to talk, I wouldn't say no.

"Sounds good."

We walked across the street and decided on the booth in the back. We ordered a few appetizers, and we got a couple of sodas.

Once our drinks were set down, he let out a breath. "Listen, Myles. I appreciate everything you've done for Montana, with the Murphy Ranch."

"It was a business deal. We're partners. She's going to do big things with it." I shrugged, reaching for my drink and then taking a sip.

"I've noticed that you spend a lot of time together. Hell, everyone in town knows something's been going on. You'd have to be blind not to. She said she went on a little getaway, and I noticed you were gone as well." He held up his hands to stop me from trying to make something up. I wasn't used to speaking to the father of the women I was hooking up with. This was a first. "I'm not here to judge. It's none of my business what's been going on. You're both grown-ups, and I like you, Myles. I really do."

We paused when the server set a plate of wings and sliders down in front of us. Delilah gave me a sympathetic look as if she knew this was an awkward conversation.

"I'm guessing you didn't bring me here to tell me how much you like me," I said, reaching for a slider, even though I wasn't fucking hungry. I had a pit in my stomach, and I'd been feeling off all day. I'd probably caught some shitty bug right before I needed to get home and get my ass to work.

"Yeah, I've got some concerns." He cleared his throat. "I don't get involved in Montana's personal life, hence the reason I never told her that I didn't care for that little punk Phillip. She never seemed all that happy, but who am I to judge? I haven't had a solid relationship since Montana was born. She's been my focus, and sure, I've dated, and I've got a lady friend I spend a lot of time with now, but my focus has always been my little girl."

"And you've raised an amazing woman," I said. "And I think Phillip is an asshole too. So I'm glad she got away from him."

"Yeah. Me too."

"But you're worried that I'm going to hurt her?" I finally said, because I could tell he was uncomfortable.

"Not intentionally. And I've got to tell you, I've never seen her as happy as she's been since you came to town. These last few months, I don't know, she's lighter. More confident. She laughs all the time." He sighed. "But I know you're leaving tonight. And I really do appreciate everything you've done for her and for me. Hell, for everyone in this town, with all the jobs you're going to be bringing to Blushing. But if you aren't going to be sticking around, then you need to leave and not look back, Myles."

For fuck's sake.

No one wanted me to keep in touch with her.

My God. Was I the fucking devil?

"She's already made it clear that when I leave, she doesn't want to continue speaking, even though we've become really good friends," I said.

Hell, Montana Kingsley was the best friend I'd ever had. I'd never shared as much with anyone or opened up the way I had with her.

"Listen, Myles. I've been in a relationship with someone who wasn't invested the way that I was, and I lost a lot of time waiting around. And my daughter deserves someone who wants to be there. Who makes her their priority. And I'm sure you two have been up front and honest about whatever the hell has been going on, but I'm asking you, man to man—if you're leaving with no intention of coming back more than once or twice a year, don't string her along. I see the way she looks at you. And I can't stand the idea of her being hurt. So right now, no one has done anything wrong. You'll leave, and she'll be stoic and strong for everyone like she always is, and probably cry when she's alone like she used to do as a kid. She never let me see her cry because she once told me she'd rather hurt alone than hurt me." He shook his head and blew out a breath, looking away for a few beats before turning his attention back to me. "Maybe you'll hurt a little too. But everyone will recover eventually. But if you drag this out. If you call her or visit every few months and string her along. You and I will have a problem. I don't care if you own the business I'm going to be working at. I will kick your ass without hesitation."

I raised a brow. He was a fairly big dude. Somewhat fit. But there was no world where Daniel Kingsley was going to kick my ass, unless I just threw my hands up and let him do it.

And if I was being honest, I would let him kick the shit out of me if I hurt her.

Hell, I already had.

And the idea of Montana crying in her house alone—it did something to me.

Something I had no idea how to deal with.

"I understand, Daniel. I want the best for her. I, er, I . . ." I couldn't find the words I needed to say. "I care about her a lot. She's somehow become my favorite person. But I know that what I have to offer isn't enough for her, and I'll respect it."

"Thank you. I really didn't want to drag your ass out back and kick the shit out of you."

I smirked. "I appreciate that."

My phone vibrated, and I glanced down at the text from his daughter.

Honey Badger: Hey. I know you were going to swing by and say
goodbye on your way to the airport, but I'm not feeling well. I've
got a fever, and I don't want to get you sick, if I haven't already.
So, I think it's best you don't come by.

I blew out a breath and told Daniel that she was sick.

"She's protecting herself. You just spent three days with her. I'm
sure you've both said your goodbyes in your own way. Don't make this
harder for her than it has to be."

I nodded. A sharp pain hit my stomach, and I cleared my throat.
"All right. But I'm going to order her some soup and bread and just
drop it on her porch on my way out of town."

I called Delilah over and placed an order to go.

"Myles," he said, his voice quiet. "I'll take it over to her. You should
just head to the airport from here."

I agreed, and he excused himself to use the restroom as I paid the bill.

I quickly typed out a text.

Me: I'm sorry you're sick. I'm sorry I didn't get to say goodbye.
I'm sorry if I've made this hard on you.

I thought of the song she loved. Those words flooded my head at
the moment. I knew I shouldn't say anything, but she'd put herself out
there and told me that she loved me. I owed her more than what I'd
given her.

Me: Montana. I remember everything.

Honey Badger: I love you too, Myles.

She knew what my words meant.

That I was a coward, incapable of loving her the way she deserved.

That sick feeling in my stomach lingered as I handed Daniel the bag of food to take to his daughter.

And when I boarded the plane home, I stared out the window and hoped the feeling would pass.

I just needed to get back to my routine.

Back to my way of living.

Once I was home, I would stop thinking about Blushing, Alaska.

About her.

CHAPTER TWENTY-FIVE

Montana

The next two weeks were ridiculously busy. I'd spent my days getting ready for our next wedding and choosing finishes for the renovation out at the ranch. We'd decided to name the boutique hotel the Blushing Inn. Violet and I liked that it had the name of our town, as well as our business. Connor thought it was a perfect fit as well.

I spoke to Myles's assistant almost daily, and I refused to ask how his boss was doing, even if I was dying to know.

Even if every night since he'd left, I cried myself to sleep. I didn't cry once when Phillip and I broke up. Hell, I didn't even cry when I'd learned that he'd cheated on me with his now fiancée.

But the loss of Myles St. James from my life had been massive. Painful.

I'd started feeling it the day we'd returned from Banff. I knew I couldn't say goodbye to him without falling apart, so I'd said I was sick. And maybe in the traditional sense I'd stretched the truth to protect my already broken heart. But I'd been physically ill, knowing the time had come.

Somewhere along the way, I'd fallen deeply in love with a man I couldn't keep.

He'd sent my father over to my house with food, and I'd pretended that I didn't want to get him sick. I took the food and insisted he head home.

I'd always been someone who liked to deal with my sadness on my own. Well, aside from Violet, who didn't care if I told her not to come over.

She came anyway.

She'd spent that first night at my house, letting me cry it out. She didn't remind me once that I'd done this to myself. She didn't shame me for getting myself into this situation.

She'd just let me cry.

And the next day I'd insisted I was fine, and I threw myself into work. *But I'm anything but fine.*

So, when I spoke to Connor, which was almost daily, I made a point to keep it all about business.

And that's the way I wanted to keep it.

We worked well together, and I was grateful that I had a contact other than Myles.

"You've been working such long hours," Violet said as she drove out toward the Blushing Inn so that we could check on the renovations, since it had been a few days since we'd been out there. Charlie said they'd had a bunch done for us to come see, and the hope was that we would be open for business in a few weeks.

"I could have done this on my own. You need to sleep, Monny. You look exhausted," Violet said.

"I thrive when I'm exhausted. I'm in wedding mode, and I can rest after this weekend." I'd forced myself to put a smile on my face every day. I would not wear my sadness with me.

"Blakely told me that Tracy Wright called the office looking for you this morning." She pulled into the driveway and put the car in park. "Her wedding is over. Her honeymoon is over. What could she possibly want now?"

"You wouldn't believe it if I told you," I said as I pushed out of the car. It was cold this morning, and we were both dressed in sweaters and jeans. The sun was out, but the breeze made it chilly.

"Tell me. I need some entertainment."

We walked up the cobblestone path to the front porch and saw several trucks parked out front. The crew was trying to get this done for us as quickly as possible.

"She asked me to go buy her whitening strips and drop them off. Then she called because she started her period, and she asked if I had a way to make it go away."

I couldn't make this shit up.

"You have got to be kidding me," Violet said before she broke out into a fit of laughter. "The wedding is over. Why is she calling her wedding planner and not her husband?"

"She said she had bad cramps, and she just assumed I could run and do a quick favor to help her out. I told her to call Bryan because I was swamped at work."

"Bad cramps, huh? It's called karma, bitch. If you treat everyone like shit, the universe is going to deliver Aunt Flo with a side of cramps every month for the rest of your life."

I chuckled as we stepped inside.

Charlie was there, bent down as he worked on the banister. His arms flexed as he used the nail gun to secure one end, with two of his guys holding it in place.

"Hey," I said. "I didn't know we were changing out the banister."

"Yes. This is unexpected, Charles," Violet said as she studied the wood railing and glared at our contractor, whom she seemed annoyed by most of the time.

"Well, it was kind of a surprise." He cleared his throat before stepping to the other side of the staircase and motioning for me to follow. "Myles asked me to bring this over from the Seaside Inn. I think it's got yours and your dad's initials engraved here."

A lump lodged in my throat. The one I'd fought so hard the last two weeks to push away. I nodded and blinked multiple times as my fingers traced over our initials carved into the gorgeous dark wood. There were little nail holes where we'd hung our stockings every year.

"You brought the banister from the Seaside Inn over here and switched them out?" Violet asked as she strode from one side to the other, admiring the woodwork.

"Yep. We'll use the banister from this place on another project at some point. But he thought you'd like it if we could salvage the one that holds a lot of memories for you," he said, and his gaze was filled with empathy.

Charlie was normally a pretty serious guy, but he'd been checking in with me more than usual lately. I assumed it was because we were working on this project together.

I nodded.

No words came.

He'd remembered that the banister meant something to me.

Damn you, Myles St. James.

I wanted to be angry at him for leaving. But the anger had yet to come.

I swallowed several times as I continued nodding, making a promise to myself that I could let it all out when I got home tonight.

I would give myself an hour to fall apart.

To grieve. To be sad. To feel all of these things that I was desperately trying not to feel.

"Fuck," Charlie said under his breath.

"Is that a proposition?" Violet asked.

"What?"

"Oh, I thought you were being suggestive." She smirked. Violet loved to mess with people, but Charlie was not the kind of man you messed with.

"No idea what the fuck that means," he grumped. "But there's one more thing to show you, and I feel like it's going to upset you now that I'm seeing the way you reacted to the banister."

"Did the billionaire send a clay molding of his magic dick?" Violet said as if she were discussing the weather.

Charlie shook his head with irritation. "No. There are no clay dicks."

"Good to know, Charles."

He ignored the comment, since she'd refused to call him "Charlie" after he'd asked her to stop calling him "Charles" multiple times over the last two weeks. Which only made her do it more.

"Come on. Let's get this over with." He directed his guys to go help the painters upstairs, and he led us to the kitchen. They were putting in the new cabinets, and the countertops were going in tomorrow. We'd removed a wall between the kitchen and the dining room, as we wanted to expand the kitchen, and they'd framed the new wall several feet away from where it originally stood. It was on the side of the kitchen, so I was anxious to see how it would all look with the change.

"It's so much larger," Violet said as we both turned at the same time. "What the motherfucking mind blow is going on?"

Charlie actually laughed at her response before straightening his face and looking at me. "What do you think?"

The lump in my throat was no longer stable.

My bottom lip started shaking, and it didn't matter how many times I blinked, the tears were too thick.

The dam broke, and I couldn't fight it.

Tears blurred my vision as I stared at the wall that I'd painted years ago for Howard and Lydia. Turquoise and pink butterflies and flowers swirled in the design.

I turned to look at Charlie, who startled when he saw the tears coming down my face.

"For fuck's sake, Charles!" Violet said. "You could have given her a heads-up."

"What? I didn't know she'd be upset by it."

"Oh really, genius. She painted that goddamn wall." She fumed, and I wanted to make her stop, but I couldn't take my eyes off the wall.

"I'm very aware. I'm the dude who had to take a wall down without damaging it and move it a mile away, keeping it intact, and then build it into the remodel. I'm more than fucking aware that she painted the wall, Violet. I thought she'd be happy that we salvaged it."

I didn't even care that they were arguing.

"Of course you did. You have a penis!" she shouted. "You don't have a clue how our minds work. Good luck to you when Harper's a teenager. She's going to hate you."

I turned because she shouldn't have brought Harper into it.

"Stop," I said, my voice shaky, as I swiped at my cheeks and my nose, trying to pull myself together. "I do like it. It was just unexpected."

"Well then, let's not bring my kid hating me into the conversation if she's okay with the wall." He glared at the woman beside me.

"Of course she's okay with the wall," she groaned. "She thought it was demolished. Which means that she's already grieved the wall, and then you go and surprise her with it. Next time . . . just do better, Charles."

"I'll keep that in mind when I'm using every bit of manpower I have to get this gigantic fucking wall over here in one piece." He didn't hide his sarcasm.

"Thank you. I appreciate that effort." Violet plastered a very fake smile on her face.

"Thank you, Charlie," I said, my voice quiet and shaky.

He sighed. "It wasn't my idea. But he really wanted it salvaged for you. He was very impressed with it."

"Oh, he who shall not be named." Violet glared at Charlie once again. I didn't know why she was blaming him when he was just doing his job.

He ran a hand over his face. "Trust me, I don't want to be the middleman."

"Well, we all know that you penises like to stick together, don't you?"

"Again. I have no idea what you're talking about." He narrowed his gaze at her. "Yes, Violet. I have a dick. A rather large one, if I'm being honest. But that has nothing to do with the fact that I was hired to do a job, and that's what I'm doing."

"Typical. Do you have any more surprises for my girl, Charles? Perhaps you could prepare her for whatever you've got left in that bag of dicks you seem to be carting around." She glared at him, arms folded across her chest, her eyes fuming. "Let me guess. Did he find her first baby footprint out in the garden and have it gold plated? Or did he find her first baby tooth and have it made into a pearl necklace that you're going to present to her next?"

He laughed. "You're absolutely insane."

"You have no idea. I haven't even gotten started." She smirked.

My phone vibrated relentlessly in my back pocket, and I pulled it out to see several texts from Monica, who was getting married this coming weekend. I pinched the bridge of my nose. "Vi, I'm begging you to tone it down. I'm good. We've got to get over to the bridal shop. Monica is having dress issues."

"It's your lucky day, Huxley. I wasn't finished with my wrath just yet," Violet grumped.

"Thanks for doing all this, Charlie. I'm honestly overcome with emotion, in a good way. I worked hard on this wall, and I just assumed it was gone. And the banister . . ." I placed a hand on my heart. "I can't tell you how much it means to me."

"Thank you, Montana. That makes it all worth it," he said before turning and raising a brow at Violet.

"What? You don't seriously think I'm going to apologize for being a protective best friend, do you?" Violet chuckled. "See you around, Charles."

He grunted something under his breath, but I couldn't make it out, and we walked outside together and got in her car.

"You okay?" she asked as she started driving toward downtown.

"Yes. You shouldn't have been rude to Charlie. It was really sweet of him to make sure it got moved over correctly. He's doing his job, Vi."

"I know that," she sang out dramatically. "But I like giving Charles shit because he's so . . . edgy. And he gets all worked up. A girl can have some fun. Plus, you cried. You never cry. So I would have attacked anyone that was the cause of it in the moment."

"I can't believe Myles did that," I said.

"Yeah, he's clearly the world's worst fling," she said, putting the car in park after she pulled into the Blooming Bride's parking lot. "This was supposed to be light and fun for you. You were supposed to have a one-nighter, let the man rock your world, and realize what a dud of a douche Phillip was before going off into the dating world. Your fling lasted for months, took you on trips, and salvaged your childhood memories. What kind of bullshit is that?"

"Of course I even failed at having a fling. It was supposed to be fun—I wasn't supposed to fall for the guy." I pushed out of the car.

"Love sucks!" Violet yelled, and I turned around and used my hand to cover her mouth.

"We're wedding planners. You can't say that out loud." I held my hand there as I waited for her to nod.

"Don't remind me. Let's go see what today's problem is." She looped her arm through mine.

I pulled the door open, and we both straightened and plastered smiles on our faces.

"I'm so glad you're here," Monica said. She had a look of panic on her face. She looked around at her mom and her bridesmaids and added, "We're having issues getting the back zipped."

Her dress looked like it was made for her.

A white satin princess-style gown.

"I took the measurements and was certain I got them right," Beatrice said. She was the local seamstress, and she took a lot of pride in her work. I was certain she was still recovering from her experience with Tracy, as she'd been really tough on the older woman about her alterations.

I stepped in front of her and raised a brow. "It fits perfectly everywhere else."

"I know. I'm not sure what's happening up here." Monica looked down at her chest.

"This isn't a shotgun wedding, is it?" Connie, Monica's mother, said, her voice all tease as she sipped her champagne on the couch. A couple of Monica's bridesmaids giggled.

"Oh my gosh, Mom. I'm not pregnant."

The strapless gown was gorgeous, and her boobs did look notably larger than they had at the last fitting; they were bursting out of the top.

I stepped up on the podium and studied her from head to toe. "Did you wear a different bra when you got your last fitting done?"

Monica chuckled. "Oh, I did just buy this new bra. It's supposed to work wonders for us less-endowed girls."

I tried not to laugh. "Violet, unzip the back a little bit for me."

She moved up onto the podium and did as I asked. "Hold the top away so I can see what's going on."

Monica held the fabric away from her body as I tipped my head down and looked. "May I make an adjustment?"

"Yes. Have at it."

I reached into the cleavage area, found the little opening on the inside of each cup, and tugged the unusually thick padding out of the bra. I held the two pads in my hand and asked Violet to zip the dress up.

"Oh. Ohhhhhh. Look at that. It fits perfectly," Monica said, and her bridesmaids all relaxed on the couch as her mother moved to her feet and got teary eyed as she took in her daughter. "Thank you so much, Montana. You both are little wedding ninjas, the way you just jump into gear."

"Yes," Connie said. "Monica told me that Violet worked some magic getting her the wedding cake that she wanted, even though it was slightly out of budget. Somehow, she got them to bend on the price."

I chuckled. Violet was a fabulous negotiator, and I'd heard her on the phone, mentioning how many weddings we refer to this particular bakery a year. She'd also mentioned that there was another baker in town who was eager to get new business. And they immediately took 20 percent off the cake that Monica had really wanted.

"We're here to make your lives easier on your special day." I smiled.

Beatrice looked relieved as she widened her eyes at Violet and me.

"Here, Bea, have a little champagne," Violet said as she handed a flute to the older woman, while everyone else was gushing over Monica's dress.

We said our goodbyes and made our way outside, just as my phone rang. I groaned when I saw Tracy's name light up my screen.

"Put her on speaker. I want to hear what she has to say this time."

I chuckled and then answered before moving her to speakerphone. "Hey, Tracy."

"Montana, I just called your office looking for you and Violet, and Blakely said you were together."

"We are. We're dealing with some wedding stuff. What's up?"

"Well, it's your lucky day. We're going back to my place to watch the video my parents had made of me as a little girl, from birth all the way to my wedding day. It's got everything on it. It's like a movie. It's three hours long, and all my bridesmaids are heading over now to watch with me. You and Violet have to come join us."

The look on Violet's face was giving me *I will murder you slowly if you agree to this* vibes.

"Oh, I wish we could, Tracy. We've got to get over to the venue to see how setup is going for the Berry wedding this weekend."

She whined a little but said she understood. "Some brides are so high maintenance," Tracy said.

I chuckled, because she just might have been the least self-aware person I'd ever met.

"Okay, well, have fun," I said. "Take care."

"I'll record some of it and send it to you so you don't feel like you missed out."

Violet threw her hands in the air, and I thanked Tracy and ended the call quickly.

After we slipped into the car, Violet turned to me. "Do we really have to go to the venue again? We already checked everything earlier today. We still have all day tomorrow to get things done."

"No. We're dropping the car at the office, grabbing Blakely, and walking to the Moose Brew. I think we've earned some cocktails."

"Yes! She's back!" Violet fist-pumped the sky.

I wasn't back. Not by a long shot.

But drowning my emotions in a few martinis felt necessary at the moment.

CHAPTER TWENTY-SIX

Myles

"Next time you and your crew decide to show up late, you won't be employed here," I told the foreman.

He nodded and apologized for the third time.

I'd been back in the city for several weeks now, and I was sick and tired of being a fucking babysitter.

"Myles," Connor said, his voice low and even so only I would hear. "How about we take it down a notch."

I came to an abrupt stop, tugging my black overcoat closed at the collar. "Take it down a notch? They've been late multiple times. That's not how you make a good name for yourself."

Connor pushed the door open, and we stepped out onto the busy street. "They were four minutes late."

"I clocked them at a hell of a lot later than that."

"You arrived thirty minutes early. That doesn't count toward them being late. They were actually four minutes late, Myles. And they've been working late every day. We're making good progress, and we're ahead of schedule."

"Whatever. They shouldn't be four minutes late. We pay them well. I'm never late. I expect the people who work for me to show the same respect." We walked side by side as we made our way to the coffee shop next door.

Our coffees were waiting for us, as Connor had used the app to place our order. Samuel was meeting us here, and we found a table for three in the back where we normally sat.

I took a sip of my coffee and let out an irritated huff. "Damn it. This coffee tastes like shit again."

"You've said that every day for a month. Perhaps you should order something different."

Connor was an even-keeled dude, but I could tell he was annoyed with me, even if he did his best to try to hide it.

We were friends, but at the end of the day, I was his boss, and he worked for me. He didn't know where that line was. And with me being as moody as I'd been lately, I didn't blame him for treading lightly.

Samuel came through the door, and Connor waved him over. My assistant almost had a look of relief on his face as my brother made his way over to the table.

As if sitting here with just me was that painful?

Fuck him.

Fuck everyone, as far as I'm concerned.

Samuel gave us each a pound of his fist as he slipped his coat off and took the seat across from me. He reached for his coffee and took a sip before setting it back down. "Damn. They really do have the best coffee in New York City."

"Well, you and I are the only two who agree on that," Connor snipped, and I glared at him.

"Oh, let me guess. We're still hating the coffee. The traffic. The noise. The weather." He chuckled.

"The construction crew. The doorman at his building. Anyone who has a dog attached to their leash. Cyclists who ride on city streets. The mailman, because how dare he think he should deliver the mail during the workday." Connor smirked before taking another sip of his coffee.

Apparently, he isn't afraid of pissing me off.

"Fuck both of you. And what the hell is going on today? Why the fuck is that dude dressed like a fucking pirate? And that kid over there who keeps giving me attitude looks like a goddamn pumpkin. Has everyone lost their fucking minds?" I grumped.

Both Connor and Samuel laughed, which irritated me even more.

"Myles," my brother said, his eyes suddenly filled with empathy, even though I wasn't the asshole dressed like a moron. "It's Halloween. And the kid giving you attitude is maybe two years old and doesn't know how to shit in a toilet. He doesn't know you exist, nor does he care. He's just checking the place out."

"I hate Halloween."

"Of course you do. Why would you enjoy seeing people dressed up, eating candy, and having a good time one day a year? It's a ludicrous concept." He oozed sarcasm and tried to cover his smile by taking a sip of coffee.

"What's going on with you?" Samuel asked. "You've been a miserable asshole ever since you came back to the city. The project is ahead of schedule. I'm coming on board starting Monday. Mom is happier than we've ever seen her. Dad is eating a big dose of humble pie. You should be on cloud nine."

"The crew was late today, again. The coffee has been fucked up ever since I returned home and doesn't taste the same. My doorman follows me around the lobby, talking incessantly. And I find it off putting when grown adults wear costumes." I shrugged. "And trust me, Dad has not eaten nearly enough humble pie. He invited me to dinner last night, and he brought a woman. I haven't seen the man since their anniversary party. We haven't discussed the divorce, and he brings a date to our dinner. Far from humble, brother."

"I don't think this has anything to do with Mom or Dad or your doorman," Samuel said, and of course Connor nodded in agreement.

"Hell, I don't think you give a shit about some stranger wearing a pirate costume or your construction team being a few minutes late."

The fucking traitor.

"What are you, a therapist now? I thought you were tired of being a doctor?"

"No. I'm tired of working seven days a week and not spending time with my girlfriend, smart-ass. But yes, I'm also a qualified medical doctor who is happy to tell you that you're being an asshole."

"I'm an asshole?"

"No. I said you're *being* an asshole." He laughed. "You're suffering, and you don't want to admit it."

"I agree with Dr. St. James," Connor said.

"Of course you do."

"Myles, why don't you just call the girl. See how she's doing?" Samuel asked.

I hadn't talked to Montana since I left Blushing. She'd asked me not to reach out, and I'd respected her wishes.

Had I texted Charlie and asked about her? Sure.

Apparently, she was doing great.

She was out there living her best life, and I was fucking miserable, and it pissed me the hell off.

"She asked me not to call her." I shrugged.

"Well, I ask you daily not to be an asshole, and that's never stopped you," my brother said, receiving a boisterous laugh from Connor.

"That's not what this is about. I've got a lot going on."

"You know what I've come to realize since making my decision to leave medicine?" Samuel said.

"Well, your last day was yesterday, so what have you learned in the last twelve hours?" I smirked.

"Life is short, brother. You can choose what you want out of this life. And you're allowed to change course whenever the fuck you want. So if you aren't happy with the original plan, do something about it."

"Those are some wise words," Connor said, and I rolled my eyes.

"Is this why you wanted to meet this morning? To tell me that I'm an asshole before you start work on Monday?"

"No. I wanted to let you know that I'm going to propose to Brianna. I'm done fucking around, and I'm ready to start living." He leaned forward, his gaze locking with mine. "You know what, Myles? You like the girl. You like her a lot. And that scares the shit out of you. But avoiding relationships because our parents had a shitty one—well, that doesn't make any sense. Because at the end of the day, not letting anyone in means you end up alone. Focusing all your energy on work means you end up alone. And that's just as bad as being in a bad relationship, as far as I'm concerned. I almost lost the woman I love, and I'm not letting her go this time."

The door opened, and a woman wearing a Tinkerbell costume with her face covered in glitter stepped inside, followed by a man in a Chewbacca costume.

It was like the universe was intentionally fucking with me.

"I'm happy for you, Samuel. But you want a relationship; you always have. You were just neglecting it, and you figured it out. I've never wanted that life."

"So you've just been a dick since you got home because you suddenly don't have the patience for New York City?" Connor asked.

I glared at him. He'd been pissing me off ever since I'd returned. He worked directly with Montana, and every time I inquired about her, he would give me lame, single-word answers.

He knew I wanted to know more, but he wasn't going to give me anything until I outright asked.

"Correct." I cleared my throat. "Now tell me about this proposal. How are you going to do it? And are you sure she'll say yes?"

"Fuck you," my brother said. "You know she'll say yes. She's already moved back in to the house. It was never about us not being happy; it was about me not prioritizing our relationship. So yes, I feel very confident. And I'm going to keep it simple."

"The St. James brothers never keep anything simple. You are the most over-the-top, bougie motherfuckers I know. Let's hear it." Connor tipped one shoulder up and chuckled.

"I'm doing it tonight. I rented out Francois's French restaurant for the evening. It's her favorite, and they canceled all the reservations and relocated them to their other location, and I offered to cover their dinner tabs for the inconvenience."

"You needed an entire restaurant?" Connor asked.

"Of course I do. Peter Arquette is over there now, setting up a makeshift jewelry store with his best engagement rings. I hired Mom's party planner, Penny, and she's currently over there covering every square inch in twinkle lights. And I flew in that blues band that she loves to play while we eat."

"Very subtle," I said with a laugh. Connor gaped at him.

"You know what, Myles?" my brother asked.

"No, but I'm guessing you and your new zest for life are going to tell me."

"Life is short. We have more money than we will ever need. So why are we spending our lives working and not living? I'm all about balance now."

"Oh, wonderful. You come on board to work for the St. James Corporation, right when you decide to be more balanced? Lucky me." I rolled my eyes.

He nodded, giving me this look that was filled with empathy. "Our past doesn't have to define us. Our parents' fucked-up relationship doesn't have to define us. We can learn from the mistakes they made. Just because it didn't work for them does not mean it can't work for us. Dad's a selfish prick. We're not like him."

"Well, Myles has his moments." Connor smirked. "But I agree. There's a big teddy bear under that gruff heart of yours."

"What the hell is this meeting even about? I thought we were going to discuss the high-rise. I have a meeting with Jackson this afternoon to go over the drawings. I didn't know I was coming to some sort of fucked-up therapy session."

"I guess we're having an intervention. You've been a dick to everyone at the office ever since you got back. With Samuel coming on board, I thought the two of us could talk to you about it."

"Holy shit," I whisper-hissed. "I was kidding. This really is an intervention?"

"Well, I also wanted to share the news about my engagement. But yes, even Brianna noticed when we had dinner with you last week. She said you don't seem like yourself. I think you need to deal with it, brother. You can't run from it."

What the fuck is happening?

"I haven't been that bad," I said, glancing between them.

"On a scale from one to ten, one being the best behavior you've ever had and ten being the worst, you're at a solid one hundred and seventy-five, Myles. And you need to figure it out." Connor shrugged. "All joking aside, at the end of the day, you're the best guy I know. And I can see that you're miserable, and I don't want that for you."

Samuel had a big grin on his face. He loved this sappy shit. "Agreed," he said. "You went to Blushing to buy a hotel, and you found the love of your life. Just fucking own it. You can make this work. People do it all the time. But we don't want to see you lose the one person who you finally have actual feelings for—because trust me when I tell you, I thought you were too closed off to ever allow it to happen. And if you just act like an asshole for another couple of months, it'll be too late. Because she'll move on. And then you won't have anyone to blame but yourself."

I pushed to my feet abruptly and pointed at each of them. "Fuck you both. You don't know what you're talking about. I've got a meeting."

Time was all I needed.

This would pass.

So I'd tone down my asshole behavior and just fake it until this feeling went away so these sensitive pricks would stop analyzing me.

It was time to stop thinking about Montana Kingsley every goddamn second of the day.

CHAPTER TWENTY-SEVEN

Montana

"Okay, we need to brainstorm," Violet said, snapping her fingers in front of me to get my attention. "Come on, girl. We need a hashtag for Leigh and Scotty Lee."

She stood at the whiteboard, marker in hand, ready to write.

"I'll start," Blakely said as she sipped her latte from the Brown Bear Diner. "'Two Lees in a pod.'"

I chuckled. "That's cute. How about 'happi-Lee ever after,' spelled with his last name, Lee."

"Nice one." Violet wrote them out on the board. "I was thinking maybe 'probab-Lee shouldn't marry a guy who has the same last name as my first name'?"

Blakely and I both made buzzing noises to let her know it was not going on the board.

"She's going to be Leigh Lee," Violet said. "Come on, that's not going to bother her?"

"She's in love. She hardly cares. How often do you call someone by their full name?" Blakely asked, tearing off a piece of muffin and popping it in her mouth.

"That's because Leigh is normal," Violet said. "And nice. I'm just relieved that we survived Tracy's wedding from hell. She'll go down as the worst bride in history."

I shook my head and forced a smile. "Yeah. We're lucky we made it through that one."

Tracy was by far the worst bride we'd ever worked with thus far. She'd made her mother cry. She'd made all of her bridesmaids cry. Her mother-in-law had left the wedding before they even made it down the aisle. But weddings were unpredictable, in the best way. You just never knew what was going to come up.

But at the end of the day, weddings were all about love and hope and happily ever after.

I still believed in it.

"You okay?" Violet asked. It had been six weeks since Myles left. Six weeks since I'd heard his voice or seen his face, outside of the hours when I scrolled through the photos I'd taken of him on my phone.

"Yeah, yeah, of course. I'm good." I gave her a thumbs-up. I'd done everything in my power to put on a happy face these last few weeks. Convincing the people I was closest to that I was fine was exhausting.

"Are you excited for our double date tonight?" Violet waggled her brows.

"That's right. You guys are going out with the hot tourists tonight," Blakely said.

"Yes. It's time for our girl to get out there. And Christopher is hot, and he insisted his best friend was a great guy. So, we'll go to the Moose Brew and have some drinks and forget about the billionaire."

"Pfft, I hardly even think about that man," I said in my most convincing voice, but they shared a look that told me they weren't buying it. "I'm looking forward to getting dressed up and meeting this guy."

I wasn't looking forward to it at all.

I preferred going home alone and allowing myself to be sad. In the comfort of my own home, where I didn't have to hear anyone tell me that I needed to get over it.

Get over him.

A part of me hated myself for making things so final. For drawing such a firm line in the sand. Because right now, seeing Myles once or twice a year didn't sound like a bad thing.

I missed him. I missed his voice.

I missed his smart-ass smirk. His laugh. His face.

His snarky comments.

The way he kissed me.

The way he touched me.

"Hello, earth to Monny," Blakely said, pulling me from my daze. Her eyes were sympathetic when I met her gaze. "Is this you not thinking about the billionaire?"

"Of course I'm not. I was thinking about laundry. I need to do a few loads this weekend." I cleared my throat.

"Sure you were. Listen, Monny, the best way to forget a man is to distract yourself with another one." Violet walked over and wrapped her arms around me. "We'll have fun tonight, okay?"

"Yeah. It'll be great."

"Oh boy," Blakely said under her breath. "Look who just walked in."

I turned to see Phillip standing in the front office, and I internally groaned. He'd texted me so many times, and I just didn't have the energy to deal with him.

Nor should I have to.

I walked out to the front office and crossed my arms over my chest. "What are you doing here, Phillip?"

"I wanted to talk to you," he said, glancing over at Violet and Blakely, who'd followed me out to the front.

"Oh, it's my favorite narcissist," Violet said. "Let me guess, you want Montana to plan your wedding to the woman you cheated on her with? That would be very on brand for you."

He sighed and then looked over at me with pleading eyes. "Can you just give me five minutes?"

I shook my head and motioned for him to follow me to my office. I moved to sit behind my desk, and he took the seat across from me.

"You have to stop texting me, Phillip. We aren't together anymore, and you're engaged to another woman. It's inappropriate, even for you."

"Oh, so now I'm the devil, huh? I made some mistakes, Montana. I'm not perfect."

"Why are you doing this? I'm not upset with you at this point. I'm over it. I don't think about it at all. So why are you pushing this so hard?" My words were harsh, but I didn't want to hear his bullshit anymore.

"Because I miss you," he whispered. "I think I really fucked up, Montana. I think about you all the time. I'm engaged to another woman, but it's you who I think about when I close my eyes at the end of the day."

"Then perhaps you should open them and look at your fiancée," I said, suddenly overcome with anger. "You're never happy, Phillip. That's your problem. You always want what you can't have. When you were with me, you were thinking about her. Figure your shit out, and leave me out of it."

"So you're saying you can't forgive me?" he asked, acting completely wounded.

A maniacal laugh escaped my lips. "I'm saying I have no desire to forgive you."

"Because you're angry."

"No, that's not it. Listen, Phillip, our relationship ran its course. You weren't wrong for ending things. I know that, because I now know what it means to love someone deeply. We didn't have that. We had a history, and it's the reason that we both hung on for so long. Too long. But that's not love. And I think we could have remained friends after everything was all said and done, but you ruined that because we both know that you were unfaithful. And now you have the audacity to come to me and see if I'll take you back while you're engaged to another woman? So, listen to me when I say this to you." I paused, waiting for his gaze to meet mine as I folded my hands on my desk. "You can fuck off, Phillip. Because I deserve better. And you don't deserve my friendship."

He just sat there gaping at me. "Wow. You've changed a lot, Montana."

"Thank God for that. If you were looking for a doormat, I believe you came to the wrong place."

"I didn't mean that in a negative way." He held his hands up. "You've changed a lot, but I admire it. And I'm happy for you, if you're happy. I'm happy that you know what it means to love someone now, even if it stings to hear it. Are you still with that rich guy?"

What part of "I don't want to be friends with you" did you miss?

"Phillip," I said as I pushed to my feet. "I do know what it means to love someone. And to be loved by someone in a way that makes you love yourself even more. And that's as much as I'm going to share with you. I wish you the best, and I hope you figure things out. But I need to get back to work now."

I walked out of the office, and Violet and Blakely were both watching as he walked past me and moved toward the door.

"Thanks for hearing me out." He shrugged. "I'm happy for you, Montana. You deserve the best, and it sounds like you've found it."

I did. I just couldn't hold on to it.

I nodded. "Take care, Phillip."

And when he stepped outside, I felt like I was a stronger person than I used to be.

I just wished I could thank the person who'd helped me realize it.

"Okay, so our code word is 'blue balls.' If either of us say it, we get the hell out of there," Violet said.

"I feel like you picked a code word that is obviously a code word. Because why would we ever just drop that in a conversation?" I said as I pulled the door open to the Moose Brew.

"'Hey, have you heard from our old friend Bill Blue Balls lately?' Or, 'Have you ever tried the blue balls cocktail?'" She laughed. "That's some talent to put 'blue balls' and 'cock' in the same sentence. You're welcome."

"Fine. We'll stick with 'blue balls.'" I rolled my eyes. We made our way toward the bar when two men stood and waved us over where they sat at a table.

"Oh, that's Christopher," she whispered close to my ear. "And look at Ray. He's hot too."

He was good looking by any standard. Blond hair, tall, sort of a surfer guy look. But I felt nothing when I approached. No butterflies. No excitement.

I didn't want to be there.

I was forcing myself to be there.

Christopher did the quick introductions, and we all did the whole awkward hug thing before taking our seats: Violet and me on one side of the table and Christopher and Ray on the other. Benji appeared out of thin air, just like he always did, and he gave me the strangest look. Maybe because I'd come to the Moose Brew a few weeks ago and cried to him over a few shots of tequila. I knew he'd take it to the grave. There were very few people I could break down to right now, and Benji just happened to be one of them.

"Who do we have here?" he asked, clearly unsure if we were using our real names.

"We aren't doing the aliases tonight. We're using our real names," Violet said with a laugh as she introduced Benji to Ray and Christopher.

We ordered a few martinis and some appetizers and settled into our own conversations with the two men.

Violet and Christopher seemed to be having a great time laughing and talking about his travels. Ray was more focused on me.

"So who was the last guy you used an alias on?" He smirked as he reached for a chicken finger.

"I've actually only done it once." I shrugged.

"Did he ever find out that you hadn't told him your real name?"

"Yes, I did eventually tell him." I sipped my cocktail.

"You went out with him more than once?"

"Yes, actually. I went out with him for several months."

His eyes widened. "So I guess he forgave you for lying about your name."

Violet said, "Umm . . . Monny, why don't you tell Ray about the Blushing Bride." She shot me a look, clearly not impressed with my topic of conversation. "I was just telling Christopher how busy we are."

"I want to hear what happened with the dude she dated for a few months after giving him a fake name," Ray said, smiling. "Is he going to show up here and try to kick my ass because you dumped him?"

"No. He's not from here. And he's long gone," Violet said with a smirk.

"Ahhh . . . good to know that I've got a real shot, then. Because you're fucking beautiful, Montana." He had one of those all-American smiles that reached his eyes, and his teeth were perfectly white. This guy belonged in a toothpaste commercial.

"Thank you. But I should tell you that you don't have a real shot, Ray. And it's not because you aren't great. I'm sure you are. You've got the looks, the smile, the charisma."

"Wow. I sound like the whole package. So what's the problem?" he asked, taking a pull from his beer bottle.

"The truth is, I'm deeply in love with another man." I reached for a french fry and bit the top off.

"Blue balls," Violet said in my ear. "Blue fucking balls, Montana Kingsley."

"Why is she saying 'blue balls' in her ear?" Christopher asked Ray.

"It's got to be their code word. I think the wheels might be coming off the cart." Ray chuckled.

"It is our code word. How did you know that?" Violet asked, looking between the two men, as I continued eating. It felt good to get it off my chest. To make sure he knew this was going nowhere so now I could just enjoy myself, eat some bar food, and take the pressure off.

"Because we have one too," Christopher said.

"What is it?" I asked.

"'Pussy cat.'" Ray laughed.

"Damn. Yours is as bad as ours," I said.

"Why are you using your code word?" Ray asked. "We can finish dinner. We didn't come here thinking we had to take you home for it to be a win. You two are vibing, and I like Montana. Even if she's in love with another man. We can still enjoy some food and drinks, right?"

"Yeah. We can." I turned to Violet. "Hold the blue balls for later and enjoy chatting with Christopher. I'm good."

She sighed. "Fine. But if you start crying, we are out of here."

"She's not going to cry." Ray smirked. "She just needs someone to let her vent. I'm guessing she isn't allowed to do that much."

He shot a look at Violet, but she was already deep in conversation with Christopher again. They all ordered another cocktail, but I switched to water. I hadn't been sleeping much, and more than one cocktail would have me falling apart.

"You seem to know a lot about broken hearts, huh?"

"Yeah. My girlfriend and I called it quits a few months ago. This is the first time I've been out on an actual date since. Christopher dragged me here to Blushing for a few days because we've been working a lot. And I guess I've been feeling sorry for myself."

"What happened?"

"I was the asshole," he said.

"No. You don't give off asshole vibes."

"Thank you. I'm working on it. I was an idiot. I was unfaithful, and she kicked my ass to the curb."

"Ah . . . well, good for her." I chuckled.

"Yep. So the guy you were dating doesn't live here?"

"Nope. He lives in New York."

"Did he cheat on you?"

"No." I rolled my eyes. "He's not like that. He's the best."

His eyes widened. "Did you cheat on him?"

"No. I would never do something like that." I winced. "No offense."

"None taken." He sipped his beer. "So you were ridiculously in love, and you dated for months, and what happened?"

"He doesn't really date. He's more of a fling type of guy," I said, thinking back to the night we met.

The way he came to my rescue with the guy hitting on me.

My chest ached at the thought.

I missed him so much that it physically hurt.

"But you two were together for months?"

"Yeah. He was here from out of town. And we just hung out every day, you know? It's probably ridiculous that I'm a mess over him, right?"

"Well, I don't know this dude. But for a guy who doesn't date, it's a little strange to date you for months while he was here. Sounds like he was all in too. So maybe he's missing you the way you're missing him. Have you asked him?"

"No. I cut off all contact. I can't be chatting with a man I'm in love with on the phone every day while dating other men."

His head tipped back with a laugh. "Maybe you bend the 'no contact' rule, and just see if he's having a hard time the way you are, you know?"

"No, I can't open that door, because it'll be too easy to fall back into that same pattern with him again. Sometimes rules are necessary, Ray. Hence the 'no cheating' rule."

His hand landed on his chest, feigning like he'd just been shot there. "Touché. But I think you're the kind of girl a guy would change his rules for."

But he didn't.

I took a sip of my water and thought over his words. "Thank you, Ray."

As if she knew what I was thinking, Violet smiled at me. "Blue balls?"

"Yep. I need to go home." I could feel all that emotion bubbling up. Ray and Christopher were very understanding, and we said our goodbyes. And I walked home hand in hand with Violet as I let it all out.

I cried and sobbed and told her how much I'd been struggling.

And we sat up on the couch talking all night, and she just hugged me over and over and promised it would pass.

But a little part of me knew it never would.

Because Myles St. James had left town—and he'd taken my heart with him.

CHAPTER TWENTY-EIGHT

Myles

"You look tired," my mother said as she reached for her iced tea.

"I've just been putting in long hours at the office."

"Well, thank you for taking time to meet with me, Myles. I know how busy you are, and I appreciate it."

"Always. You know that." I paused when the server set down our plates in front of us.

We'd met at my mother's favorite French restaurant in the city. I remembered coming here with her when I was young, and we'd spend some one-on-one time together.

"So the divorce is going to be final soon. Your father wants to keep the house in the city, and I'll live full time in the country."

"That's kind of how it's been for a while anyway, right?" I asked, because their marriage had been broken for a very long time.

"Yes." She cleared her throat before folding her hands where they rested on the table. "I'm sorry, Myles. I'm sorry that I didn't do this sooner. I thought I was doing the right thing keeping our family together, but I was wrong."

"You did the best you could, Mom. I don't blame you."

I didn't blame her. She wasn't the one who'd been off having affairs and babies with other people. She hadn't forced me to keep a secret and threatened me about it for years.

"I should have done better. And that's what I'm trying to do now. I know the damage it did to you, keeping your father's secret for all those years. I know that you and Samuel are aware that Caleb is your father's son. I don't know, maybe I just thought that if we never discussed it, it wouldn't be real. I'm in therapy now, and that's really helped me to work through the choices I've made. It's also helped me to make decisions for myself now."

"I'm happy you're prioritizing yourself, Mom. You always deserved better. So you know about Caleb?" I asked, because she'd always been nice to him, and she'd never said a word about it to me or Samuel.

"Yes. I confronted Wendy years ago. She admitted that Samuel was his son." She shook her head. "And that's why I allowed them to continue living on the property. I couldn't very well put them out on the street. It wasn't Caleb's fault that they did what they did."

"You're a much bigger person than I am, Mom. I hope you at least called him out."

"Yes. That's when I took you and Samuel on that surprise vacation to the Amalfi Coast. But your father told me that if I left him, he'd make all of our lives difficult. He said it was a onetime thing, but I knew differently. And I just pulled away from him over the years, until I realized that we had more of a business relationship. I can't even call it a friendship. We don't like one another, or at least I don't like him all that much. I wasted so much time, Myles." A sad laugh escaped her mouth.

I'd always wanted to know why she stayed, and since we were being honest with one another, it seemed like an okay time to ask.

"Why would you stay for all those years, knowing he was having a full-blown affair with a woman who worked for you? A woman you considered a friend?"

"I met your father when I was eighteen years old. You know that I grew up without money, without things. And I met this man who gave me this fairy-tale life. Yes, he was difficult and selfish at times, but he wanted to give his family everything he could. I loved your father for a long time. And a little part of me will always love him because he gave me the two greatest gifts of my life—you and Samuel. But I should have left a long time ago. I spent many years feeling incredibly lonely. And that's when my friendship started with Gino. I never cheated on your father, and I never would. He may not have respected our vows, but I always have. You have to remember that Papa and Nana didn't have a great marriage. I didn't have a great example, and that's not an excuse, but it's the truth. But I'm making changes now, Myles, and I want that for you as well."

"Mom, you are not the bad guy here. I don't blame you. I wish you'd left sooner, just because I want you to have everything you deserve. You deserve to be loved and cherished. He never deserved you."

She reached for my hand and squeezed it. "Gino and I have a very special friendship, and he's always told me that I deserve better. I'm going to pursue that, because I've pushed these feelings for him away for a long time, and I don't have to do that anymore. None of us do." She shrugged. "Look at Samuel. He's engaged now. He's working with you and making decisions for his life that are based around making himself happy. He took your father out of the equation and decided what kind of life he wanted. That's what I've done as well. And I want that for you."

"That man has been out of the equation for me for a very long time. That's why I left medical school. That's why I'm doing what I love. Even if he calls it playing with LEGOs, I know that I'm doing what I love. I don't base my decisions on him anymore."

Her thumb moved soothingly over the back of my hand. "You don't seem happy, Myles. I know that your profession is something that you chose, and I'm proud of you for that. But your personal life is a different story. And I couldn't live with myself if I was the reason you don't experience love in your life. Real love, Myles. You're an amazing man, and you deserve that. Don't let our mistakes cost you someone you love."

Fucking Samuel. The dude has a big mouth.

"Mom, I'm fine."

"Myles, you aren't fine. Ever since you returned home, you've seemed like a zombie every time I see you. Every time I speak to you. You are a shell of yourself, and I recognize that because I lived that way for a very long time. I was angry and I didn't know how to express it. I buried it deep inside myself and put on a brave face and suffered in silence. I ended up becoming a mom that my boys didn't respect. A woman that I didn't respect. And I'm changing that now, and I don't want you to do that."

Now it was my turn to squeeze her hand. "I never blamed you. It killed me that you stayed with him, but I never blamed you. You were a wonderful mother. I just always felt that you deserved better."

"And you don't think that you deserve better?"

"I have everything that I want, Mom." I pulled my hand away and reached for my water. This lunch had turned into a much heavier conversation than I'd anticipated, and I wanted to stop talking about it.

"Your father has had multiple affairs, Myles. Wendy is not going to stay with him. She and I may not be close friends, but we share a similar experience of being in a relationship with a toxic man that we both happened to have loved at some point. But the truth is, he's a lonely man. He's messed up in his own way, and he uses his money and his power to bully people. But you aren't sticking it to your father by being alone. Because you're just doing what I did all those years."

My gaze locked with hers. "How am I doing what you did? I hardly talk to the man. I made a decision to do what I wanted professionally. He doesn't decide what I do any longer."

"Because of the trauma that you experienced as a young boy and young man, I think you're afraid to open your heart. I think you were brave when you took over the company from your grandfather. It was a bold move." Another tear slipped down her cheek. "But you are afraid to let yourself love and be loved, Myles. So you throw yourself into work, just like he did. You may not have chosen medicine, but you are choosing a career over a family. And Samuel told me that he believes you have real feelings for Montana. So why would you walk away?"

I groaned. "That brother of mine sure has a big fucking mouth."

"It doesn't matter who told me. Samuel loves you. We've both noticed a huge change in you since you've returned home. It's been two months. You're miserable, and for what? You can have it all, Myles. I was afraid to leave my marriage for a very long time, and fear can steal years of your life. I don't want that for you. Tell me why you're so afraid to love someone and let them love you back?"

I leaned back in my chair. The question had my skin prickling and my heart pounding in my ears. I didn't respond. I didn't know what to say.

She repeated the question. "Why are you so afraid?"

"I don't know."

"Do you love her?" she pressed, and I wanted to shout at her for pushing me. For turning our lunch into a goddamn therapy session.

I looked away, letting out a long breath.

Her words played over and over in my head.

"She lives there, and I live here."

"That wasn't the question."

"I wouldn't even know how to be in a relationship, Mom," I said as a pain settled in my chest. "She can do a hell of a lot better than me. Chances of me failing her are high. She deserves better. She deserves—everything."

"Myles, you are the best son and the best brother. Your grandfather adored you. You know how to be in a relationship. You're just afraid of failing. Because you've seen what that looks like. But you are not a coward. You are a fighter. And I'm going to ask you this one more time, and I want you to be brave enough to answer me." Her gaze locked with mine. "Do you love her?"

I didn't hesitate this time. "Yes."

"Then do something about it. Do not waste years being unhappy. I've been there. You can't get that time back."

"I don't know how to do this, Mom." I cleared my throat. "I've never done it before."

"Did you know how to be a brother when Samuel was born? No. You figured it out because you loved him, and you're the best damn brother I've ever known. Did you know how to handle your father's affair when you were young? No. But you did what you could to protect me, because you love me. Did you know how to run your grandfather's business when he passed away? No. But you figured it out because you loved him. You're a smart man, Myles. You spent months with her. Every time I spoke to you, you were with her. That's all it is. Time and care and love. You know how to do it. You're just afraid of failing. Dig deep, my brave boy." Tears were streaming down her face now, and I didn't even care if we were making a scene in this restaurant.

She was right.

I was afraid.

And that pissed me the hell off.

"Okay." I nodded. "I'm going to fix this. And if it's too late, I'm going to fight harder."

She swiped at her face and smiled through her tears. "I love you, Myles."

"I love you, too, Mom."

"What are you going to do?" she said, her voice still wobbly from the conversation.

"I'm going to fucking figure it out."

I pulled out my phone and sent a text message to my brother first.

Me: I need your help. I'll meet you at the office in twenty minutes. Tell Connor to meet us there, it's going to take a village.

Samuel: I've got you, brother. See you soon.

I paid the bill and walked my mother out to her waiting car as her driver opened the back door.

I chuckled, because this was one fucked-up lunch. "Thanks for the talk."

"It was years late, but I'm glad we had it. You deserve to be loved, and you deserve to be happy. No more fear, okay?"

I nodded and kissed her cheek. "I'll keep you posted."

After she drove off, I walked the few short blocks to the office and dialed Charlie.

"Hey. What did I do to deserve a call? You usually text," he said with a laugh.

"And you give me those lame one-word answers when I text."

"When you want to man up and actually ask the question instead of asking bullshit questions about Montana and the renovations, you'll get more."

"All right. I'm asking."

"I'm listening," he said.

"How is she? Is she dating anyone?"

"She was pretty down in the dumps for a while. Hell, she probably still is. The girl tries to be stoic, but she wears her heart on her sleeve. Hasn't seemed like herself since you left. But Benji told me she and Violet were there on a double date not too long ago, so I don't know, Myles."

"I'm going to fucking fix this."

"It's about time you pulled your head out of your ass. Do you have a plan?"

"No. I just know that I'm miserable, and something needs to change," I said. "But she told me not to reach out to her, and for all I know, she hates me now."

"You're no stranger to people hating you, are you?" He laughed, and I rolled my eyes.

"Fuck off. I'm going to fix this."

"I knew you were a sappy bastard beneath it all."

"You're lucky you aren't standing in front of me right now," I said, not hiding the sarcasm from my voice.

"Myles," he said.

"Yep."

"Only come back if you're going to stay. Don't string her along. She's one of the good ones."

"I know. That's why I've been a miserable fuck ever since I came home."

"Yeah, Connor may have mentioned that." He chuckled. "I'm glad you figured it out. I guess this means you'll be back in Blushing soon."

I missed my girl. Everything about her. I missed her falling asleep beside me. I missed the sound of her voice. The way her lips turned up in the corners when I was being a smart-ass. Hell, I even missed small-town living. The peacefulness. The easiness. All of it.

"Yep. I've got to take care of a few things, but I'll be in touch."

"Got you, buddy. Let me know what you need."

"Thank you." I ended the call and made my way into the building and up to the top floor.

My brother and Connor were in the conference room, both with goofy smiles on their faces. And for the first time in two months, I felt hopeful.

I rolled my eyes. "Don't get fucking cocky. But I need your help."

"Of course you do. And you're going to need to put your ego aside and go big," Connor said.

"Lucky for you, I'm the king of grand gestures," my brother said. "Let's brainstorm." He sat down at the table, and I took the seat beside him, with Connor across from us.

I didn't know what I needed to do, but I knew I'd figure it out.

Because I was done staying away.

I wanted her, and it was time I let her know.

CHAPTER TWENTY-NINE

Montana

"Do you think it's weird that my name is going to be Leigh Lee?" my client asked as she shook her head with a smile on her face.

"You know what?"

"What?"

"I've seen people walk down the aisle with the perfect last name, and they weren't happy. And I see the way Scotty looks at you. He's so crazy about you, and that's what everyone dreams of. When you two are together, you can feel all that love. So who cares what your last name is? If it bothers you, you could hyphenate your maiden name, or Scotty could take your last name. But that just comes down to what makes you both happy. Anyone focusing on your name at the wedding is just envious of what you two have. Because it's rare. And I don't think you should go into this weekend with anything but joy, because you're lucky," I said honestly, and I startled when I realized a tear was rolling down my cheek.

Will I ever get a freaking break?

Leigh turned her chair to face me in the conference room, taking my hands in hers. "Montana, you've literally made my wedding dreams come true, and we haven't even walked down the aisle yet. You're amazing, and you deserve all the happiness too." She sniffed and smiled up at me. "I never liked Phillip for you. Do you know that everyone in town used to say that he was dating out of his class, because he was never good enough for you? But you sure seemed happy whenever I'd see you with Myles around town. You two were always laughing and smiling and looking at one another like there was no one else around. You never seemed like that with Phillip. And I don't know if you were dating Myles or what was going on; it's not my business. But I know you deserve to feel like that all the time."

A lump so thick formed in my throat, and I shook my head. "I'm the wedding planner. I'm supposed to be making you cry. Not vice versa."

"You're so much more than a wedding planner to me, Montana. You're a friend. And you feel like family. And I just want you to know how much I appreciate you. So I'm going to rock being Mrs. Leigh Lee for the rest of my life. And if anyone has something to say about it, I'll just think of you and smirk, knowing that they're just envious."

"Damn straight, girl. You're living the whole fairy tale." I pushed to my feet, and she did the same as we hugged. After we'd pulled apart, we made our way back out to the office. She waved goodbye, and I turned to see the seating chart that Blakely had printed out for us.

"Oh, this is perfect," I said, looking it over. "Yes. Keeping a few tables between her parents will make it a little less stressful for Leigh."

Her parents had gone through a brutal divorce a few years back. Her father had remarried, and there was no love between them anymore. So Leigh had been worried about it, but a thoughtful seating chart could alleviate a lot of that anxiety.

"Hey," Violet said, emerging from her office. "Do you want to head over to the farmhouse and check it out? Apparently, it's all done."

"Yes. Why don't we close up early so the three of us can head over there and see it together," I said as the bells on the door chimed, and I turned around.

My mouth gaped open at the sight of him.

Myles St. James.

He stood there in dark jeans, a dress shirt, and a camel-colored dress coat. His hair was cut short on the sides and a little longer on top. Peppered facial hair dusted his jaw, and his sage green eyes found mine.

I couldn't speak. I wanted to lunge at him and wrap my arms around him.

But I was frozen.

Afraid to let those feelings free again.

He was probably visiting. Here for a quick trip and just passing by.

"Hey," he said, his voice gruff.

"Hi." My voice sounded more like a squeak, and I glanced over at Violet and Blakely, who were both gaping at the man as if they couldn't believe he was here either.

"I wanted to see if you had a free minute to speak." He took a step closer, and I sucked in a breath.

"What are you doing here? I thought Connor was handling everything for the business?" I squared my shoulders, suddenly remembering that I needed to protect myself where this man was concerned.

"Do you want to do this right here?" he asked.

"Yes, please," Violet and Blakely said at the same time, and I tried to ignore them.

"Is this business related?" I asked.

"Montana," he said, moving another step closer. "It's never been business related with us, has it?"

I shook my head, unsure what to say.

"I fucked up when I left here and agreed not to speak to you."

"Why?" I asked, my voice trembling.

"Because I think about you every day when I wake up. I think about you all day when I'm at work. I think about you when I eat dinner alone, because I don't want to be with anyone but you."

"So you just want to stroll into town and have dinner with me, and then leave again?" I asked, taking a step back because I'd never be able to move on if I let him come in and out of my life whenever he felt like it.

"Nope. That's not what I'm saying."

"What are you saying?" Violet asked.

"I'm saying that I'm madly in love with you, Montana Kingsley. And I'm saying that . . ." He paused and cleared his throat. His voice was low and deep as he bent down and looked me right in the eyes. "'I Remember Everything.'"

My heart pounded in my ears at his words. He'd remembered the song. I blinked rapidly several times, trying to keep the tears away.

"'I Remember Everything' too," I whispered. "But what does this change?"

"Well, it changes everything. I want you. I want us, Montana. And I'll do whatever it takes to make that work."

"But you don't live here," I said, my voice shaking.

He slipped his coat off and dropped it on the desk. And then he reached for the buttons on his dress shirt and started unbuttoning them one at a time, his eyes never leaving mine.

"Oh, hell yes!" Violet called out as she reached for a handful of Skittles from the candy jar.

Blakely took a few pieces of candy from Violet's hand as she watched Myles open his shirt.

His six-pack abs were on full display, and then he pushed his shirt off his left shoulder, exposing dark ink.

You, Me, and Forever.

He'd tattooed those words over his heart.

I couldn't speak. I couldn't breathe.

"Samuel is going to take on a larger role at the company, and I am going to spend a lot of time here. I can work remotely most of the time, and I'll travel for meetings and to check on projects. We can have three homes. One here, one in Banff, and one in New York. You can't be throwing weddings when it's dark for twenty hours a day. So we'll be in the city, together, when you aren't working. And when you need to be here, I'll be here beside you." He placed his hand over his chest just beneath the ink. "You, me, and forever, baby."

I lunged forward, throwing myself into his arms. Tears ran down my face as I hugged him.

"You, me, and forever, Moneybags," I whispered against his ear.

He set me down on my feet and placed a hand on each side of my face. "I missed you, Honey Badger."

"I've missed you too," I croaked.

"I've actually missed you too," Violet said with a laugh. "My girl has been a real sad sack, and I was about done with it."

"She tried to put on a brave face," Blakely said. "But some things you can't hide."

"Okay, I appreciate the commentating, but I'd like to take my man to my office and kiss him properly in private," I said as I grabbed his coat and led him away.

"What fun is that?" Violet shouted from behind us.

Once we were inside my office, I closed the door and wrapped my hands around his neck.

Emotion was thick as I looked up at him. My bottom lip shook. "I can't believe you're here. And you really want to make this work."

"It's not an option," he said as his thumb stroked my bottom lip. "I don't want to live without you, Montana. I have never told a woman outside of my mother and grandmother that I loved them. But I fucking love you. I love you in a way I never knew I was capable of loving another person. I knew I loved you the day you told me how you felt, and I let fear stop me from saying it back to you. I was afraid that I wasn't going to be able to give you what you deserve. But I'm over that bullshit. Because I will do whatever it takes to make this work. If that means I live in a small town with a moose with giant balls and a porcupine who camps out on my doorstep, so fucking be it. I. Love. You. All of you. Every inch of you."

"I love you too." Tears streamed down my face.

"No more tears, baby. It's you and me now."

"You and me forever, huh?" I sniffed.

"Yes. And forever starts right fucking now."

"Where are you going to live?" I asked, still trying to wrap my head around the fact that the man I loved was moving to Blushing, Alaska, so we could be together.

He tugged me close as his arms came around me, and his hands found my ass before lifting me off the ground. My legs wrapped around his waist as my fingers tangled in his hair.

"I don't do anything half-assed; you should know that. So I'm coming here because I want to be with you. I want you by my side. I made a very generous offer on that Airbnb I was staying in, and they've already accepted verbally, and we're just getting the paperwork filed."

My head tipped back on a laugh. "You don't mess around, Moneybags."

"Buckle up, baby. I plan on convincing you to move in with me as soon as possible, but I figured it would take you a little time to process all of this."

"You could have just moved in to my house, you know?"

"It's the size of a postage stamp, and we can't have Porky living alone, right? Plus, I want to have plenty of space for us each to have a home office, and lots of rooms to grow into."

My eyes widened. "Wow. You had me at 'porcupine.'"

"And you had me the minute I laid eyes on you, Montana Kingsley. I may not know what I'm doing, but I'm going to try like hell to show you that I can do this. Do you trust me?"

"I mean, I did go home with you the very first night we met. I'd never done that before. And that was before I even knew you. I just had this feeling about you," I said, my teeth sinking into my bottom lip.

"What feeling, baby?"

"Like I'd met the man I was going to spend my life with. Like he was going to be worth all the heartache."

He smiled. "No more heartache. We're together now, and that's all that matters."

"I love you, Myles St. James."

"I love you." He tugged my head down and kissed me.

It was needy and fevered and desperate.

Like two souls that had been kept apart and finally reunited.

My fingers tangled in his hair as I tried to pull him closer.

Wanting.

Needing.

Mine.

CHAPTER THIRTY

Myles

"I can't say I've ever gone around the table saying what my hopes are for the new year, but I like it," Samuel said as he flashed me that cocky smirk of his.

Yes, I was hosting Christmas dinner with my girlfriend.

Hello, my name is Myles St. James, and I am no longer an eternal bachelor. I have a girlfriend.

A woman I love so fiercely, I'd throw my body in front of hers if she was in danger.

Mind you, I prefer to keep us both alive so I can continue making her cry out my name every fucking night.

But I'm that sappy guy now. I don't even mind hosting holiday dinners for family and friends. I even spend time thinking about the perfect gift to get her.

Montana Kingsley is the epitome of "my better half."

She completed me in a way I didn't know I needed.

She made me want to be a better man and all that corny bullshit.

"Just answer the damn question," I grumped.

"And clearly the Grinch has arrived at the table," Samuel said as laughter filled the room.

We were in the dining room at the home I'd purchased, one I was trying to convince Montana to move in to with me.

"My hopes for the new year are easy. I'm marrying the love of my life." He paused and kissed Brianna on the cheek. "So making this woman my wife is at the top of the list, and I don't know, maybe she'll agree to let us start filling our home with miniature versions of her."

Everyone oohed and aahed. I pretended to gag, because Samuel had become quite the sappy pussy since he'd quit his doctoring gig.

As much as I teased him and gave him a hard time—I loved seeing my brother so happy. He was doing an amazing job at the St. James Corp., and our partnership had proved to be the best decision for both of us.

"Okay, only one person left to go," Montana said as she beamed up at me.

I smirked, looking around the table at all the people who'd come to celebrate with us. My mother and Gino, who were now officially dating and had flown in this morning with Samuel and Brianna. And then we had Daniel, Howard, and Lydia, who were now retired and thrilled that Montana had taken over hosting the holidays. Benji had finally agreed to come and close the bar for the night, after I'd threatened to drive over there and drag him here. Charlie was here with his little girl, Harper. Blakely and her sister, Brynn, were here to round out the group.

Violet had flown home for the holidays, but she and Montana had already FaceTimed multiple times today, because they couldn't go long without speaking.

I'd never experienced a holiday like this.

One that I didn't dread with awkward, forced family dynamics.

"My hope for the new year is more of this," I said, motioning around the table. "The fact that my girlfriend agreed to move in with me this morning means this is going to be a good year."

Montana's cheeks pinked, and she smiled. "I even got us matching key chains."

"Well, you've asked her every day since you moved to Blushing, so it was bound to happen," Daniel said over his laughter.

"Yes. I will now be carrying a porcupine key chain." A loud laugh escaped me as I kissed her on the forehead. "You make me a very happy man, baby."

"Oh boy," Samuel said. "Mom's crying."

"No, I'm fine. I'm totally fine." She used her napkin to dab her eyes. "It just makes me emotional to see both of my boys so happy. And that you've both found such amazing women to love."

Gino kissed my mom on the cheek.

"Happy for you, too, Mom," I said, and I meant it.

Montana had insisted on inviting my father to come here for the holidays as well. He and my mother were officially divorced, and he was dating a new woman who was twenty years his junior, but he appeared happy with her, so I wouldn't judge. He wasn't cheating on my mother, so he could do whatever he wanted now. He'd declined the offer, though, because he and his girlfriend were going to Paris for the holidays.

I'd be lying if I didn't admit that I was relieved that he wasn't here.

We were slowly repairing our relationship, but it wasn't going to happen overnight. But we'd made progress, and I'd just take it one day at a time.

Now that my brother and I were both running the business, he didn't have much to say about it.

Both of his sons had chosen a different path from his, and I think he'd realized berating us for our choices wasn't going to change anything.

"So you two are moving in together. That's a big step," Charlie said with a ridiculous grin on his face.

I rolled my eyes. "Moving to Blushing was the big step. Living with my girl will be as easy as breathing."

"Just don't leave dirty dishes in the sink or forget to put your laundry away," Daniel said with a laugh. "I lived with her for eighteen years. She runs a tight ship."

"You loved living with me," Montana said.

"I did, sweetheart. The house has never been as clean as when you lived there." He smirked. "All joking aside, I'm happy for you. But if you're shacking up with my little girl, you better think about putting a ring on it soon."

"Did you just quote Beyoncé?" Blakely laughed hysterically.

"Trust me. I think about it all the time," I admitted, and Montana just smiled up at me.

We'd talked about it.

I'd made this decision to move here because I wanted to be with her. So marrying her was a no-brainer.

This was the woman I wanted to spend my life with.

I was just waiting for the perfect time to ask her.

We finished up dinner, and Brianna was busy talking to Montana, Blakely, and Brynn about her wedding plans. My mom was playing cards with Harper and Gino as Daniel, Howard, and Lydia watched.

I moved behind the dark wood bar and poured a whiskey for Samuel, Charlie, and Benji.

"Happy for you, brother," Samuel said as he held up his glass.

"I'm just glad I don't have to get those daily text messages from you pretending to ask about the jobsite when you just wanted to know about your girl," Charlie teased before taking a sip.

"You weren't very helpful," I reminded him.

"I wasn't supposed to be. I wanted you to pull your head out of your ass. Looks like my plan worked out."

"I mean, they started off with her using an alias. They've come a long way." Benji clinked his glass to mine again.

"He's a stubborn ass," Samuel said, winking at me. "But he always figures it out. I'm just wondering what the plan is for that fucking porcupine who lives on the front porch."

"Oh, didn't he tell you? He has me building Porky a house of his own in the side yard that will match this one," Charlie said, shaking his head.

"That fucker can't stay on the front porch forever, and I can't just put him out on the street. It'll be a mini version of this house, and he can come and go as he pleases."

"And that was a giant moose in the road that we passed driving here today, right?" Samuel asked for the fifteenth time.

"Ahhh . . . yes, welcome to Blushing. That would be Clifford Wellhung," Charlie said, his voice laced with humor. "Just don't make eye contact. He's got some giant balls, but he'll keep to himself if you don't mess with him."

"I want to have swagger like that moose. He just moves through town like his shit doesn't stink, with testicles the size of bowling balls," Benji said as laughter erupted from all of us.

I glanced around the room and found my girl intently listening to Brianna.

As if she felt me watching her, her head turned slowly, her dark eyes locking with mine. Her lips turned up in the corner, and she smiled, her teeth sinking into that juicy bottom lip.

"How long are you fuckers going to stick around?" I grumped, suddenly wanting everyone to go home.

"Your girl smiles at you, and you want to kick us all to the curb?" Charlie laughed.

"Damn straight. We passed out gifts. We fed you. You had dessert. How long are you going to linger?" I tried to hide my smile, because I loved giving these guys shit.

"I'm happy for you," Samuel said, his eyes slightly wet with emotion. Maybe it was from the booze. Maybe it was because he'd feared I'd never find this kind of happiness.

"Yeah, me too, brother."

Holiday music piped through the speakers as we all moved around the room chatting with one another.

Howard and Lydia were the first to say they were going to head home, and slowly but surely everyone followed.

When my mother, Samuel, and Gino left to head to the hotel, we were finally alone.

I pushed the door closed and locked it before grabbing Montana and throwing her over my shoulder.

"What are you doing?" she squealed.

"I thought they'd never leave."

"You're ridiculous, Moneybags," she said as I walked down the hallway and dropped her on the bed, and she bounced a little.

I hovered above her. "I'm ridiculous when it comes to you."

"I'm ridiculous when it comes to you too."

My mouth crashed into hers, and I kissed her hard. She pushed me back, and we were both frantic to get the other undressed, all while our lips never lost contact. I kicked off my shoes, and she was unbuckling my jeans before she shoved my pants and boxers down my legs, and I stepped out of them. My hands found the zipper on the back of her dress, and I rolled onto my back with her on top of me. She unclasped her bra and let it fall from her shoulders, exposing her perfect tits. My mouth watered at the sight as I teased her nipples with my thumbs. Her dark hair tumbled around her shoulders, and she looked sexy as hell. I couldn't wait one more second, so I tore the lace panties at her hip and tugged them free, tossing them on the floor.

"You're lucky you bought me all those replacements for Christmas," she said as she positioned my tip at her entrance.

"I am lucky, baby. I don't doubt that for one fucking second."

She smiled as she slowly slid down my erection. My hands gripped her hips as I guided her up and down.

Taking our time to find our rhythm.

She rode me slowly at first.

And then I pushed up, wrapping my lips around her hard peak, before moving to the other side. She groaned as she moved faster.

Our breaths loud and labored.

Filling the room around us.

I could feel her tighten around me, and I pulled back to watch her.

There was nothing better than watching my woman fall apart with me buried deep inside her.

Faster.

Harder.

She met me thrust for thrust.

"Come for me, beautiful," I said as her body started to shake, and I watched her in awe as she went over the edge.

Eyes wild. Lips plump. Tits bouncing.

Fucking perfection.

My name left her lips on a cry, and it was all it took.

I followed her right over the edge.

Just like I always would.

EPILOGUE

Montana

"So how do you feel about closing on your house?" he asked as we walked toward the Moose Brew.

"I mean, the fact that Violet bought it sort of feels like it's still in the family, you know?"

"Yeah, that worked out well." He cleared his throat. He'd been a little off today. Very distracted, which wasn't like Myles. But the Seaside Inn was almost completed, and he'd had to travel to New York a few times over the last two months for work.

"Are you sure you want to go get dinner? We can just go home. I'm sure you're exhausted. You've been going nonstop."

"Baby, I don't get exhausted. I want to take my girl to dinner." He squeezed my hand in his as he glanced over at Clifford, lying in the snow in the center of town. "I don't know how long it'll take me to get used to seeing that dude just hanging out wherever the hell he feels like it."

I laughed. "We have some breaks in the upcoming wedding season, and I'm looking forward to spending some long weekends in New York soon."

"Me too." He pulled the door open, and I heard the song playing immediately: "I Remember Everything," by Zach Bryan.

The lights were turned off, which didn't catch me off guard at first because it was still dark outside. But the entire place was lit up with twinkle lights. They were strung from the ceiling, running from one end to the other. Candles were lit on every single table, and tall pillars lined a walkway along the floor. There wasn't anyone here.

Just Myles and me.

"Oh my gosh. What is this?" I whispered as tears pricked my eyes.

"This is where it all happened, Dominique." He chuckled as he led me down the candlelit walkway to the bar.

The place where we first met.

There were vases filled with red roses covering the bar top, and my legs shook as we continued to move closer.

"Myles," I whispered when we stopped in front of the bar.

Zach Bryan was singing my favorite song.

"So, I found myself a great diamond dealer from Chicago," he teased.

"Oh yeah? I've heard they do a lot of imports and exports."

"Oh yes. This woman, she's the queen of imports and exports." He smiled as he stroked the hair away from my face. His thumb moved to my cheek, swiping away the single tear that had escaped. "Don't cry, baby."

"I'm just really happy," I croaked.

He nodded. "I've never been happier."

And then he dropped to his knee, my hand in his, and I could no longer keep the tears at bay. I looked down at him through blurred vision.

"Me either."

"Montana, you are the love of my life. The love that I never knew existed. I want to spend my life with you. I want to travel and see the world with you. I want to fill our home with as many babies as you want. I want to grow old in this small town with you," he said as he looked up at me, his voice deep and even. "You, me, and forever, baby."

"Me too." My words were barely audible as I dropped down on my knees to be closer to him.

"Montana Kingsley, will you marry me?" He pulled a black velvet ring box from his coat pocket and opened it.

I gaped at the large stunning princess-cut diamond set on a platinum band.

"Yes." I fell forward, wrapping my arms around his neck. "I love you so much."

"I love you," he said against my ear. "Thanks for making me the happiest man in the world."

I pulled back to look at him. He smiled as his thumbs swiped at the liquid beneath my eyes. And then he took the ring from the box and slipped it onto my finger. "Wow. You must have found yourself the best diamond dealer in town. This is stunning."

"So are you, Mrs. St. James." He stared down at my hand.

"Mrs. St. James," I whispered. "So we're really doing this? We're getting married?"

"I mean, we have the song, and we have the hashtag, right?" he said as he pulled me up to stand.

"You, me, and forever, Myles St. James."

"You, me, and forever, baby." He leaned down and kissed me.

My hands tangled in his hair, and I was lost in the moment.

Because I'd been selling happily ever after for the last five years, but I'd never truly believed in it for myself.

Until this man strolled into town and swept me off my feet.

I'd found my forever, and I was never letting go.

Myles and I had slept in because it was Saturday, and the snow made me want to stay inside with my fiancé wrapped around me. But the call from Violet was so frantic that we'd thrown on clothes and hurried over to her house.

My old house that she'd just bought a few weeks ago.

I couldn't believe my eyes as I took in the place. It had completely flooded and was an absolute mess.

"I mean, you lived here for a few years and had no issues. I buy the place and the pipes burst? What kind of fucked-up deal is that?" Violet said as she threw her hands in the air for the millionth time.

Myles had immediately called Charlie, who was currently walking from room to room assessing the damage as his daughter held his hand and walked beside him.

"Vi, I'm so sorry about this. I can't believe this happened."

"Well, she went out of town, and she didn't turn off the water to the house," Charlie said as he came down the hallway and back into the flooded kitchen and family room. Harper moved to stand between me and Violet as she beamed up at us.

"Who turns their water off when they go out of town?" Violet screeched at him.

"I do." He shrugged. "Anyway, insurance will cover the cost, but it's going to be a gut job. You've got to rip up all the floors and replace the whole kitchen, and the bathrooms are probably unsalvageable."

She groaned. "Aren't you supposed to make me feel better, Charles? This is a nightmare. How long do you think it will take to get this place put back together?"

"Assuming we can get the materials quickly, I would say you're looking at around three months."

"Where am I supposed to live until then?"

"You can stay with us," I said, wrapping an arm around her.

"I love you, Monny, but you two are all over each other. I don't want to be hiding in a guest room when you're climbing your man like a tree." She glanced down at Harper and winced, but the little girl was busy looking around at the mess.

"You're being ridiculous. It would be great. Just like our old college days, minus the ball and chain." I chuckled as I glanced at my fiancé, who didn't look pleased with the idea.

"Hey, didn't your cousin just move out of your guesthouse?" Myles asked Charlie.

"Yes. And she smelled like broccoli and toothpaste," Harper said, and I couldn't help but laugh.

"Yes, Jordan just moved to be closer to her boyfriend. The place is small, but it's in good shape."

"How much is it a month?" Violet crossed her arms over her chest.

"Well, I didn't charge her rent. She just agreed to help me with Harper. You know, getting her to school if I have to be on a jobsite early, or picking her up and getting her started on her homework until I get home. So that's more what I was looking for."

"Yay. Violet can take me to school. She smells like birthday cake and flowers." Harper looked up at Violet, who gaped at her as if she had no idea what she was talking about.

"I mean, if I'm going to smell like cake, I suppose birthday cake would be the best option."

Harper covered her mouth and chuckled. "It's the best kind of cake ever. I'm hungry, Daddy," she said as Charlie scooped her up and held her on his hip.

"I've got to get this one some food. We ran out of the house when you called, Myles." Charlie moved toward the door. "I'll get the estimates to you by the end of the day, and we'll have to sit down and go over the pricing and some options for replacing everything. Why don't we meet Monday morning at my office?"

"Monday morning? It's Saturday morning and I have a flooded house, Charles."

He rolled his eyes. "We can't order anything before Monday, Violet. And you'll need to call your insurance company today. If you want to stay in the guesthouse until the renovation is done, it's yours. Just stay out of my hair, and I'll stay out of yours."

"I thought you wanted help with Harper?" Violet narrowed her gaze as she looked at him.

"Not sure how I feel about that."

"Not sure how you feel about that? Are you kidding me? I have four siblings, you jackass—er, jackass-uming man," she corrected for Harper's sake. "You should be so lucky to have me help out."

"Fine, Violet." He pinched the bridge of his nose as his daughter clapped her hands together. "Meet me at my house in an hour. I'm taking Harps to the Brown Bear Diner for some pancakes."

"Yay for pancakes!" Harper cheered, and I couldn't help but smile at how adorable she was. Her long hair hung down her back, and she had these pink little cherub cheeks.

"I'll be there, unless I find a free place to live in the next half hour that isn't with a couple who can't keep their hands to themselves," Violet said. "Feel free to bring leftover pancakes home, roomie."

"Yeah, room service doesn't come with the house," Charlie grumped before walking out the door.

"That man can be a real jackass," Violet huffed, moving toward her bedroom. "I can't believe I have to pack up and move out."

I flashed Myles my best apologetic smile and told him I was going to go help Violet get her clothes packed up. We agreed to come back tomorrow and grab some dishes and a few other things from her kitchen.

"I'm so sorry about this, Vi," I said as we pulled clothing from her closet.

"It's fine. Thankfully the moodiest bastard in town has an opening at the inn," she said, oozing sarcasm.

"I can't believe you won't just stay with me." I loaded a few sweaters into a duffel bag.

"I'm a grown-up, Monny. You know how I am about having my own space. And what if I meet a hot tourist? I can't bring him home to my friend's house."

"When was the last time you brought a hot tourist home? Everyone seems to bug you pretty quickly lately."

A pair of socks hit me in the face, and I chuckled.

"Hey, I can't help it if the male species is annoying. But do you think he was joking about me taking care of Harper? Because I'm not really into babysitting."

"Yet you got defensive when he said he didn't think it was a good idea."

"Correct. How dare he question my capabilities? I'm quite capable. I just don't necessarily want to be tied down to taking care of a kid I hardly know."

"Listen, I offered you a room in my home, and you turned it down. You wanted the guesthouse at Charlie's so you'd have a place of your own, so I suggest you just say thank you and do whatever he needs you to do."

"Whatever he needs me to do, huh? You make it sound so dirty," she said over a fit of laughter.

"No, you made it sound dirty." I rolled my eyes and slung the duffel over my shoulder. I walked out to find Myles placing a few things on her kitchen counter to bring to Charlie's place, while Violet packed up her bathroom and makeup products.

"Almost done?" he asked as he maneuvered around a puddle to stay on an area that had less water on the floor.

"Yep. I can ride with Violet over there if you want to go home."

"Not a chance, Honey Badger. We can follow her over. Maybe we can even get her to stop for pancakes on the way."

"Ahhh . . . you're hungry, huh?"

"Hungry for you," he whispered against my ear.

"And this is why I can't live with you two. It's like a porno, twenty-four seven. I'm in a bit of a rut lately, so I can't be living with two horndogs." Violet set her bag and hangers on the counter.

Myles laughed and grabbed the duffel and the hangers and piled them over his forearm. "I'll start loading the cars. But we're getting pancakes on the way. I need fuel before we move you in."

"I can live with that!" Violet shouted after him.

We spent the next hour loading both Violet's car and Myles's car with her stuff, and she called the insurance company to get the process started.

We told Violet we'd meet her at the Brown Bear Diner, and I slipped into the passenger seat beside my fiancé. "Thanks for helping her."

"She's your best friend. Of course I'll help her. I already told Charlie I'd be happy to cover the rent for her while she's living there. I just didn't want to say it in front of her, because she tends to get a little . . . hostile." He chuckled.

"She's go
t a lot more bark than bite to her."

"Damn, woman. You made that sound sexy too," he said.

I shook my head with a laugh as he drove toward the diner. The snow was falling, and we'd rushed out of the house before we'd even had time to do much to ourselves. But here he was, stepping right into my messy little life.

This man who'd lived in the city just a few months ago was wearing a pair of sexy-as-sin gray joggers, a flannel shirt, and some snow boots.

And he was doing it all for me.

He pulled in to the lot beside the diner and put the car in park. "What's going on in that head of yours?"

I turned to look at him as I unbuckled my seat belt. "Thank you for being the man of my dreams."

"Happy to oblige, beautiful." He smirked as I climbed over the seat and onto his lap.

"I love you."

"I love you. It's you, me, and forever," he said before he tugged my head down and kissed me.

The End

BONUS SCENE

Myles

New York City

"That wasn't so bad, was it?" Montana asked when we got back to the apartment.

She'd adjusted to the city with ease, and she'd somehow brought my dysfunctional family together.

"That was probably the most bearable family dinner we've ever had." I shrugged as I dropped my keys on the counter.

My father and his new girlfriend, Mandy, had joined my mother, Gino, Samuel, Brianna, Caleb, Montana, and myself for dinner.

Yes, Montana had encouraged me to reach out to Caleb, who'd actually visited us in Blushing because he was interested in seeing the hotel I'd built there.

My father was now acknowledging the fact that he had three sons, and this weird weight was lifted from my shoulders now that everything was out in the open. My parents were getting along a lot better now that they weren't together.

"And Caleb seems really happy to be part of the family. He really worships you, you know?" she said as we both settled on the couch.

"He does not. He's just an awkward kid." I chuckled, because he'd asked me no less than thirty questions about the business during dinner.

"He looks up to you, Myles. It's sweet." She ran her fingers through my hair as my phone vibrated, and I pulled it from my back pocket.

"Sweet, huh? This is him calling. We just had dinner, and there can't possibly be anything left for him to ask me."

"Answer the phone. It could be important."

I put it on speaker after I answered. "Hey, Caleb. What's up?"

"Myles. Hi. I wasn't sure you would answer," he said.

I glanced at Montana as she settled on my lap, facing me, and listening like this was the most important phone call she'd ever been lucky enough to listen in on.

"I'm here. Everything okay?"

"I, um, I wanted to ask you a favor," he said, sounding nervous.

"All right. What is it?"

"My fraternity is having father-son day, and you know, your father, well, I guess he's technically our father now . . ." He cleared his throat. "But I just don't feel super comfortable around him just yet. Some of the guys are having their brothers come instead. And I just wondered if you and Samuel would consider coming. I thought I'd ask you first."

Montana smiled at me, and I nodded. I didn't need her to tell me I should do this. I knew I would do it.

Hell, I wanted to do it.

He was a good kid, and as much as I joked about it, I liked him.

He was family.

"Yeah. I'd be happy to come," I said.

"Really?" His voice was nineteen octaves higher now.

I chuckled. "You're my brother, Caleb. I wouldn't miss it. Text me the details, and I'll be there."

He was quiet for a few beats, and Montana's head rested on my shoulder.

"Thanks, Myles. It means a lot."

"You got it, buddy. Talk soon." I ended the call, and she lifted her head and smiled.

"I have a surprise for you," she said, pushing off my lap and hurrying down the hall.

"I hope you're coming out of that room naked," I said.

"Nope." She held a large bag in her hands, and she came to sit beside me on the couch. "I have something that I think you're going to like."

I took the bag and pulled out a large LEGO box, then chuckled. "You got me LEGOs?"

"My fiancé likes to build things, and what does this place look like to you?"

I studied the box. "It kind of looks like our place in Banff."

"It does, right?"

"I love it. You going to help me build it?" I asked, because this woman was everything good in my life.

"Well, you know how you keep asking when we're going to make this engagement official?"

"That's an understatement." I wanted to marry her the day I proposed to her. And I'd brought it up every day since.

"So we both want to have a small wedding, right?"

"Oh, is it small now? I thought you only wanted it to be you and me?" I teased, because I didn't give a damn what kind of wedding we had; I just wanted to make it official.

"I know. I'm sticking to the song and the hashtag, and I don't want anything big, but I thought maybe it could just be me and you, and our families, and just our closest friends. I feel like my dad and your mom and brothers would want to be there. I know Violet and Blakely would want to be there, and Connor and Jackson and Charlie and Benji. We could get married in Banff at the house, and keep it real small, but a little bigger than I originally planned."

She handed me two small boxes. I opened them up to find a bride and groom who looked very similar to us. The names MONEYBAGS and HONEY BADGER were written on their shirts.

"What do we have here?"

"It's you and me."

"Did you have these made?" I asked, completely fascinated by them.

"I sure did. Who knew that you could customize your LEGO figurines?" she said as she climbed back on my lap.

"My future wife did. And it was very thoughtful."

"So what do you think? A wedding in Banff in two weeks? Nothing fancy, just family and friends, and you and me."

I placed a hand on each side of her face. "I'd marry you right now. I'd marry you tomorrow. And I'll marry you in two weeks. I just want you to be my wife."

"Well, we have the custom figurines, so I feel like we have to go through with it now." She chuckled.

"Thank you," I said, a lump forming in my throat as my gaze locked with hers.

"For what? The figurines?" She smiled down at me.

I ran my thumb along her jawline and shook my head. "For showing me how much I was missing. For showing me how good life could be."

"Well, I never believed in fairy tales before I met you." Her voice cracked a little on the last word. "But you showed me that they're very real."

"I'm just getting started, baby."

And I meant it.

Forever may have just started the day I rolled into Blushing, Alaska . . . but we had a lifetime to go.

ACKNOWLEDGMENTS

Greg, you inspire every hero I write. Love you!

Chase and Hannah, thank you for always being my biggest cheerleaders. Love you!

Tiffany Adams, thank you for all of your support with writing my first small-town-Alaska romance! Your photos, voice messages, and input were more helpful than I can even put into words. So thankful for you!! Xo

Willow, Catherine, and Kandi, I am so grateful to be on this journey with you. Thank you for listening, for cheering me on, for making me laugh on the days I need it most. So thankful for your friendship!

Pathi, thank you for believing in me from the start, and for giving me the push I needed.

Nat, I am SO INCREDIBLY thankful to have you in my corner. I'd be lost without you.

Lauren Plude and Lindsey Faber, thank you for believing in me and in the Blushing Bride world. Thank you for being so incredibly supportive and kind throughout the process. Cheers to our first book together! I'm so grateful for you both!

Nina, thank you for making my wildest dreams come true. I am forever grateful for YOU!

Kim Cermak, thank you for all that you do for me. I'm endlessly thankful for you!

Christine Miller, Kelley Beckham, Tiffany Bullard, Sarah Norris, Valentine Grinstead, Meagan Reynoso, Amy Dindia, Josette Ochoa, and Ratula Roy, I am endlessly thankful for YOU!

Tatyana (Bookish Banter), Logan Chisolm, Kayla Compton, thank you for all that you do for me to support every release and keep me on track!

Abi Mehrholz, thank you for all your support and encouragement. I'm so grateful for you!

Paige, forever grateful for your friendship. You brighten Mother's Days! LOL!

Stephanie Hubenak, thank you for always reading my words early! So grateful for your friendship! Thank you for finding this gorgeous couple for the cover, and for always supporting me!!

Doo, Annette, Abi, Meagan, Diana, Jennifer, Pathi, Natalie, and Caroline, thank you for being the BEST beta readers EVER! Your feedback means the world to me. I am so thankful for you!

Natasha, Corinne, and Lauren, thank you for pushing me every day and for being the best support system! Love you!

Amy, I love sprinting with you so much! So grateful for your friendship! Love you!

Gianna Rose, Rachel Parker, Janelle Pegram, Kelly Yates, Rachel Baldwin, Sarah Sentz, Ashley Anastasio, Kayla Compton, Tiara Cobillas, Tori Ann Harris, and Erin O'Donnell, thank you for your friendship and your support. It means the world to me!

Mom, thank you for being my biggest cheerleader and reading everything I write! Love you!

Dad, you really are the reason that I keep chasing my dreams! Thank you for teaching me to never give up. Love you!

Sandy, thank you for reading and supporting me throughout this journey! Love you!

To all the bloggers, Bookstagrammers, and ARC readers who have posted, shared, and supported me—I can't begin to tell you how much it means to me. I love seeing the graphics you make and the gorgeous posts you share. I am forever grateful for your support!

To all the readers who take the time to pick up my books and take a chance on my words . . . THANK YOU for helping to make my dreams come true!

KEEP UP ON NEW RELEASES

Linktree: Laurapavlovauthor

Newsletter: Laurapavlov.com

FOLLOW ME

Website: laurapavlov.com

Goodreads: @laurapavlov

Instagram: @laurapavlovauthor

Facebook: @laurapavlovauthor

Pav-Love's Readers: @pav-love's readers

Amazon: @laurapavlov

BookBub: @laurapavlov

TikTok: @laurapavlovauthor

ABOUT THE AUTHOR

Photo © 2020 Chase Pavlov

Laura Pavlov is best known for writing swoony, emotional stories with a side of angst and a dash of humor. A hopeless romantic at heart, she likes to take her characters on a journey that always leads to happily ever after. Pavlov is happily married to her college sweetheart and devoted to her two amazing kids, who are now adulting. She's also a dog whisperer to one temperamental Yorkie and one wild Bernedoodle. The author resides in Las Vegas, Nevada, where she is currently living her own happily ever after.